Alice Munro

The Beggar Maid

STORIES OF FLO AND ROSE

Penguin Books
in association with Allen Lane

Penguin Books Ltd, Harmondsworth, Middlesex, England
Penguin Books, 625 Madison Avenue, New York, New York 10022, U.S.A.
Penguin Books Australia Ltd, Ringwood, Victoria, Australia
Penguin Books Canada Ltd, 2801 John Street, Markham, Ontario, Canada L3R 1B4
Penguin Books (N.Z.) Ltd, 182-190 Wairau Road, Auckland 10, New Zealand

First published by Allen Lane 1980
Published by Penguin Books in association with Allen Lane 1980
Copyright © Alice Munro, 1979

Made and printed in Great Britain by
Richard Clay (The Chaucer Press) Ltd, Bungay, Suffolk

PENGUIN BOOKS IN ASSOCIATION WITH ALLEN LANE

THE BEGGAR MAID

Alice Munro was born in Wingham, Ontario and went to the University of Western Ontario. She is the author of three other novels, *Dance of the Happy Shades, Lives of Girls and Women,* and *Something I've Been Meaning to Tell You.* She now lives in Clinton, Ontario.

To G. Fn.

Contents

THE BEGGAR MAID

Royal Beatings

Royal *Beating.* That was Flo's promise. You are going to get one Royal Beating.

The word Royal lolled on Flo's tongue, took on trappings. Rose had a need to picture things, to pursue absurdities, that was stronger than the need to stay out of trouble, and instead of taking this threat to heart she pondered: how is a beating royal? She came up with a tree-lined avenue, a crowd of formal spectators, some white horses and black slaves. Someone knelt, and the blood came leaping out like banners. An occasion both savage and splendid. In real life they didn't approach such dignity, and it was only Flo who tried to supply the event with some high air of necessity and regret. Rose and her father soon got beyond anything presentable.

Her father was king of the royal beatings. Those Flo gave never amounted to much; they were quick cuffs and slaps dashed off while her attention remained elsewhere. You get out of my road, she would say. You mind your own business. You take that look off your face.

They lived behind a store in Hanratty, Ontario. There were four of them: Rose, her father, Flo, Rose's young half brother Brian. The store was really a house, bought by Rose's father and mother when they married and set up here in the furniture and upholstery repair business. Her mother could do upholstery. From both parents Rose should have inherited clever hands, a quick sympathy with materials, an eye for the nicest turns of mending, but she hadn't. She was

3

clumsy, and when something broke she couldn't wait to sweep it up and throw it away.

Her mother had died. She said to Rose's father during the afternoon, "I have a feeling that is so hard to describe. It's like a boiled egg in my chest, with the shell left on." She died before night, she had a blood clot on her lung. Rose was a baby in a basket at the time, so of course could not remember any of this. She heard it from Flo, who must have heard it from her father. Flo came along soon afterward, to take over Rose in the basket, marry her father, open up the front room to make a grocery store. Rose, who had known the house only as a store, who had known only Flo for a mother, looked back on the sixteen or so months her parents spent here as an orderly, far gentler and more ceremonious time, with little touches of affluence. She had nothing to go on but some egg cups her mother had bought, with a pattern of vines and birds on them, delicately drawn as if with red ink; the pattern was beginning to wear away. No books or clothes or pictures of her mother remained. Her father must have got rid of them, or else Flo would. Flo's only story about her mother, the one about her death, was oddly grudging. Flo liked the details of a death: the things people said, the way they protested or tried to get out of bed or swore or laughed (some did those things), but when she said that Rose's mother mentioned a hard-boiled egg in her chest she made the comparison sound slightly foolish, as if her mother really was the kind of person who might think you could swallow an egg whole.

Her father had a shed out behind the store, where he worked at his furniture repairing and restoring. He caned chair seats and backs, mended wickerwork, filled cracks, put legs back on, all most admirably and skillfully and cheaply. That was his pride: to startle people with such fine work, such moderate, even ridiculous charges. During the Depression people could not afford to pay more, perhaps, but he continued the practice through the war, through the years of prosperity after the war, until he died. He never discussed with Flo what he charged or what was owing. After he died she had to go out and unlock the shed and take all sorts of scraps of paper and torn envelopes from the big wicked-looking hooks that were his files. Many of these she found were not accounts or receipts at all but records of the weather, bits of information about the garden, things he had been moved to write down.

Ate new potatoes 25th June. Record.
Dark Day, 1880's, nothing supernatural. Clouds of ash from forest fires.
Aug 16, 1938. Giant thunderstorm in evng. Lightning str. Pres. Church,
Turberry Twp. Will of God?
Scald strawberries to remove acid.
All things are alive. Spinoza.

Flo thought Spinoza must be some new vegetable he planned to grow,
like broccoli or eggplant. He would often try some new thing. She
showed the scrap of paper to Rose and asked, did she know what
Spinoza was? Rose did know, or had an idea—she was in her teens by
that time—but she replied that she did not. She had reached an age
where she thought she could not stand to know any more, about her
father, or about Flo; she pushed any discovery aside with embarrassment and dread.

There was a stove in the shed, and many rough shelves covered with
cans of paint and varnish, shellac and turpentine, jars of soaking
brushes and also some dark sticky bottles of cough medicine. Why
should a man who coughed constantly, whose lungs took in a whiff of
gas in the War (called, in Rose's earliest childhood, not the First, but
the Last, War) spend all his days breathing fumes of paint and turpentine? At the time, such questions were not asked as often as they
are now. On the bench outside Flo's store several old men from the
neighborhood sat gossiping, drowsing, in the warm weather, and some
of these old men coughed all the time too. The fact is they were dying,
slowly and discreetly, of what was called, without any particular sense
of grievance, "the foundry disease." They had worked all their lives at
the foundry in town, and now they sat still, with their wasted yellow
faces, coughing, chuckling, drifting into aimless obscenity on the subject of women walking by, or any young girl on a bicycle.

From the shed came not only coughing, but speech, a continual
muttering, reproachful or encouraging, usually just below the level at
which separate words could be made out. Slowing down when her father was at a tricky piece of work, taking on a cheerful speed when he
was doing something less demanding, sandpapering or painting. Now
and then some words would break through and hang clear and nonsensical on the air. When he realized they were out, there would be a
quick bit of cover-up coughing, a swallowing, an alert, unusual silence.

"Macaroni, pepperoni, Botticelli, beans—"

What could that mean? Rose used to repeat such things to herself. She could never ask him. The person who spoke these words and the person who spoke to her as her father were not the same, though they seemed to occupy the same space. It would be the worst sort of taste to acknowledge the person who was not supposed to be there; it would not be forgiven. Just the same, she loitered and listened.

The cloud-capped towers, she heard him say once.

"The cloud-capped towers, the gorgeous palaces."

That was like a hand clapped against Rose's chest, not to hurt, but astonish her, to take her breath away. She had to run then, she had to get away. She knew that was enough to hear, and besides, what if he caught her? It would be terrible.

This was something the same as bathroom noises. Flo had saved up, and had a bathroom put in, but there was no place to put it except in a corner of the kitchen. The door did not fit, the walls were only beaverboard. The result was that even the tearing of a piece of toilet paper, the shifting of a haunch, was audible to those working or talking or eating in the kitchen. They were all familiar with each other's nether voices, not only in their more explosive moments but in their intimate sighs and growls and pleas and statements. And they were all most prudish people. So no one ever seemed to hear, or be listening, and no reference was made. The person creating the noises in the bathroom was not connected with the person who walked out.

They lived in a poor part of town. There was Hanratty and West Hanratty, with the river flowing between them. This was West Hanratty. In Hanratty the social structure ran from doctors and dentists and lawyers down to foundry workers and factory workers and draymen; in West Hanratty it ran from factory workers and foundry workers down to large improvident families of casual bootleggers and prostitutes and unsuccessful thieves. Rose thought of her own family as straddling the river, belonging nowhere, but that was not true. West Hanratty was where the store was and they were, on the straggling tail end of the main street. Across the road from them was a blacksmith shop, boarded up about the time the war started, and a house that had been another store at one time. The Salada Tea sign had never been taken out of the front window; it remained as a proud and interesting decoration though there was no Salada Tea for sale inside. There was just a bit of sidewalk, too cracked and tilted for roller-skating, though Rose longed for roller skates and often pictured herself whizzing along in a plaid skirt, agile and fashionable. There was one street light, a tin flower; then the amenities gave up and there were dirt roads and boggy places, front-yard dumps and strange-looking houses. What made the houses strange-looking were the attempts to keep them from going completely to ruin. With some the attempt had never been made. These were gray and rotted and leaning over, falling into a landscape of scrub hollows, frog ponds, cattails and nettles. Most houses, however, had been patched up with tarpaper, a few fresh shingles, sheets of tin, hammered-out stovepipes, even cardboard. This was, of course, in the days before the war, days of what would later be legendary poverty, from which Rose would remember mostly low-down things—serious-looking anthills and wooden steps, and a cloudy, interesting, problematical light on the world.

There was a long truce between Flo and Rose in the beginning. Rose's nature was growing like a prickly pineapple, but slowly, and secretly, hard pride and skepticism overlapping, to make something surprising even to herself. Before she was old enough to go to school, and while Brian was still in the baby carriage, Rose stayed in the store with both of them—Flo sitting on the high stool behind the counter, Brian asleep by the window; Rose knelt or lay on the wide creaky floorboards working with crayons on pieces of brown paper too torn or irregular to be used for wrapping.

People who came to the store were mostly from the houses around. Some country people came too, on their way home from town, and a few people from Hanratty, who walked across the bridge. Some people were always on the main street, in and out of stores, as if it was their duty to be always on display and their right to be welcomed. For instance, Becky Tyde.

Becky Tyde climbed up on Flo's counter, made room for herself beside an open tin of crumbly jam-filled cookies.

"Are these any good?" she said to Flo, and boldly began to eat one. "When are you going to give us a job, Flo?"

"You could go and work in the butcher shop," said Flo innocently. "You could go and work for your brother."

"Roberta?" said Becky with a stagey sort of contempt. "You think I'd work for him?" Her brother who ran the butcher shop was named Robert but often called Roberta, because of his meek and nervous ways. Becky Tyde laughed. Her laugh was loud and noisy like an engine bearing down on you.

She was a big-headed loud-voiced dwarf, with a mascot's sexless swagger, a red velvet tam, a twisted neck that forced her to hold her head on one side, always looking up and sideways. She wore little polished high-heeled shoes, real lady's shoes. Rose watched her shoes, being scared of the rest of her, of her laugh and her neck. She knew from Flo that Becky Tyde had been sick with polio as a child, that was why her neck was twisted and why she had not grown any taller. It was hard to believe that she had started out differently, that she had ever been normal. Flo said she was not cracked, she had as much brains as anybody, but she knew she could get away with anything.

"You know I used to live out here?" Becky said, noticing Rose. "Hey! What's-your-name! Didn't I used to live out here, Flo?"

"If you did it was before my time," said Flo, as if she didn't know anything.

"That was before the neighborhood got so downhill. Excuse me saying so. My father built his house out here and he built his slaughterhouse and we had half an acre of orchard."

"Is that so?" said Flo, using her humoring voice, full of false geniality, humility even. "Then why did you ever move away?"

"I told you, it got to be such a downhill neighborhood," said Becky. She would put a whole cookie in her mouth if she felt like it, let her cheeks puff out like a frog's. She never told any more.

Flo knew anyway, and who didn't. Everyone knew the house, red brick with the veranda pulled off and the orchard, what was left of it, full of the usual outflow—car seats and washing machines and bedsprings and junk. The house would never look sinister, in spite of what had happened in it, because there was so much wreckage and confusion all around.

Becky's old father was a different kind of butcher from her brother according to Flo. A bad-tempered Englishman. And different from Becky in the matter of mouthiness. His was never open. A skinflint, a family tyrant. After Becky had polio he wouldn't let her go back to school. She was seldom seen outside the house, never outside the yard. He didn't want people gloating. That was what Becky said, at the trial. Her mother was dead by that time and her sisters married. Just Becky and Robert at home. People would stop Robert on the road and ask him, "How about your sister, Robert? Is she altogether better now?"

"Yes."

"Does she do the housework? Does she get your supper?"

"Yes."

"And is your father good to her, Robert?"

The story being that the father beat them, had beaten all his children and beaten his wife as well, beat Becky more now because of her deformity, which some people believed he had caused (they did not understand about polio). The stories persisted and got added to. The reason that Becky was kept out of sight was now supposed to be her pregnancy, and the father of the child was supposed to be her own father. Then people said it had been born, and disposed of.

"What?"

"Disposed of," Flo said. "They used to say go and get your lamb chops at Tyde's, get them nice and tender! It was all lies in all probability," she said regretfully.

Rose could be drawn back—from watching the wind shiver along the old torn awning, catch in the tear—by this tone of regret, caution, in Flo's voice. Flo telling a story—and this was not the only one, or even the most lurid one, she knew—would incline her head and let her face go soft and thoughtful, tantalizing, warning.

"I shouldn't even be telling you this stuff."

More was to follow.

Three useless young men, who hung around the livery stable, got together—or were got together, by more influential and respectable men in town—and prepared to give old man Tyde a horsewhipping, in the interests of public morality. They blacked their faces. They were provided with whips and a quart of whiskey apiece, for courage. They were: Jelly Smith, a horse-racer and a drinker; Bob Temple, a ball-player and strongman; and Hat Nettleton, who worked on the town dray, and had his nickname from a bowler hat he wore, out of vanity as much as for the comic effect. He still worked on the dray, in fact; he had kept the name if not the hat, and could often be seen in public—

almost as often as Becky Tyde—delivering sacks of coal, which blackened his face and arms. That should have brought to mind his story, but didn't. Present time and past, the shady melodramatic past of Flo's stories, were quite separate, at least for Rose. Present people could not be fitted into the past. Becky herself, town oddity and public pet, harmless and malicious, could never match the butcher's prisoner, the cripple daughter, a white streak at the window: mute, beaten, impregnated. As with the house, only a formal connection could be made.

The young men primed to do the horsewhipping showed up late, outside Tyde's house, after everybody had gone to bed. They had a gun, but they used up their ammunition firing it off in the yard. They yelled for the butcher and beat on the door; finally they broke it down. Tyde concluded they were after his money, so he put some bills in a handkerchief and sent Becky down with them, maybe thinking those men would be touched or scared by the sight of a little wry-necked girl, a dwarf. But that didn't content them. They came upstairs and dragged the butcher out from under his bed, in his nightgown. They dragged him outside and stood him in the snow. The temperature was four below zero, a fact noted later in court. They meant to hold a mock trial but they could not remember how it was done. So they began to beat him and kept beating him until he fell. They yelled at him, *Butcher's meat!* and continued beating him while his nightgown and the snow he was lying in turned red. His son Robert said in court that he had not watched the beating. Becky said that Robert had watched at first but had run away and hid. She herself had watched all the way through. She watched the men leave at last and her father make his delayed bloody progress through the snow and up the steps of the veranda. She did not go out to help him, or open the door until he got to it. Why not? she was asked in court, and she said she did not go out because she just had her nightgown on, and she did not open the door because she did not want to let the cold into the house.

Old man Tyde then appeared to have recovered his strength. He sent Robert to harness the horse, and made Becky heat water so that he could wash. He dressed and took all the money and with no explanation to his children got into the cutter and drove to Belgrave where he left the horse tied in the cold and took the early morning train to

Toronto. On the train he behaved oddly, groaning and cursing as if he was drunk. He was picked up on the streets of Toronto a day later, out of his mind with fever, and was taken to a hospital, where he died. He still had all the money. The cause of death was given as pneumonia.

But the authorities got wind, Flo said. The case came to trial. The three men who did it all received long prison sentences. A farce, said Flo. Within a year they were all free, had all been pardoned, had jobs waiting for them. And why was that? It was because too many higher-ups were in on it. And it seemed as if Becky and Robert had no interest in seeing justice done. They were left well-off. They bought a house in Hanratty. Robert went into the store. Becky after her long seclusion started on a career of public sociability and display.

That was all. Flo put the lid down on the story as if she was sick of it. It reflected no good on anybody.

"Imagine," Flo said.

Flo at this time must have been in her early thirties. A young woman. She wore exactly the same clothes that a woman of fifty, or sixty, or seventy, might wear: print housedresses loose at the neck and sleeves as well as the waist; bib aprons, also of print, which she took off when she came from the kitchen into the store. This was a common costume at the time, for a poor though not absolutely poverty-stricken woman; it was also, in a way, a scornful deliberate choice. Flo scorned slacks, she scorned the outfits of people trying to be in style, she scorned lipstick and permanents. She wore her own black hair cut straight across, just long enough to push behind her ears. She was tall but fine-boned, with narrow wrists and shoulders, a small head, a pale, freckled, mobile, monkeyish face. If she had thought it worthwhile, and had the resources, she might have had a black-and-pale, fragile, nurtured sort of prettiness; Rose realized that later. But she would have to have been a different person altogether; she would have to have learned to resist making faces, at herself and others.

Rose's earliest memories of Flo were of extraordinary softness and hardness. The soft hair, the long, soft, pale cheeks, soft almost invisible fuzz in front of her ears and above her mouth. The sharpness of her knees, hardness of her lap, flatness of her front.

When Flo sang:

> Oh the buzzin' of the bees in the cigarette trees
> And the soda-*water* fountain . . .

Rose thought of Flo's old life before she married her father, when she worked as a waitress in the coffee shop in Union Station, and went with her girl friends Mavis and Irene to Centre Island, and was followed by men on dark streets and knew how pay phones and elevators worked. Rose heard in her voice the reckless dangerous life of cities, the gum-chewing sharp answers.

And when she sang:

> Then slowly, slowly, she got up
> And slowly she came nigh him
> And all she said, that she ever did say,
> Was young man I think, you're dyin'!

Rose thought of a life Flo seemed to have had beyond that, earlier than that, crowded and legendary, with Barbara Allen and Becky Tyde's father and all kinds of outrages and sorrows jumbled up together in it.

The royal beatings. What got them started?

Suppose a Saturday, in spring. Leaves not out yet but the doors open to the sunlight. Crows. Ditches full of running water. Hopeful weather. Often on Saturdays Flo left Rose in charge of the store—it's a few years now, these are the years when Rose was nine, ten, eleven, twelve—while she herself went across the bridge to Hanratty (going uptown they called it) to shop and see people, and listen to them. Among the people she listened to were Mrs. Lawyer Davies, Mrs. Anglican Rector Henley-Smith, and Mrs. Horse-Doctor McKay. She came home and imitated their flibberty voices. Monsters, she made them seem; of foolishness, and showiness, and self-approbation.

When she finished shopping she went into the coffee shop of the Queen's Hotel and had a sundae. What kind? Rose and Brian wanted to know when she got home, and they would be disappointed if it was only pineapple or butterscotch, pleased if it was a Tin Roof, or Black and White. Then she smoked a cigarette. She had some ready-rolled, that she carried with her, so that she wouldn't have to roll one in public. Smoking was the one thing she did that she would have called showing off in anybody else. It was a habit left over from her working days, from Toronto. She knew it was asking for trouble. Once the Catholic priest came over to her right in the Queen's Hotel, and flashed his lighter at her before she could get her matches out. She thanked him but did not enter into conversation, lest he should try to convert her.

Another time, on the way home, she saw at the town end of the bridge a boy in a blue jacket, apparently looking at the water. Eighteen, nineteen years old. Nobody she knew. Skinny, weakly looking, something the matter with him, she saw at once. Was he thinking of jumping? Just as she came up even with him, what does he do but turn and display himself, holding his jacket open, also his pants. What he must have suffered from the cold, on a day that had Flo holding her coat collar tight around her throat.

When she first saw what he had in his hand, Flo said, all she could think of was, what is he doing out here with a baloney sausage?

She could say that. It was offered as truth; no joke. She maintained that she despised dirty talk. She would go out and yell at the old men sitting in front of her store.

"If you want to stay where you are you better clean your mouths out!"

Saturday, then. For some reason Flo is not going uptown, has decided to stay home and scrub the kitchen floor. Perhaps this has put her in a bad mood. Perhaps she was in a bad mood anyway, due to people not paying their bills, or the stirring-up of feelings in spring. The wrangle with Rose has already commenced, has been going on forever, like a dream that goes back and back into other dreams, over hills and through doorways, maddeningly dim and populous and familiar and elusive. They are carting all the chairs out of the kitchen preparatory to the scrubbing, and they have also got to move some extra provisions for the store, some cartons of canned goods, tins of maple syrup, coal-oil cans, jars of vinegar. They take these things out to the woodshed. Brian who is five or six by this time is helping drag the tins.

"Yes," says Flo, carrying on from our lost starting point. "Yes, and that filth you taught to Brian."

"What filth?"

"And he doesn't know any better."

There is one step down from the kitchen to the woodshed, a bit of carpet on it so worn Rose can't ever remember seeing the pattern. Brian loosens it, dragging a tin.

"Two Vancouvers," she says softly.

Flo is back in the kitchen. Brian looks from Flo to Rose and Rose says again in a slightly louder voice, an encouraging sing-song, "Two Vancouvers—"

"Fried in snot!" finishes Brian, not able to control himself any longer.

"Two pickled arseholes—"

"—tied in a knot!"

There it is. The filth.

> Two Vancouvers fried in snot!
> Two pickled arseholes tied in a knot!

Rose has known that for years, learned it when she first went to school. She came home and asked Flo, what is a Vancouver?

"It's a city. It's a long ways away."

"What else besides a city?"

Flo said, what did she mean, what else? How could it be fried, Rose said, approaching the dangerous moment, the delightful moment, when she would have to come out with the whole thing.

"Two Vancouvers fried in snot!/Two pickled arseholes tied in a knot!"

"You're going to get it!" cried Flo in a predictable rage. "Say that again and you'll get a good clout!"

Rose couldn't stop herself. She hummed it tenderly, tried saying the innocent words aloud, humming through the others. It was not just the words snot and arsehole that gave her pleasure, though of course they did. It was the pickling and tying and the unimaginable Vancouvers. She saw them in her mind shaped rather like octopuses, twitching in the pan. The tumble of reason; the spark and spit of craziness.

Lately she has remembered it again and taught it to Brian, to see if it has the same effect on him, and of course it has.

"Oh, I heard you!" says Flo. "I heard that! And I'm warning you!"

So she is. Brian takes the warning. He runs away, out the woodshed door, to do as he likes. Being a boy, free to help or not, involve himself or not. Not committed to the household struggle. They don't need him anyway, except to use against each other, they hardly notice his going. They continue, can't help continuing, can't leave each other alone. When they seem to have given up they really are just waiting and building up steam.

Flo gets out the scrub pail and the brush and the rag and the pad for her knees, a dirty red rubber pad. She starts to work on the floor. Rose sits on the kitchen table, the only place left to sit, swinging her legs. She can feel the cool oilcloth, because she is wearing shorts, last summer's tight faded shorts dug out of the summer-clothes bag. They smell a bit moldy from winter storage.

Flo crawls underneath, scrubbing with the brush, wiping with the rag. Her legs are long, white and muscular, marked all over with blue veins as if somebody had been drawing rivers on them with an indelible pencil. An abnormal energy, a violent disgust, is expressed in the chewing of the brush at the linoleum, the swish of the rag.

What do they have to say to each other? It doesn't really matter. Flo speaks of Rose's smart-aleck behavior, rudeness and sloppiness and conceit. Her willingness to make work for others, her lack of gratitude. She mentions Brian's innocence, Rose's corruption. Oh, don't you think you're somebody, says Flo, and a moment later, Who do you think you are? Rose contradicts and objects with such poisonous reasonableness and mildness, displays theatrical unconcern. Flo goes beyond her ordinary scorn and self-possession and becomes amazingly theatrical herself, saying it was for Rose that she sacrificed her life. She saw her father saddled with a baby daughter and she thought, what is that man going to do? So she married him, and here she is, on her knees.

At that moment the bell rings, to announce a customer in the store. Because the fight is on, Rose is not permitted to go into the store and wait on whoever it is. Flo gets up and throws off her apron, groaning—but not communicatively, it is not a groan whose exasperation Rose is allowed to share—and goes in and serves. Rose hears her using her normal voice.

"About time! Sure is!"

She comes back and ties on her apron and is ready to resume.

"You never have a thought for anybody but your ownself! You never have a thought for what I'm doing."

"I never asked you to do anything. I wish you never had. I would have been a lot better off."

Rose says this smiling directly at Flo, who has not yet gone down on her knees. Flo sees the smile, grabs the scrub rag that is hanging on the side of the pail, and throws it at her. It may be meant to hit her in the face but instead it falls against Rose's leg and she raises her foot and catches it, swinging it negligently against her ankle.

"All right," says Flo. "You've done it this time. All right."

Rose watches her go to the woodshed door, hears her tramp through the woodshed, pause in the doorway, where the screen door hasn't yet been hung, and the storm door is standing open, propped with a brick. She calls Rose's father. She calls him in a warning, summoning voice, as if against her will preparing him for bad news. He will know what this is about.

The kitchen floor has five or six different patterns of linoleum on it. Ends, which Flo got for nothing and ingeniously trimmed and fitted together, bordering them with tin strips and tacks. While Rose sits on the table waiting, she looks at the floor, at this satisfying arrangement of rectangles, triangles, some other shape whose name she is trying to remember. She hears Flo coming back through the woodshed, on the creaky plank walk laid over the dirt floor. She is loitering, waiting, too. She and Rose can carry this no further, by themselves.

Rose hears her father come in. She stiffens, a tremor runs through her legs, she feels them shiver on the oilcloth. Called away from some peaceful, absorbing task, away from the words running in his head, called out of himself, her father has to say something. He says, "Well? What's wrong?"

Now comes another voice of Flo's. Enriched, hurt, apologetic, it seems to have been manufactured on the spot. She is sorry to have called him from his work. Would never have done it, if Rose was not driving her to distraction. How to distraction? With her back talk and impudence and her terrible tongue. The things Rose has said to Flo are such that, if Flo had said them to her mother, she knows her father would have thrashed her into the ground.

Rose tries to butt in, to say this isn't true.

What isn't true?

Her father raises a hand, doesn't look at her, says, "Be quiet."

When she says it isn't true, Rose means that she herself didn't start this, only responded, that she was goaded by Flo, who is now, she believes, telling the grossest sort of lies, twisting everything to suit herself. Rose puts aside her other knowledge that whatever Flo has said or done, whatever she herself has said or done, does not really matter at all. It is the struggle itself that counts, and that can't be stopped, can never be stopped, short of where it has got to, now.

Flo's knees are dirty, in spite of the pad. The scrub rag is still hanging over Rose's foot.

Her father wipes his hands, listening to Flo. He takes his time. He is slow at getting into the spirit of things, tired in advance, maybe, on the verge of rejecting the role he has to play. He won't look at Rose, but at any sound or stirring from Rose, he holds up his hand.

"Well we don't need the public in on this, that's for sure," Flo says, and she goes to lock the door of the store, putting in the store window the sign that says BACK SOON, a sign Rose made for her with a great deal of fancy curving and shading of letters in black and red crayon. When she comes back she shuts the door to the store, then the door to the stairs, then the door to the woodshed.

Her shoes have left marks on the clean wet part of the floor.

"Oh, I don't know," she says now, in a voice worn down from its emotional peak. "I don't know what to do about her." She looks down and sees her dirty knees (following Rose's eyes) and rubs at them viciously with her bare hands, smearing the dirt around.

"She humiliates me," she says, straightening up. There it is, the explanation. "She humiliates me," she repeats with satisfaction. "She has no respect."

"I do not!"

"Quiet, you!" says her father.

"If I hadn't called your father you'd still be sitting there with that grin on your face! What other way is there to manage you?"

Rose detects in her father some objections to Flo's rhetoric, some embarrassment and reluctance. She is wrong, and ought to know she is wrong, in thinking that she can count on this. The fact that she knows about it, and he knows she knows, will not make things any better. He is beginning to warm up. He gives her a look. This look is at first cold and challenging. It informs her of his judgment, of the hopelessness of her position. Then it clears, it begins to fill up with something else, the way a spring fills up when you clear the leaves away. It fills with hatred and pleasure. Rose sees that and knows it. Is that just a description of anger, should she see his eyes filling up with anger? No. Hatred is right. Pleasure is right. His face loosens and changes and grows younger, and he holds up his hand this time to silence Flo.

"All right," he says, meaning that's enough, more than enough, this part is over, things can proceed. He starts to loosen his belt.

Flo has stopped anyway. She has the same difficulty Rose does, a difficulty in believing that what you know must happen really will happen, that there comes a time when you can't draw back.

"Oh, I don't know, don't be too hard on her." She is moving around nervously as if she has thoughts of opening some escape route. "Oh, you don't have to use the belt on her. Do you have to use the belt?"

He doesn't answer. The belt is coming off, not hastily. It is being grasped at the necessary point. *All right you.* He is coming over to Rose. He pushes her off the table. His face, like his voice, is quite out of character. He is like a bad actor, who turns a part grotesque. As if he must savor and insist on just what is shameful and terrible about this. That is not to say he is pretending, that he is acting, and does not mean it. He is acting, and he means it. Rose knows that, she knows everything about him.

She has since wondered about murders, and murderers. Does the thing have to be carried through, in the end, partly for the effect, to prove to the audience of one—who won't be able to report, only register, the lesson—that such a thing can happen, that there is nothing that can't happen, that the most dreadful antic is justified, feelings can be found to match it?

She tries again looking at the kitchen floor, that clever and comforting geometrical arrangement, instead of looking at him or his belt. How can this go on in front of such daily witnesses—the linoleum, the calendar with the mill and creek and autumn trees, the old accommodating pots and pans?

Hold out your hand!

Those things aren't going to help her, none of them can rescue her.

They turn bland and useless, even unfriendly. Pots can show malice, the patterns of linoleum can leer up at you, treachery is the other side of dailiness.

At the first, or maybe the second, crack of pain, she draws back. She will not accept it. She runs around the room, she tries to get to the doors. Her father blocks her off. Not an ounce of courage or of stoicism in her, it would seem. She runs, she screams, she implores. Her father is after her, cracking the belt at her when he can, then abandoning it and using his hands. Bang over the ear, then bang over the other ear. Back and forth, her head ringing. Bang in the face. Up against the wall and bang in the face again. He shakes her and hits her against the wall, he kicks her legs. She is incoherent, insane, shrieking. *Forgive me! Oh please, forgive me!*

Flo is shrieking too. *Stop, stop!*

Not yet. He throws Rose down. Or perhaps she throws herself down. He kicks her legs again. She has given up on words but is letting out a noise, the sort of noise that makes Flo cry, *Oh, what if people can hear her?* The very last-ditch willing sound of humiliation and defeat it is, for it seems Rose must play her part in this with the same grossness, the same exaggeration, that her father displays, playing his. She plays his victim with a self-indulgence that arouses, and maybe hopes to arouse, his final, sickened contempt.

They will give this anything that is necessary, it seems, they will go to any lengths.

Not quite. He has never managed really to injure her, though there are times, of course, when she prays that he will. He hits her with an open hand, there is some restraint in his kicks.

Now he stops, he is out of breath. He allows Flo to move in, he grabs Rose up and gives her a push in Flo's direction, making a sound of disgust. Flo retrieves her, opens the stair door, shoves her up the stairs.

"Go on up to your room now! Hurry!"

Rose goes up the stairs, stumbling, letting herself stumble, letting herself fall against the steps. She doesn't bang her door because a gesture like that could still bring him after her, and anyway, she is weak. She lies on the bed. She can hear through the stovepipe hole Flo snuffling and remonstrating, her father saying angrily that Flo should have kept quiet then, if she did not want Rose punished she should not have recommended it. Flo says she never recommended a hiding like that.

They argue back and forth on this. Flo's frightened voice is growing stronger, getting its confidence back. By stages, by arguing, they are being drawn back into themselves. Soon it's only Flo talking; he will not talk anymore. Rose has had to fight down her noisy sobbing, so as to listen to them, and when she loses interest in listening, and wants to sob some more, she finds she can't work herself up to it. She has passed into a state of calm, in which outrage is perceived as complete and final. In this state events and possibilities take on a lovely simplicity. Choices are mercifully clear. The words that come to mind are not the quibbling, seldom the conditional. Never is a word to which the right is suddenly established. She will never speak to them, she will never look at them with anything but loathing, she will never forgive them. She will punish them; she will finish them. Encased in these finalities, and in her bodily pain, she floats in curious comfort, beyond herself, beyond responsibility.

Suppose she dies now? Suppose she commits suicide? Suppose she runs away? Any of these things would be appropriate. It is only a matter of choosing, of figuring out the way. She floats in her pure superior state as if kindly drugged.

And just as there is a moment, when you are drugged, in which you feel perfectly safe, sure, unreachable, and then without warning and right next to it a moment in which you know the whole protection has fatally cracked, though it is still pretending to hold soundly together, so there is a moment now—the moment, in fact, when Rose hears Flo step on the stairs—that contains for her both present peace and freedom and a sure knowledge of the whole down-spiraling course of events from now on.

Flo comes into the room without knocking, but with a hesitation that shows it might have occurred to her. She brings a jar of cold cream. Rose is hanging on to advantage as long as she can, lying face down on the bed, refusing to acknowledge or answer.

"Oh come on," Flo says uneasily. "You aren't so bad off, are you? You put some of this on and you'll feel better."

She is bluffing. She doesn't know for sure what damage has been done. She has the lid off the cold cream. Rose can smell it. The intimate, babyish, humiliating smell. She won't allow it near her. But in order to avoid it, the big ready clot of it in Flo's hand, she has to move. She scuffles, resists, loses dignity, and lets Flo see there is not really much the matter.

"All right," Flo says. "You win. I'll leave it here and you can put it on when you like."

Later still a tray will appear. Flo will put it down without a word and go away. A large glass of chocolate milk on it, made with Vita-Malt from the store. Some rich streaks of Vita-Malt around the bottom of the glass. Little sandwiches, neat and appetizing. Canned salmon of the first quality and reddest color, plenty of mayonnaise. A couple of butter tarts from a bakery package, chocolate biscuits with a peppermint filling. Rose's favorites, in the sandwich, tart and cookie line. She will turn away, refuse to look, but left alone with these eatables will be miserably tempted, roused and troubled and drawn back from thoughts of suicide or flight by the smell of salmon, the anticipation of crisp chocolate, she will reach out a finger, just to run it around the edge of one of the sandwiches (crusts cut off!) to get the overflow, get a taste. Then she will decide to eat one, for strength to refuse the rest. One will not be noticed. Soon, in helpless corruption, she will eat them all. She will drink the chocolate milk, eat the tarts, eat the cookies. She will get the malty syrup out of the bottom of the glass with her finger, though she sniffles with shame. Too late.

Flo will come up and get the tray. She may say, "I see you got your appetite still," or, "Did you like the chocolate milk, was it enough syrup in it?" depending on how chastened she is feeling, herself. At any rate, all advantage will be lost. Rose will understand that life has started up again, that they will all sit around the table eating again, listening to the radio news. Tomorrow morning, maybe even tonight. Unseemly and unlikely as that may be. They will be embarrassed, but rather less than you might expect considering how they have behaved. They will feel a queer lassitude, a convalescent indolence, not far off satisfaction.

One night after a scene like this they were all in the kitchen. It must have been summer, or at least warm weather, because her father spoke of the old men who sat on the bench in front of the store.

"Do you know what they're talking about now?" he said, and nodded his head toward the store to show who he meant, though of course they were not there now, they went home at dark.

"Those old coots," said Flo. "What?"

There was about them both a geniality not exactly false but a bit more emphatic than was normal, without company.

Rose's father told them then that the old men had picked up the idea somewhere that what looked like a star in the western sky, the first star that came out after sunset, the evening star, was in reality an airship hovering over Bay City, Michigan, on the other side of Lake Huron. An American invention, sent up to rival the heavenly bodies. They were all in agreement about this, the idea was congenial to them. They believed it to be lit by ten thousand electric light bulbs. Her father had ruthlessly disagreed with them, pointing out that it was the planet Venus they saw, which had appeared in the sky long before the invention of an electric light bulb. They had never heard of the planet Venus.

"Ignoramuses," said Flo. At which Rose knew, and knew her father knew, that Flo had never heard of the planet Venus either. To distract them from this, or even apologize for it, Flo put down her teacup, stretched out with her head resting on the chair she had been sitting on and her feet on another chair (somehow she managed to tuck her dress modestly between her legs at the same time), and lay stiff as a board, so that Brian cried out in delight, "Do that! Do that!"

Flo was double-jointed and very strong. In moments of celebration or emergency she would do tricks.

They were silent while she turned herself around, not using her arms at all but just her strong legs and feet. Then they all cried out in triumph, though they had seen it before.

Just as Flo turned herself Rose got a picture in her mind of that airship, an elongated transparent bubble, with its strings of diamond lights, floating in the miraculous American sky.

"The planet Venus!" her father said, applauding Flo. "Ten thousand electric lights!"

There was a feeling of permission, relaxation, even a current of happiness, in the room.

Years later, many years later, on a Sunday morning, Rose turned on the radio. This was when she was living by herself in Toronto.

Well sir.

It was a different kind of place in our day. Yes it was.

It was all horses then. Horses and buggies. Buggy races up and down the main street on the Saturday nights.

"Just like the chariot races," says the announcer's, or interviewer's, smooth encouraging voice.

I never seen a one of them.

"No sir, that was the old Roman chariot races I was referring to. That was before your time."

Musta been before my time. I'm a hunerd and two years old.

"That's a wonderful age, sir."

It is so.

She left it on, as she went around the apartment kitchen, making coffee for herself. It seemed to her that this must be a staged interview, a scene from some play, and she wanted to find out what it was. The old man's voice was so vain and belligerent, the interviewer's quite hopeless and alarmed, under its practiced gentleness and ease. You were surely meant to see him holding the microphone up to some toothless, reckless, preening centenarian, wondering what in God's name he was doing here, and what would he say next?

"They must have been fairly dangerous."

What was dangerous?

"Those buggy races."

They was. Dangerous. Used to be the runaway horses. Used to be a-plenty of accidents. Fellows was dragged along on the gravel and cut their face open. Wouldna matter so much if they was dead. Heh.

Some of them horses was the high-steppers. Some, they had to have the mustard under their tail. Some wouldn step out for nothin. That's the thing it is with the horses. Some'll work and pull till they drop down dead and some wouldn pull your cock out of a pail of lard. Hehe.

It must be a real interview after all. Otherwise they wouldn't have put that in, wouldn't have risked it. It's all right if the old man says it. Local color. Anything rendered harmless and delightful by his hundred years.

Accidents all the time then. In the mill. Foundry. Wasn't the precautions.

"You didn't have so many strikes then, I don't suppose? You didn't have so many unions?"

Everybody taking it easy nowadays. We worked and we was glad to get it. Worked and was glad to get it.

"You didn't have television."

Didn't have no TV. Didn't have no radio. No picture show.

"You made your own entertainment."

That's the way we did.

"You had a lot of experiences young men growing up today will never have."

Experiences.

"Can you recall any of them for us?"

I eaten groundhog meat one time. One winter. You wouldna cared for it. Heh.

There was a pause, of appreciation, it would seem, then the announcer's voice saying that the foregoing had been an interview with Mr. Wilfred Nettleton of Hanratty, Ontario, made on his hundred and second birthday, two weeks before his death, last spring. A living link with our past. Mr. Nettleton had been interviewed in the Wawanash County Home for the Aged.

Hat Nettleton.

Horsewhipper into centenarian. Photographed on his birthday, fussed over by nurses, kissed no doubt by a girl reporter. Flash bulbs popping at him. Tape recorder drinking in the sound of his voice. Oldest resident. Oldest horsewhipper. Living link with our past.

Looking out from her kitchen window at the cold lake, Rose was longing to tell somebody. It was Flo who would enjoy hearing. She thought of her saying *Imagine!* in a way that meant she was having her worst suspicions gorgeously confirmed. But Flo was in the same place Hat Nettleton had died in, and there wasn't any way Rose could reach her. She had been there even when that interview was recorded, though she would not have heard it, would not have known about it. After Rose put her in the Home, a couple of years earlier, she had stopped talking. She had removed herself, and spent most of her time sitting in a corner of her crib, looking crafty and disagreeable, not answering anybody, though she occasionally showed her feelings by biting a nurse.

Privilege

Rose knew a lot of people who wished they had been born poor, and hadn't been. So she would queen it over them, offering various scandals and bits of squalor from her childhood. The Boys' Toilet and the Girls' Toilet. Old Mr. Burns in his Toilet. Shortie McGill and Franny McGill in the entrance to the Boys' Toilet. She did not deliberately repeat the toilet locale, and was a bit surprised at the way it kept cropping up. She knew that those little dark or painted shacks were supposed to be comical—always were, in country humor—but she saw them instead as scenes of marvelous shame and outrage.

The Girls' Toilet and the Boys' Toilet each had a protected entryway, which saved having a door. Snow blew in anyway through the cracks between the boards and the knotholes that were for spying. Snow piled up on the seat and on the floor. Many people, it seemed, declined to use the hole. In the heaped snow under a glaze of ice, where the snow had melted and frozen again, were turds copious or lonesome, preserved as if under glass, bright as mustard or grimy as charcoal, with every shading in between. Rose's stomach turned at the sight; despair got hold of her. She halted in the doorway, could not force herself, decided she could wait. Two or three times she wet on the way home, running from the school to the store, which was not very far. Flo was disgusted.

"Wee-pee, wee-pee," she sang out loud, mocking Rose. "Walking home and she had a wee-pee!"

Flo was also fairly pleased, because she liked to see people brought down to earth, Nature asserting itself; she was the sort of woman who will make public what she finds in the laundry bag. Rose was mortified, but didn't reveal the problem. Why not? She was probably afraid that Flo would show up at the school with a pail and shovel, cleaning up, and lambasting everybody into the bargain.

She believed the order of things at school to be unchangeable, the rules there different from any that Flo could understand, the savagery incalculable. Justice and cleanliness she saw now as innocent notions out of a primitive period of her life. She was building up the first store of things she could never tell.

She could never tell about Mr. Burns. Right after she started to school, and before she had any idea what she was going to see—or, indeed, of what there was to see—Rose was running along the school fence with some other girls, through the red dock and goldenrod, and crouching behind Mr. Burns's toilet, which backed on the schoolyard. Someone had reached through the fence and yanked the bottom boards off, so you could see in. Old Mr. Burns, half-blind, paunch, dirty, spirited, came down the backyard talking to himself, singing, swiping at the tall weeds with his cane. In the toilet, too, after some moments of strain and silence, his voice was heard.

> There is a green hill far away
> Outside a city wall
> Where the dear Lord was crucified
> Who died to save us all.

Mr. Burns's singing was not pious but hectoring, as if he longed, even now, for a fight. Religion, around here, came out mostly in fights. People were Catholics or fundamentalist Protestants, honor-bound to molest each other. Many of the Protestants had been—or their families had been—Anglicans, Presbyterians. But they had got too poor to show up at those churches, so had veered off to the Salvation Army, the Pentecostals. Others had been total heathens until they were saved. Some were heathens yet, but Protestant in fights. Flo said the Anglicans and the Presbyterians were snobs and the rest were Holy Rollers, while the Catholics would put up with any two-facedness or debauching, as long as they got your money for the Pope. So Rose did not have to go to any church at all.

All the little girls squatted to see, peered in at that part of Mr. Burns that sagged through the hole. For years Rose thought she had seen testicles but on reflection she believed it was only bum. Something like a cow's udder, which looked to have a prickly surface, like the piece of tongue before Flo boiled it. She wouldn't eat that tongue, and after she told him what it was Brian wouldn't eat it either, so Flo went into a temper and said they could live on boiled baloney.

The older girls didn't get down to look, but stood by, several making puking noises. Some of the little girls jumped up and joined them, eager to imitate, but Rose remained squatting, amazed and thoughtful. She would have liked to contemplate, but Mr. Burns removed himself, came out buttoning and singing. Girls sneaked along the fences to call to him.

"Mr. Burns! Good morning Mr. Burns! Mr. Burns-your-balls!"

He came roaring at the fence, chopping with his cane, as if they were chickens.

Younger and older, boys and girls and everybody—except the teacher, of course, who locked the door at recess and stayed in the school, like Rose holding off till she got home, risking accidents and enduring agonies—everybody gathered to look in the entryway of the Boys' Toilet when the word went round: Shortie McGill is fucking Franny McGill!

Brother and sister.

Relations performing.

That was Flo's word for it: *perform*. Back in the country, back on the hill farms she came from, Flo said that people had gone dotty, been known to eat boiled hay, and performed with their too-close relations. Before Rose understood what was meant she used to imagine some makeshift stage, some rickety old barn stage, where members of a family got up and gave silly songs and recitations. *What a performance!* Flo would say in disgust, blowing out smoke, referring not to any single act but to everything along that line, past and present and future, going on anywhere in the world. People's diversions, like their pretensions, could not stop astounding her.

Whose idea was this, for Franny and Shortie? Probably some of the big boys dared Shortie, or he bragged and they challenged him. One thing was certain: the idea could not be Franny's. She had to be caught for this, or trapped. You couldn't say caught, really, because she wouldn't run, wouldn't put that much faith in escaping. But she showed unwillingness, had to be dragged, then pushed down where they wanted her. Did she know what was coming? She would know at least that nothing other people devised for her ever turned out to be pleasant.

Franny McGill had been smashed against the wall, by her father, drunk, when she was a baby. So Flo said. Another story had Franny falling out of a cutter, drunk, kicked by a horse. At any rate, smashed. Her face had got the worst of it. Her nose was crooked, making every breath she took a long, dismal-sounding snuffle. Her teeth were badly bunched together, so that she could not close her mouth and never could contain her quantities of spit. She was white, bony, shuffling, fearful, like an old woman. Marooned in Grade Two or Three, she could read and write a little, was seldom called on to do so. She may not have been so stupid as everybody thought, but simply stunned, bewildered, by continual assault. And in spite of everything there was something hopeful about her. She would follow after anybody who did not immediately attack and insult her; she would offer bits of crayon, knots of chewed gum pried off seats and desks. It was necessary to fend her off firmly, and scowl warningly whenever she caught your eye.

Go away Franny. Go away or I'll punch you. I will. I really will.

The use Shortie was making of her, that others made, would continue. She would get pregnant, be taken away, come back and get pregnant again, be taken away, come back, get pregnant, be taken away again. There would be talk of getting her sterilized, getting the Lions Club to pay for it, there would be talk of shutting her up, when she died suddenly of pneumonia, solving the problem. Later on Rose would think of Franny when she came across the figure of an idiotic, saintly whore, in a book or a movie. Men who made books and movies seemed to have a fondness for this figure, though Rose noticed they would clean her up. They cheated, she thought, when they left out the breathing and the spit and the teeth; they were refusing to take into account the aphrodisiac prickles of disgust, in their hurry to reward themselves with the notion of a soothing blankness, undifferentiating welcome.

The welcome Franny gave Shortie was not so saintly, after all. She let out howls, made ripply, phlegmy, by her breathing problems. She kept jerking one leg. Either the shoe had come off, or she had not been wearing shoes to start with. There was her white leg and bare foot, with muddy toes—looking too normal, too vigorous and self-respecting, to belong to Franny McGill. That was all of her Rose could see. She was small, and had got shoved to the back of the crowd. Big boys were around them, hollering encouragement, big girls were hovering behind, giggling. Rose was interested but not alarmed. An act performed on Franny had no general significance, no bearing on what could happen to anyone else. It was only further abuse.

When Rose told people these things, in later years, they had considerable effect. She had to swear they were true, she was not exaggerating. And they were true, but the effect was off-balance. Her schooling seemed deplorable. It seemed she must have been miserable, and that was not so. She was learning. She learned how to manage in the big fights that tore up the school two or three times a year. Her inclination was to be neutral, and that was a bad mistake; it could bring both sides down on you. The thing to do was to ally yourself with people living near you, so you would not be in too much danger walking home. She was never sure what fights were about, and she did not have a good instinct for fighting, did not really understand the necessity. She would always be taken by surprise by a snowball, a stone, a shingle whacked down from behind. She knew she would never flourish, never get to any very secure position—if indeed there was such a thing—in the world of school. But she was not miserable, except in the matter of not being able to go to the toilet. Learning to survive, no matter with what cravenness and caution, what shocks and forebodings, is not the same as being miserable. It is too interesting.

She learned to fend off Franny. She learned never to go near the school basement which had all the windows broken and was black, dripping, like a cave; to avoid the dark place under the steps and the place between the woodpiles; not to attract in any way the attention of the big boys, who seemed like wild dogs to her, just as quick and strong, capricious, jubilant in attack.

A mistake she made early and would not have made later on was in telling Flo the truth instead of some lie when a big boy, one of the Morey boys, tripped and grabbed her as she was coming down the fire escape, tearing the sleeve of her raincoat out at the armhole. Flo came to the school to raise Cain (her stated intention) and heard witnesses swear Rose had torn it on a nail. The teacher was glum, would not declare herself, indicated Flo's visit was not welcome. Adults did not come to the school, in West Hanratty. Mothers were strongly partisan in fights, would hang over their gates, and yell; some would even rush out to tug hair and flail shingles, themselves. They would abuse the teacher behind her back and send their children off to school with instructions not to take any lip from her. But they would never have behaved as Flo did, never have set foot on school property, never have carried a complaint to that level. They would never have believed, as Flo seemed to believe (and here Rose saw her for the first time out of her depth, mistaken) that offenders would confess, or be handed over, that justice would take any form but a ripping and tearing of a Morey coat, in revenge, a secret mutilation in the cloakroom.

Flo said the teacher did not know her business.

But she did. She knew it very well. She locked the door at recess and let whatever was going to happen outside happen. She never tried to make the big boys come up from the basement or in from the fire escape. She made them chop kindling for the stove and fill the drinking pail; otherwise they were at liberty. They didn't mind the wood-chopping or pumping, though they liked to douse people with freezing water, and came near murder with the axe. They were just at school because there was no place else for them to be. They were old enough for work but there were no jobs for them. Older girls could get jobs, as maids at least; so they did not stay in school, unless they were planning to write the Entrance, go to high school, maybe someday get jobs in stores or banks. Some of them would do that. From places like West Hanratty girls move up more easily than boys.

The teacher had the big girls, excepting those in the Entrance Class, kept busy bossing the younger children, petting and slapping them, correcting spelling, and removing for their own use anything interesting in the way of pencil boxes, new crayons, Cracker Jack jewelry.

What went on in the cloakroom, what lunchpail-robbing or coat-slashing or pulling down pants there was, the teacher did not consider her affair.

She was not in any way enthusiastic, imaginative, sympathetic. She walked over the bridge every day from Hanratty, where she had a sick husband. She had come back to teaching in middle age. Probably this was the only job she could get. She had to keep at it, so she kept at it. She never put cutouts up on the windows or pasted gold stars in the workbooks. She never did drawings on the board with colored chalk. She had no gold stars, there was no colored chalk. She showed no love of anything she taught, or anybody. She must have wished, if she wished for anything, to be told one day she could go home, never see any of them, never open a spelling book, again.

But she did teach things. She must have taught something to the people who were going to write the Entrance, because some of them passed it. She must have made a stab at teaching everybody who came into that school to read and write and do simple arithmetic. The stair railings were knocked out, desks were wrenched loose from the floor, the stove smoked and the pipes were held together with wire, there were no library books or maps, and never enough chalk; even the yardstick was dirty and splintered at one end. Fights and sex and pilferage were the important things going on. Nevertheless. Facts and tables were presented. In the face of all that disruption, discomfort, impossibility, some thread of ordinary classroom routine was maintained; an offering. Some people learned to spell.

She took snuff. She was the only person Rose had ever seen do that. She would sprinkle a bit on the back of her hand and lift the hand to her face, give a delicate snort. Her head back, her throat exposed, she looked for a moment contemptuous, challenging. Otherwise she was not in the least eccentric. She was plump, gray, shabby.

Flo said she had probably fogged her brain with the snuff. It was like being a drug addict. Cigarettes only shot your nerves.

One thing in the school was captivating, lovely. Pictures of birds. Rose didn't know if the teacher had climbed up and nailed them above the blackboard, too high for easy desecration, if they were her first and last hopeful effort, or if they dated from some earlier, easier time in the school's history. Where had they come from, how had they arrived there, when nothing else did, in the way of decoration, illustration?

A red-headed woodpecker; an oriole; a blue jay; a Canada goose. The colors clear and long-lasting. Backgrounds of pure snow, of blossoming branches, of heady summer sky. In an ordinary classroom they would not have seemed so extraordinary. Here they were bright and eloquent, so much at variance with everything else that what they seemed to represent was not the birds themselves, not those skies and snows, but some other world of hardy innocence, bounteous information, privileged lightheartedness. No stealing from lunchpails there; no slashing coats; no pulling down pants and probing with painful sticks; no fucking; no Franny.

There were three big girls in the Entrance Class. One was named Donna; one was Cora; one was Bernice. Those three were the Entrance Class; there was nobody else. Three queens. But when you looked closer, a queen and two princesses. That was how Rose thought of them. They walked around the schoolyard arm-in-arm, or with their arms around each other's waists. Cora in the middle. She was the tallest. Donna and Bernice leaning against and leading up to her.

It was Cora Rose loved.

Cora lived with her grandparents. Her grandmother went across the bridge to Hanratty, to do cleaning and ironing. Her grandfather was the honey-dumper. That meant he went around cleaning out toilets. That was his job.

Before she had the money saved up to put in a real bathroom Flo had gotten a chemical toilet to put in a corner of the woodshed. A better arrangement than the outhouse, particularly in the wintertime. Cora's grandfather disapproved. He said to Flo, "Many has got these chemicals in and many has wished they never."

He pronounced the *ch* in *chemicals* like the *ch* in *church*.

Cora was illegitimate. Her mother worked somewhere, or was married. Perhaps she worked as a maid, and she was able to send castoffs. Cora had plenty of clothes. She came to school in fawn-colored satin, rippling over the hips; in royal-blue velvet with a rose of the same material flopping from one shoulder; in dull rose crepe loaded with fringe. These clothes were too old for her (Rose did not think so), but not too big. She was tall, solid, womanly. Sometimes she did her hair in a roll on top of her head, let it dip over one eye. She and Donna and Bernice often had their hair done in some grown-up style, their lips richly painted, their cheeks cakily powdered. Cora's features were heavy. She had an oily forehead, lazy brunette eyelids, the ripe and indolent self-satisfaction that would soon go hard and matronly. But she was splendid at the moment, walking in the schoolyard with her attendants (it was actually Donna with the pale oval face, the fair frizzy hair, who came closest to being pretty), arms linked, seriously talking. She did not waste any attention on the boys at school, none of those girls did. They were waiting, perhaps already acquiring, real boyfriends. Some boys called to them from the basement door, wistfully insulting, and Cora turned and yelled at them.

"Too old for the cradle, too young for the bed!"

Rose had no idea what that meant, but she was full of admiration for the way Cora turned on her hips, for the taunting, cruel, yet lazy and unperturbed sound of her voice, her glossy look. When she was by herself she would act that out, the whole scene, the boys calling, Rose being Cora. She would turn just as Cora did, on her imaginary tormentors, she would deal out just such provocative scorn.

Too old for the cradle, too young for the bed!

Rose walked around the yard behind the store, imagining the fleshy satin rippling over her own hips, her own hair rolled and dipping, her lips red. She wanted to grow up to be exactly like Cora. She did not want to wait to grow up. She wanted to be Cora, now.

Cora wore high heels to school. She was not light-footed. When she walked around the schoolroom in her rich dresses you could feel the room tremble, you could hear the windows rattle. You could smell her, too. Her talcum and cosmetics, her warm dark skin and hair.

The three of them sat at the top of the fire escape, in the first warm weather. They were putting on nail polish. It smelled like bananas, with a queer chemical edge. Rose had meant to go up the fire escape into the school, as she usually did, avoiding the everyday threat of the main entrance, but when she saw those girls she turned back, she did not dare expect them to shift over.

Cora called down.

"You can come up if you want to. Come on up!"

She was teasing her, encouraging her, as she would a puppy.

"How would you like to get your nails done?"

"Then they'll all want to," said the girl named Bernice, who as it turned out owned the nail polish.

"We won't do them," said Cora. "We'll just do her. What's your name? Rose? We'll just do Rose. Come on up, honey."

She made Rose hold out her hand. Rose saw with alarm how mottled it was, how grubby. And it was cold and trembly. A small, disgusting object. Rose would not have been surprised to see Cora drop it.

"Spread your fingers out. There. Relax. Lookit your hand shake! I'm not going to bite you. Am I? Hold steady like a good girl. You don't want me to go all crooked, do you?"

She dipped the brush in the bottle. The color was deep red, like raspberries. Rose loved the smell. Cora's own fingers were large, pink, steady, warm.

"Isn't that pretty? Won't your nails look pretty?"

She was doing it in the difficult, now-forgotten style of that time, leaving the half-moon and the whites of the nails bare.

"It's rosy to match your name. That's a pretty name, Rose. I like it. I like it better than Cora. I hate Cora. Your fingers are freezing for such a warm day. Aren't they freezing, compared to mine?"

She was flirting, indulging herself, as girls that age will do. They will try out charm on anything, on dogs or cats or their own faces in the mirror. Rose was too much overcome to enjoy herself, at the moment. She was weak and dazzled, terrified by such high favor.

From that day on, Rose was obsessed. She spent her time trying to walk and look like Cora, repeating every word she had ever heard her say. Trying to *be* her. There was a charm for Rose about every gesture Cora made, about the way she stuck a pencil into her thick, coarse hair, the way she groaned sometimes in school, with imperial boredom. The way she licked her finger and carefully smoothed her eyebrows. Rose licked her own finger and smoothed her own eyebrows, longing for them to be dark, instead of sunbleached and nearly invisible.

Imitation was not enough. Rose went further. She imagined that she would be sick and Cora would somehow be called to look after her. Nighttime cuddles, strokings, rockings. She made up stories of danger and rescue, accidents and gratitude. Sometimes she rescued Cora, sometimes Cora rescued Rose. Then all was warmth, indulgence, revelations.

That's a pretty name.

Come on up, honey.

The opening, the increase, the flow, of love. Sexual love, not sure yet exactly what it needed to concentrate on. It must be there from the start, like the hard white honey in the pail, waiting to melt and flow. There was some sharpness lacking, some urgency missing; there was the incidental differences in the sex of the person chosen; otherwise it was the same thing, the same thing that has overtaken Rose since. The high tide; the indelible folly; the flash flood.

When things were flowering—lilacs, apple trees, hawthorns along the road—they had the game of funerals, organized by the older girls. The person who was supposed to be dead—a girl, because only girls played this game—lay stretched out at the top of the fire escape. The rest filed up slowly, singing some hymn, and cast down their armloads of flowers. They bent over pretending to sob (some really managed it) and took the last look. That was all there was to it. Everybody was supposed to get a chance to be dead but it didn't work out that way. After the big girls had each had their turn they couldn't be bothered playing subordinate roles in the funerals of the younger ones. Those left to carry on soon realized that the game had lost all its importance, its glamor, and they drifted away, leaving only a stubborn ragtag to finish things off. Rose was one of those left. She held out in hopes that Cora might walk up the fire escape in her procession, but Cora ignored it.

The person playing dead got to choose what the processional hymn was. Cora had chosen "How beautiful Heaven must be." She lay heaped with flowers, mostly lilacs, and wore her rose crepe dress. Also some beads, a brooch that said her name in green sequins, heavy face powder. Powder was trembling in the soft hairs at the corners of her mouth. Her eyelashes fluttered. Her expression was concentrated, frowning, sternly dead. Sadly singing, laying down lilacs, Rose was close enough to commit some act of worship, but could not find any. She could only pile up details to be thought over later. The color of Cora's hair. The under-strands shone where it was pulled up over her ears. A lighter caramel, warmer, than the hair on top. Her arms were bare, dusky, flattened out, the heavy arms of a woman, fringe lying on them. What was her real smell? What was the statement, frowning and complacent, of her plucked eyebrows? Rose would strain over these things afterward, when she was alone, strain to remember them, know them, get them for good. What was the use of that? When she thought of Cora she had the sense of a glowing dark spot, a melting center, a smell and taste of burnt chocolate, that she could never get at.

What can be done about love, when it gets to this point, of such impotence and hopelessness and crazy concentration? Something will have to whack it.

She made a bad mistake soon. She stole some candy from Flo's store, to give to Cora. An idiotic, inadequate thing to do, a childish thing, as she knew at the time. The mistake was not just in the stealing, though that was stupid, and not easy. Flo kept the candy up behind the counter, on a slanted shelf, in open boxes, out of reach but not out of sight of children. Rose had to watch her chance, then climb up on the stool and fill a bag with whatever she could grab—gum drops, jelly beans, licorice allsorts, maple buds, chicken bones. She didn't eat any of it herself. She had to get the bag to school, which she did by carrying it under her skirt, the top of it tucked into the elastic top of her underpants. Her arm was pressed tightly against her waist to hold everything in place. Flo said, "What's the matter, have you got a stomachache?" but luckily was too busy to investigate.

Rose hid the bag in her desk and waited for an opportunity, which didn't crop up as expected.

Even if she had bought the candy, obtained it legitimately, the whole thing would have been a mistake. It would have been all right at the beginning, but not now. By now she required too much, in the way of gratitude, recognition, but was not in the state to accept anything. Her heart pounded, her mouth filled with the strange coppery taste of longing and despair, if Cora even happened to walk past her desk with her heavy, important tread, in her cloud of skin-heated perfumes. No gesture could match what Rose felt, no satisfaction was possible, and she knew that what she was doing was clownish, unlucky.

She could not bring herself to offer it, there was never a right time, so after a few days she decided to leave the bag in Cora's desk. Even that was difficult. She had to pretend she had forgotten something, after four, run back into the school, with the knowledge that she would have to run out again later, alone, past the big boys at the basement door.

The teacher was there, putting on her hat. Every day for that walk across the bridge she put on her old green hat with a bit of feather stuck in it. Cora's friend Donna was wiping off the boards. Rose tried to stuff the bag into Cora's desk. Something fell out. The teacher didn't bother, but Donna turned and yelled at her, "Hey, what are you doing in Cora's desk?"

Rose dropped the bag on the seat and ran out.

The thing she hadn't foreseen at all was that Cora would come to Flo's store and turn the candy in. But that was what Cora did. She did not do it to make trouble for Rose but simply to enjoy herself. She enjoyed her importance and respectability and the pleasure of grown-up exchange.

"I don't know what she wanted to give it to me for," she said, or Flo said she said. Flo's imitation was off, for once; it did not sound to Rose at all like Cora's voice. Flo made her sound mincing and whining.

"I-thought-I-better-come-and-tell-you!"

The candy was in no condition for eating, anyway. It was all squeezed and melted together, so that Flo had to throw it out.

Flo was dumbfounded. She said so. Not at the stealing. She was naturally against stealing but she seemed to understand that in this case it was the secondary evil, it was less important.

"What were you doing with it? Giving it to her? What were you giving it to her for? Are you in love with her or something?"

She meant that as an insult and a joke. Rose answered no, because she associated love with movie endings, kissing, and getting married. Her feelings were at the moment shocked and exposed, and already, though she didn't know it, starting to wither and curl up at the edges. Flo was a drying blast.

"You are so," said Flo. "You make me sick."

It wasn't future homosexuality Flo was talking about. If she had known about that, or thought of it, it would have seemed to her even more of a joke, even more outlandish, more incomprehensible, than the regular carrying-on. It was love she sickened at. It was the enslavement, the self-abasement, the self-deception. That struck her. She saw the danger, all right; she read the flaw. Headlong hopefulness, readiness, need.

"What is so wonderful about her?" asked Flo, and immediately answered herself. "Nothing. She is a far cry from good-looking. She is going to turn out a monster of fat. I can see the signs. She is going to have a mustache, too. She has one already. Where does she get her clothes from? I guess she thinks they suit her."

Rose did not reply to this and Flo said further that Cora had no father, you might wonder what her mother worked at, and who was her grandfather? The honey-dumper!

Flo went back to the subject of Cora, now and then, for years.

"There goes your idol!" she would say, seeing Cora go by the store after she had started to high school.

Rose pretended to have no recollection.

"You know her!" Flo kept it up. "You tried to give her candy! You stole that candy for her! Didn't I have a laugh."

Rose's pretense was not altogether a lie. She remembered the facts, but not the feelings. Cora turned into a big dark sulky-looking girl with round shoulders, carrying her high school books. The books were no help to her, she failed at high school. She wore ordinary blouses and a navy blue skirt, which did make her look fat. Perhaps her personality could not survive the loss of her elegant dresses. She went away, she got a war job. She joined the Air Force, and appeared home on leave, bunched into their dreadful uniform. She married an airman.

Rose was not much bothered by this loss, this transformation. Life was altogether a series of surprising developments, as far as she could learn. She only thought how out-of-date Flo was, as she went on recalling the story and making Cora sound worse and worse—swarthy, hairy, swaggering, fat. So long after, and so uselessly, Rose saw Flo trying to warn and alter her.

The school changed with the war. It dwindled, lost all its evil energy, its anarchic spirit, its style. The fierce boys went into the Army. West Hanratty changed too. People moved away to take war jobs and even those who stayed behind were working, being better paid than they had ever dreamed. Respectability took hold, in all but the stubbornest cases. Roofs got shingled all over instead of in patches. Houses were painted, or covered with imitation brick. Refrigerators were bought and bragged about. When Rose thought of West Hanratty during the war years, and during the years before, the two times were so separate it was as if an entirely different lighting had been used, or as if it was all on film and the film had been printed in a different way, so that on the one hand things looked clean-edged and decent and limited and ordinary, and on the other, dark, grainy, jumbled, and disturbing.

The school itself got fixed up. Windows replaced, desks screwed down, dirty words hidden under splashes of dull red paint. The Boys' Toilet and the Girls' Toilet were knocked down and the pits filled in. The Government and the School Board saw fit to put flush toilets in the cleaned-up basement.

Everybody was moving in that direction. Mr. Burns died in the summertime and the people who bought his place put in a bathroom. They also put up a high fence of chicken wire, so that nobody from the schoolyard could reach over and get their lilacs. Flo had put in a bathroom too by this time. She said they might as well have the works, it was wartime prosperity.

Cora's grandfather had to retire, and there never was another honey-dumper.

Half a Grapefruit

Rose wrote the Entrance, she went across the bridge, she went to high school.

There were four large clean windows along the wall. There were new fluorescent lights. The class was Health and Guidance, a new idea. Boys and girls mixed until after Christmas, when they got on to Family Life. The teacher was young and optimistic. She wore a dashing red suit that flared out over the hips. She went up and down, up and down the rows, making everybody say what they had for breakfast, to see if they were keeping Canada's Food Rules.

Differences soon became evident, between town and country.

"Fried potatoes."

"Bread and corn syrup."

"Tea and porridge."

"Tea and bread."

"Tea and fried eggs and cottage roll."

"Raisin pie."

There was some laughing, the teacher making ineffectual scolding faces. She was getting to the town side of the room. A rough sort of segregation was maintained, voluntarily, in the classroom. Over here people claimed to have eaten toast and marmalade, bacon and eggs, Corn Flakes, even waffles and syrup. Orange juice, said a few.

Rose had stuck herself on to the back of a town row. West Hanratty was not represented, except by her. She was wanting badly to align herself with towners, against her place of origin, to attach herself to those waffle-eating coffee-drinking aloof and knowledgeable possessors of breakfast nooks.

"Half a grapefruit," she said boldly. Nobody else had thought of it.

As a matter of fact Flo would have thought eating grapefruit for breakfast as bad as drinking champagne. They didn't even sell grapefruit in the store. They didn't go in much for fresh fruit. A few spotty bananas, small unpromising oranges. Flo believed, as many country people did, that anything not well-cooked was bad for the stomach. For breakfast they too had tea and porridge. Puffed Rice in the summertime. The first morning the Puffed Rice, light as pollen, came spilling into the bowl, was as festive, as encouraging a time as the first day walking on the hard road without rubbers or the first day the door could be left open in the lovely, brief time between frost and flies.

Rose was pleased with herself for thinking of the grapefruit and with the way she had said it, in so bold, yet so natural, a voice. Her voice could go dry altogether in school, her heart could roll itself up into a thumping ball and lodge in her throat, sweat could plaster her blouse to her arms, in spite of Mum. Her nerves were calamitous.

She was walking home across the bridge a few days later, and she heard someone calling. Not her name but she knew it was meant for her, so she softened her steps on the boards, and listened. The voices were underneath her, it seemed, though she could look down through the cracks and see nothing but fast-running water. Somebody must be hidden down by the pilings. The voices were wistful, so delicately disguised she could not tell if they were boys' or girls'.

"Half-a-grapefruit!"

She would hear that called, now and again, for years, called out from an alley or a dark window. She would never let on she heard, but would soon have to touch her face, wipe the moisture away from her upper lip. We sweat for our pretensions.

It could have been worse. Disgrace was the easiest thing to come by. High school life was hazardous, in that harsh clean light, and nothing was ever forgotten. Rose could have been the girl who lost the Kotex. That was probably a country girl, carrying the Kotex in her pocket or in the back of her notebook, for use later in the day. Anybody who lived at a distance might have done that. Rose herself had done it. There was a Kotex dispenser in the girls' washroom but it was always empty, would swallow your dimes but disgorge nothing in return. There was the famous pact made by two country girls to seek out the janitor at lunchtime, ask him to fill it. No use.

"Which one of you is the one that needs it?" he said. They fled. They said his room under the stairs had an old grimy couch in it, and a cat's skeleton. They swore to it.

That Kotex must have fallen on the floor, maybe in the cloakroom, then been picked up and smuggled somehow into the trophy case in the main hall. There it came to public notice. Folding and carrying had spoiled its fresh look, rubbed its surface, so that it was possible to imagine it had been warmed against the body. A great scandal. In morning assembly, the Principal made reference to a disgusting object. He vowed to discover, expose, flog and expel the culprit who had put it on view. Every girl in the school was denying knowledge of it. Theories abounded. Rose was afraid that she might be a leading candidate for ownership, so was relieved when responsibility was fixed on a big sullen country girl named Muriel Mason, who wore slub rayon housedresses to school, and had B.O.

"You got the rag on today, Muriel?" boys would say to her now, would call after her.

"If I was Muriel Mason I would want to kill myself," Rose heard a senior girl say to another on the stairs. "I *would* kill myself." She spoke not pityingly but impatiently.

Every day when Rose got home she would tell Flo about what went on in school. Flo enjoyed the episode of the Kotex, would ask about fresh developments. Half-a-grapefruit she never got to hear about. Rose would not have told her anything in which she did not play a superior, an onlooker's part. Pitfalls were for others, Flo and Rose agreed. The change in Rose, once she left the scene, crossed the bridge, changed herself into chronicler, was remarkable. No nerves anymore. A loud skeptical voice, some hip-swinging in a red and yellow plaid skirt, more than a hint of swaggering.

Flo and Rose had switched roles. Now Rose was the one bringing stories home, Flo was the one who knew the names of the characters and was waiting to hear.

Horse Nicholson, Del Fairbridge, Runt Chesterton. Florence Dodie, Shirley Pickering, Ruby Carruthers. Flo waited daily for news of them. She called them Jokers.

"Well, what did those jokers get up to today?"

They would sit in the kitchen, the door wide open to the store in case any customers came in, and to the stairs in case her father called. He was in bed. Flo made coffee or she told Rose to get a couple of Cokes out of the cooler.

This is the sort of story Rose brought home:

Ruby Carruthers was a slutty sort of girl, a redhead with a bad squint. (One of the great differences between then and now, at least in the country, and places like West Hanratty, was that squints and wall-eyes were let alone, teeth overlapped or protruded any way they liked.) Ruby Carruthers worked for the Bryants, the hardware people; she did housework for her board and stayed in the house when they went away, as they often did, to the horse races or the hockey games or to Florida. One time when she was there alone three boys went over to see her. Del Fairbridge, Horse Nicholson, Runt Chesterton.

"To see what they could get," Flo put in. She looked at the ceiling and told Rose to keep her voice down. Her father would not tolerate this sort of story.

Del Fairbridge was a good-looking boy, conceited, and not very clever. He said he would go into the house and persuade Ruby to do it with him, and if he could get her to do it with all three of them, he would. What he didn't know was that Horse Nicholson had already arranged with Ruby to meet him under the veranda.

"Spiders in there, likely," said Flo. "I guess they don't care."

While Del was wandering around the dark house looking for her, Ruby was under the veranda with Horse, and Runt who was in on the whole plan was sitting on the veranda steps keeping watch, no doubt listening attentively to the bumping and the breathing.

Presently Horse crawled out and said he was going into the house to find Del, not to enlighten him but to see how the joke was working, this being the most important part of the proceedings, as far as Horse was concerned. He found Del eating marshmallows in the pantry and saying Ruby Carruthers wasn't fit to piss on, he could do better any day, and he was going home.

Meanwhile Runt had crawled under the veranda and got to work on Ruby.

"Jesus Murphy!" said Flo.

Then Horse came out of the house and Runt and Ruby could hear him overhead, walking on the veranda. Said Ruby, who is that? And Runt said, oh, that's only Horse Nicholson. *Then who the hell are you?* said Ruby.

Jesus Murphy!

Rose did not bother with the rest of the story, which was that Ruby got into a bad mood, sat on the veranda steps with the dirt from underneath all over her clothes and in her hair, refused to smoke a cigarette or share a package of cupcakes (now probably rather squashed) that Runt had swiped from the grocery store where he worked after school. They teased her to tell them what was the matter and at last she said, "I think I got a right to know who I'm doing it with."

"She'll get what she deserves," said Flo philosophically. Other people thought so too. It was the fashion, if you picked up any of Ruby's things, by mistake, particularly her gym suit or running shoes, to go and wash your hands, so you wouldn't risk getting V.D.

Upstairs Rose's father was having a coughing fit. These fits were desperate, but they had become used to them. Flo got up and went to the bottom of the stairs. She listened there until the fit was over.

"That medicine doesn't help him one iota," she said. "That doctor couldn't put a Band-Aid on straight." To the end, she blamed all Rose's father's troubles on medicines, doctors.

"If you ever got up to any of that with a boy it would be the end of you," she said. "I mean it."

Rose flushed with rage and said she would die first.

"I hope so," Flo said.

Here is the sort of story Flo told Rose:

When her mother died, Flo was twelve, and her father gave her away. He gave her to a well-to-do farming family who were to work her for her board and send her to school. But most of the time they did not send her. There was too much work to be done. They were hard people.

"If you were picking apples and there was one left on the tree you would have to go back and pick over every tree in the entire orchard. The same when you were out picking up stones in the field. Leave one and you had to do the whole field again."

The wife was the sister of a bishop. She was always careful of her skin, rubbing it with Hinds Honey and Almond. She took a high tone with everybody and was sarcastic and believed that she had married down.

"But she was good-looking," said Flo, "and she gave me one thing. It was a long pair of satin gloves, they were a light brown color. Fawn. They were lovely. I never meant to lose them but I did."

Flo had to take the men's dinner to them in the far field. The husband opened it up and said, "Why is there no pie in this dinner?"

"If you want any pie you can make it yourself," said Flo, in the exact words and tone of her mistress when they were packing the dinner. It was not surprising that she could imitate that woman so well; she was always doing it, even practicing at the mirror. It *was* surprising she let it out then.

The husband was amazed, but recognized the imitation. He marched Flo back to the house and demanded of his wife if that was what she had said. He was a big man, and very bad-tempered. No, it is not true, said the bishop's sister, that girl is nothing but a trouble-maker and a liar. She faced him down, and when she got Flo alone she hit her such a clout that Flo was knocked across the room into a cupboard. Her scalp was cut. It healed in time without stitches (the bishop's sister didn't get the doctor, she didn't want talk), and Flo had the scar still.

She never went back to school after that.

Just before she was fourteen she ran away. She lied about her age and got a job in the glove factory, in Hanratty. But the bishop's sister found out where she was, and every once in a while would come to see her. We forgive you, Flo. You ran away and left us but we still think of you as our Flo and our friend. You are welcome to come out and spend a day with us. Wouldn't you like a day in the country? It's not very healthy in the glove factory, for a young person. You need the air. Why don't you come and see us? Why don't you come today?

And every time Flo accepted this invitation it would turn out that there was a big fruit preserving or chili sauce making in progress, or they were wallpapering or spring-cleaning, or the threshers were coming. All she ever got to see of the country was where she threw the dishwater over the fence. She never could understand why she went or why she stayed. It was a long way, to turn around and walk back to town. And they were such a helpless outfit on their own. The bishop's sister put her preserving jars away dirty. When you brought them up from the cellar there would be bits of mold growing in them, clots of fuzzy rotten fruit on the bottom. How could you help but be sorry for people like that?

When the bishop's sister was in the hospital, dying, it happened that Flo was in there too. She was in for her gall bladder operation, which Rose could just remember. The bishop's sister heard that Flo was there and wanted to see her. So Flo let herself be hoisted into a wheelchair and wheeled down the hall, and as soon as she laid eyes on the woman in the bed—the tall, smooth-skinned woman all bony and spotted now, drugged and cancerous—she began an overwhelming nosebleed, the first and last she ever suffered in her life. The red blood was whipping out of her, she said, like streamers.

She had the nurses running for help up and down the hall. It seemed as if nothing could stop it. When she lifted her head it shot right on the sick woman's bed, when she lowered her head it streamed down on the floor. They had to put her in ice packs, finally. She never got to say good-bye to the woman in the bed.

"I never did say good-bye to her."

"Would you want to?"

"Well yes," said Flo. "Oh yes. I would."

Rose brought a pile of books home every night. Latin, Algebra, Ancient and Medieval History, French, Geography. *The Merchant of Venice, A Tale of Two Cities, Shorter Poems, Macbeth.* Flo expressed hostility to them as she did toward all books. The hostility seemed to increase with a book's weight and size, the darkness and gloominess of its binding and the length and difficulty of the words in its title. *Shorter Poems* enraged her, because she opened it and found a poem that was five pages long.

She made rubble out of the titles. Rose believed she deliberately mispronounced. Ode came out Odd and Ulysses had a long shh in it, as if the hero was drunk.

Rose's father had to come downstairs to go to the bathroom. He hung on to the banister and moved slowly but without halting. He wore a brown wool bathrobe with a tasseled tie. Rose avoided looking at his face. This was not particularly because of the alterations his sickness might have made, but because of the bad opinion of herself she was afraid she would find written there. It was for him she brought the books, no doubt about it, to show off to him. And he did look at them, he could not walk past any book in the world without picking it up and looking at its title. But all he said was, "Look out you don't get too smart for your own good."

Rose believed he said that to please Flo, in case she might be listening. She was in the store at the time. But Rose imagined that no matter where Flo was, he would speak as if she might be listening. He was anxious to please Flo, to anticipate her objections. He had made a decision, it seemed. Safety lay with Flo.

Rose never answered him back. When he spoke she automatically bowed her head, tightened her lips in an expression that was secretive, but carefully not disrespectful. She was circumspect. But all her need for flaunting, her high hopes for herself, her gaudy ambitions, were not hidden from him. He knew them all, and Rose was ashamed, just to be in the same room with him. She felt that she disgraced him, had disgraced him somehow from the time she was born, and would disgrace him still more thoroughly in the future. But she was not repenting. She knew her own stubbornness; she did not mean to change.

Flo was his idea of what a woman ought to be. Rose knew that, and indeed he often said it. A woman ought to be energetic, practical, clever at making and saving; she ought to be shrewd, good at bargaining and bossing and seeing through people's pretensions. At the same time she should be naive intellectually, childlike, contemptuous of maps and long words and anything in books, full of charming jumbled notions, superstitions, traditional beliefs.

"Women's minds are different," he said to Rose during one of the calm, even friendly periods, when she was a bit younger. Perhaps he forgot that Rose was, or would be, a woman herself. "They believe what they have to believe. You can't follow their thought." He was saying this in connection with a belief of Flo's, that wearing rubbers in the house would make you go blind. "But they can manage life some ways, that's their talent, it's not in their heads, there's something they are smarter at than a man."

So part of Rose's disgrace was that she was female but mistakenly so, would not turn out to be the right kind of woman. But there was more to it. The real problem was that she combined and carried on what he must have thought of as the worst qualities in himself. All the things he had beaten down, successfully submerged, in himself, had surfaced again in her, and she was showing no will to combat them. She mooned and daydreamed, she was vain and eager to show off; her whole life was in her head. She had not inherited the thing he took pride in, and counted on—his skill with his hands, his thoroughness and conscientiousness at any work; in fact she was unusually clumsy, slapdash, ready to cut corners. The sight of her slopping around with her hands in the dishpan, her thoughts a thousand miles away, her rump already bigger than Flo's, her hair wild and bushy; the sight of the large and indolent and self-absorbed fact of her, seemed to fill him with irritation, with melancholy, almost with disgust.

All of which Rose knew. Until he had passed through the room she was holding herself still, she was looking at herself through his eyes. She too could hate the space she occupied. But the minute he was gone she recovered. She went back into her thoughts or to the mirror, where she was often busy these days, piling all her hair up on top of her head, turning part way to see the line of her bust, or pulling the skin to see how she would look with a slant, a very slight, provocative slant, to her eyes.

She knew perfectly well, too, that he had another set of feelings about her. She knew he felt pride in her as well as this nearly uncontrollable irritation and apprehension; the truth was, the final truth was, that he would not have her otherwise and willed her as she was. Or one part of him did. Naturally he had to keep denying this. Out of humility, he had to, and perversity. Perverse humility. And he had to seem to be in sufficient agreement with Flo.

Rose did not really think this through, or want to. She was as uneasy as he was, about the way their chords struck together.

When Rose came home from school Flo said to her, "Well, it's a good thing you got here. You have to stay in the store."

Her father was going to London, to the Veterans' Hospital.

"Why?"

"Don't ask me. The doctor said."

"Is he worse?"

"*I* don't know. *I* don't know anything. That do-nothing doctor doesn't think so. He came this morning and looked him over and he says he's going. We're lucky, we got Billy Pope to run him down."

Billy Pope was a cousin of Flo's who worked in the butcher shop. He used actually to live at the slaughterhouse, in two rooms with cement floors, smelling naturally of tripe and entrails and live pig. But he must have had a home-loving nature; he grew geraniums in old tobacco cans, on the thick cement windowsills. Now he had the little apartment over the shop, and had saved his money and bought a car, an Oldsmobile. This was shortly after the war, when new cars made a special sensation. When he came to visit he kept wandering to the window and taking a look at it, saying something to call attention, such as, "She's light on the hay but you don't get the fertilizer out of her."

Flo was proud of him and the car.

"See, Billy Pope's got a big back seat, if your father needs to lay down."

"Flo!"

Rose's father was calling her. When he was in bed at first he very seldom called her, and then discreetly, apologetically even. But he had got past that, called her often, made up reasons, she said, to get her upstairs.

"How does he think he'll get along without me down there?" she said. "He can't let me alone five minutes." She seemed proud of this, although often she would make him wait; sometimes she would go to the bottom of the stairs and force him to call down further details about why he needed her. She told people in the store that he wouldn't let her alone for five minutes, and how she had to change his sheets twice a day. That was true. His sheets became soaked with sweat. Late at night she or Rose, or both of them, would be out at the washing machine in the woodshed. Sometimes, Rose saw, her father's underwear was stained. She would not want to look, but Flo held it up, waved it almost under Rose's nose, cried out, "Lookit that again!" and made clucking noises that were a burlesque of disapproval.

Rose hated her at these times, hated her father as well; his sickness; the poverty or frugality that made it unthinkable for them to send things to the laundry; the way there was not a thing in their lives they were protected from. Flo was there to see to that.

Rose stayed in the store. No one came in. It was a gritty, windy day, past the usual time for snow, though there hadn't been any. She could hear Flo moving around upstairs, scolding and encouraging, getting her father dressed, probably, packing his suitcase, looking for things. Rose had her schoolbooks on the counter and to shut out the household noises she was reading a story in her English book. It was a story by Katherine Mansfield, called "The Garden Party." There were poor people in that story. They lived along the lane at the bottom of the garden. They were viewed with compassion. All very well. But Rose was angry in a way that the story did not mean her to be. She could not really understand what she was angry about, but it had something to do with the fact that she was sure Katherine Mansfield was never obliged to look at stained underwear; her relatives might be cruel and frivolous but their accents would be agreeable; her compassion was floating on clouds of good fortune, deplored by herself, no doubt, but *despised* by Rose. Rose was getting to be a prig about poverty, and would stay that way for a long time.

She heard Billy Pope come into the kitchen and shout out cheerfully, "Well, I guess yez wondered where I was."

Katherine Mansfield had no relatives who said *yez*.

Rose had finished the story. She picked up *Macbeth*. She had memorized some speeches from it. She memorized things from Shakespeare, and poems, other than the things they had to memorize for school. She didn't imagine herself as an actress, playing Lady Macbeth on a stage, when she said them. She imagined herself *being* her, being Lady Macbeth.

"I come on foot," Billy Pope was shouting up the stairs. "I had to take her in." He assumed everyone would know he meant the car. "I don't know what it is. I can't idle her, she stalls on me. I didn't want to go down to the city with anything running not right. Rose home?"

Billy Pope had been fond of Rose ever since she was a little girl. He used to give her a dime, and say, "Save up and buy yourself some corsets." That was when she was flat and thin. His joke.

He came into the store.

"Well Rose, you bein a good girl?"

She barely spoke to him.

"You goin at your schoolbooks? You want to be a schoolteacher?"

"I might." She had no intention of being a schoolteacher. But it was surprising how people would let you alone, once you admitted to that ambition.

"This is a sad day for you folks here," said Billy Pope in a lower voice.

Rose lifted her head and looked at him coldly.

"I mean, your Dad goin down to the hospital. They'll fix him up, though. They got all the equipment down there. They got the good doctors."

"I doubt it," Rose said. She hated that too, the way people hinted at things and then withdrew, that slyness. Death and sex were what they did that about.

"They'll fix him and get him back by spring."

"Not if he has lung cancer," Rose said firmly. She had never said that before and certainly Flo had not said it.

Billy Pope looked as miserable and ashamed for her as if she had said something very dirty.

"Now that isn't no way for you to talk. You don't talk that way. He's going to be coming downstairs and he could of heard you."

There is no denying the situation gave Rose pleasure, at times. A severe pleasure, when she was not too mixed up in it, washing the sheets or listening to a coughing fit. She dramatized her own part in it, saw herself clear-eyed and unsurprised, refusing all deceptions, young in years but old in bitter experience of life. In such spirit she had said *lung cancer*.

Billy Pope phoned the garage. It turned out that the car would not be fixed until suppertime. Rather than set out then, Billy Pope would stay overnight, sleeping on the kitchen couch. He and Rose's father would go down to the hospital in the morning.

"There don't need to be any great hurry, I'm not going to jump for *him*," said Flo, meaning the doctor. She had come into the store to get a can of salmon, to make a loaf. Although she was not going anywhere and had not planned to, she had put on stockings, and a clean blouse and skirt.

She and Billy Pope kept up a loud conversation in the kitchen while she got supper. Rose sat on the high stool and recited in her head, looking out the front window at West Hanratty, the dust scudding along the street, the dry puddle holes.

> Come to my woman's breasts,
> And take my milk for gall, you murdering ministers!

A jolt it would give them, if she yelled that into the kitchen.

At six o'clock she locked the store. When she went into the kitchen she was surprised to see her father there. She hadn't heard him. He hadn't been either talking or coughing. He was dressed in his good suit, which was an unusual color—a dark oily sort of green. Perhaps it had been cheap.

"Look at him all dressed up," Flo said. "He thinks he looks smart. He's so pleased with himself he wouldn't go back to bed."

Rose's father smiled unnaturally, obediently.

"How do you feel now?" Flo said.

"I feel all right."

"You haven't had a coughing spell, anyway."

Her father's face was newly shaved, smooth and delicate, like the animals they had once carved at school out of yellow laundry soap.

"Maybe I ought to get up and stay up."

"That's the ticket," Billy Pope said boisterously. "No more laziness. Get up and stay up. Get back to work."

There was a bottle of whiskey on the table. Billy Pope had brought it. The men drank it out of little glasses that had once held cream cheese. They topped it up with half an inch or so of water.

Brian, Rose's half brother, had come in from playing somewhere; noisy, muddy, with the cold smell of outdoors around him.

Just as he came in Rose said, "Can I have some?" nodding at the whiskey bottle.

"Girls don't drink that," Billy Pope said.

"Give you some and we'd have Brian whining after some," said Flo.

"Can I have some?" said Brian, whining, and Flo laughed uproariously, sliding her own glass behind the bread box. "See there?"

There used to be people around in the old days that did cures," said Billy Pope at the supper table. "But you don't hear about none of them no more."

"Too bad we can't get hold of one of them right now," said Rose's father, getting hold of and conquering a coughing fit.

"There was the one faith healer I used to hear my Dad talk about," said Billy Pope. "He had a way of talkin, he talked like the Bible. So this deaf fellow went to him and he seen him and he cured him of his deafness. Then he says to him, 'Durst hear?' "

"Dost hear?" Rose suggested. She had drained Flo's glass while getting out the bread for supper, and felt more kindly disposed toward all her relatives.

"That's it. *Dost hear?* And the fellow said yes, he did. So the faith healer says then, *Dost believe?* Now maybe the fellow didn't understand what he meant. And he says *What in?* So the faith healer he got mad, and he took away the fellow's hearing like that, and he went home deaf as he come."

Flo said that out where she lived when she was little, there was a woman who had second sight. Buggies, and later on, cars, would be parked to the end of her lane on Sundays. That was the day people came from a distance to consult with her. Mostly they came to consult her about things that were lost.

"Didn't they want to get in touch with their relations?" Rose's father said, egging Flo on as he liked to when she was telling a story. "I thought she could put you in touch with the dead."

"Well, most of them seen enough of their relations when they was alive."

It was rings and wills and livestock they wanted to know about; where had things disappeared to?

"One fellow I knew went to her and he had lost his wallet. He was a man that worked on the railway line. And she says to him, well, do you remember it was about a week ago you were working along the tracks and you come along near an orchard and you thought you would like an apple? So you hopped over the fence and it was right then you dropped your wallet, right then and there in the long grass. But a dog came along, she says, a dog picked it up and dropped it a ways further along the fence, and that's where you'll find it. Well, he'd forgot all about the orchard and climbing that fence and he was so amazed at her, he gave her a dollar. And he went and found his wallet in the very place she described. This is true, I knew him. But the money was all chewed up, it was all chewed up in shreds, and when he found that he was so mad he said he wished he never give her so much!"

"Now, you never went to her," said Rose's father. "You wouldn't put your faith in the like of that?" When he talked to Flo he often spoke in country phrases, and adopted the country habit of teasing, saying the opposite of what's true, or believed to be true.

"No, I never went actually to ask her anything," Flo said. "But one time I went. I had to go over there and get some green onions. My mother was sick and suffering with her nerves and this woman sent word over, that she had some green onions was good for nerves. It wasn't nerves at all it was cancer, so what good they did I don't know."

Flo's voice climbed and hurried on, embarrassed that she had let that out.

"I had to go and get them. She had them pulled and washed and tied up for me, and she says, don't go yet, come on in the kitchen and see what I got for you. Well, I didn't know what, but I dasn't not do it. I thought she was a witch. We all did. We all did, at school. So I sat down in the kitchen and she went into the pantry and brought out a big chocolate cake and she cut a piece and give it to me. I had to sit and eat it. She sat there and watched me eat. All I can remember about her is her hands. They were great big red hands with big veins sticking up on them, and she'd be flopping and twisting them all the time in her lap. I often thought since, she ought to eat the green onions herself, she didn't have so good nerves either.

"Then I tasted a funny taste. In the cake. It was peculiar. I dasn't stop eating though. I ate and ate and when I finished it all up I said thank you and I tell you I got out of there. I walked all the way down the lane because I figured she was watching me, and when I got to the road I started to run. But I was still scared she was following after me, invisible or something, and she might read what was in my mind and pick me up and pound my brains out on the gravel. When I got home I just flung open the door and hollered *Poison!* That's what I was thinking. I thought she made me eat a poisoned cake.

"All it was was moldy. That's what my mother said. The damp in her house and she would go for days without no visitors to eat it, in spite of the crowds she collected other times. She could have a cake sitting around too long a while.

"But I didn't think so. No. I thought I had ate poison and I was doomed. I went and sat in this sort of place I had in a corner of the granary. Nobody knew I had it. I kept all kinds of junk in there. I kept some chips of broken china and some velvet flowers. I remember them, they were off a hat that had got rained on. So I just sat there, and I waited."

Billy Pope was laughing at her. "Did they come and haul you out?"

"I forget. I don't think so. They would've had a hard time finding me, I was in behind all the feed bags. No. I don't know. I guess what happened in the end was I got tired out waiting and come out by myself."

"And lived to tell the tale," said Rose's father, swallowing the last word as he was overcome by a prolonged coughing fit. Flo said he shouldn't stay up any longer but he said he would just lie down on the kitchen couch, which he did. Flo and Rose cleared the table and washed the dishes, then for something to do they all—Flo and Billy Pope and Brian and Rose—sat around the table and played euchre. Her father dozed. Rose thought of Flo sitting in a corner of the granary with the bits of china and the wilted velvet flowers and whatever else was precious to her, waiting, in a gradually reduced state of terror, it must have been, and exaltation, and desire, to see how death would slice the day.

Her father was waiting. His shed was locked, his books would not be opened again, by him, and tomorrow was the last day he would wear shoes. They were all used to this idea, and in some ways they would be more disturbed if his death did not take place, than if it did. No one could ask what he thought about it. He would have treated such an inquiry as an impertinence, a piece of dramatizing, an indulgence. Rose believed he would have. She believed he was prepared for Westminster Hospital, the old soldiers' hospital, prepared for its masculine gloom, its yellowing curtains pulled around the bed, its spotty basins. And for what followed. She understood that he would never be with her more than at the present moment. The surprise to come was that he wouldn't be with her less.

Drinking coffee, wandering around the blind green halls of the new high school, at the Centennial Year Reunion—she hadn't come for that, had bumped into it accidentally, so to speak, when she came home to see what was to be done about Flo—Rose met people who said, "Did you know Ruby Carruthers was dead? They took off the one breast and then the other but it was all through her, she died."

And people who said, "I saw your picture in a magazine, what was the name of that magazine, I have it at home."

The new high school had an auto mechanics shop for training auto mechanics and a beauty parlor for training beauty parlor operators; a library; an auditorium; a gymnasium; a whirling fountain arrangement for washing your hands in the Ladies' Room. Also a functioning dispenser of Kotex.

Del Fairbridge had become an undertaker.

Runt Chesterton had become an accountant.

Horse Nicholson had made a lot of money as a contractor and had left that to go into politics. He had made a speech saying that what they needed was a lot more God in the classroom and a lot less French.

Wild Swans

Flo said to watch for White Slavers. She said this was how they operated: an old woman, a motherly or grandmotherly sort, made friends while riding beside you on a bus or train. She offered you candy, which was drugged. Pretty soon you began to droop and mumble, were in no condition to speak for yourself. Oh, help, the woman said, my daughter (granddaughter) is sick, please somebody help me get her off so that she can recover in the fresh air. Up stepped a polite gentleman, pretending to be a stranger, offering assistance. Together, at the next stop, they hustled you off the train or bus, and that was the last the ordinary world ever saw of you. They kept you a prisoner in the White Slave place (to which you had been transported drugged and bound so you wouldn't even know where you were), until such time as you were thoroughly degraded and in despair, your insides torn up by drunken men and invested with vile disease, your mind destroyed by drugs, your hair and teeth fallen out. It took about three years, for you to get to this state. You wouldn't want to go home, then, maybe couldn't remember home, or find your way if you did. So they let you out on the streets.

Flo took ten dollars and put it in a little cloth bag which she sewed to the strap of Rose's slip. Another thing likely to happen was that Rose would get her purse stolen.

Watch out, Flo said as well, for people dressed up as ministers. They were the worst. That disguise was commonly adopted by White Slavers, as well as those after your money.

Rose said she didn't see how she could tell which ones were disguised.

Flo had worked in Toronto once. She had worked as a waitress in a coffee shop in Union Station. That was how she knew all she knew. She never saw sunlight, in those days, except on her days off. But she saw plenty else. She saw a man cut another man's stomach with a knife, just pull out his shirt and do a tidy cut, as if it was a watermelon not a stomach. The stomach's owner just sat looking down surprised, with no time to protest. Flo implied that that was nothing, in Toronto. She saw two bad women (that was what Flo called whores, running the two words together, like badminton) get into a fight, and a man laughed at them, other men stopped and laughed and egged them on, and they had their fists full of each other's hair. At last the police came and took them away, still howling and yelping.

She saw a child die of a fit, too. Its face was black as ink.

"Well I'm not scared," said Rose provokingly. "There's the police, anyway."

"Oh, them! They'd be the first ones to diddle you!"

She did not believe anything Flo said on the subject of sex. Consider the undertaker.

A little bald man, very neatly dressed, would come into the store sometimes and speak to Flo with a placating expression.

"I only wanted a bag of candy. And maybe a few packages of gum. And one or two chocolate bars. Could you go to the trouble of wrapping them?"

Flo in her mock-deferential tone would assure him that she could. She wrapped them in heavy-duty white paper, so they were something like presents. He took his time with the selection, humming and chatting, then dawdled for a while. He might ask how Flo was feeling. And how Rose was, if she was there.

"You look pale. Young girls need fresh air." To Flo he would say, "You work too hard. You've worked hard all your life."

"No rest for the wicked," Flo would say agreeably.

When he went out she hurried to the window. There it was—the old black hearse with its purple curtains.

"He'll be after them today!" Flo would say as the hearse rolled away at a gentle pace, almost a funeral pace. The little man had been an undertaker, but he was retired now. The hearse was retired too. His sons had taken over the undertaking and bought a new one. He drove the old hearse all over the country, looking for women. So Flo said. Rose could not believe it. Flo said he gave them the gum and the candy. Rose said he probably ate them himself. Flo said he had been seen, he had been heard. In mild weather he drove with the windows down, singing, to himself or to somebody out of sight in the back.

> Her brow is like the snowdrift
> Her throat is like the swan

Flo imitated him singing. Gently overtaking some woman walking on a back road, or resting at a country crossroads. All compliments and courtesy and chocolate bars, offering a ride. Of course every woman who reported being asked said she had turned him down. He never pestered anybody, drove politely on. He called in at houses, and if the husband was home he seemed to like just as well as anything to sit and chat. Wives said that was all he ever did anyway but Flo did not believe it.

"Some women are taken in," she said. "A number." She liked to speculate on what the hearse was like inside. Plush. Plush on the walls and the roof and the floor. Soft purple, the color of the curtains, the color of dark lilacs.

All nonsense, Rose thought. Who could believe it, of a man that age?

Rose was going to Toronto on the train for the first time by herself. She had been once before, but that was with Flo, long before her father died. They took along their own sandwiches and bought milk from the vendor on the train. It was sour. Sour chocolate milk. Rose kept taking tiny sips, unwilling to admit that something so much desired could fail her. Flo sniffed it, then hunted up and down the train until she found the old man in his red jacket, with no teeth and the tray hanging around his neck. She invited him to sample the chocolate milk. She invited people nearby to smell it. He let her have some ginger ale for nothing. It was slightly warm.

"I let him know," Flo said looking around after he had left. "You have to let them know."

A woman agreed with her but most people looked out the window. Rose drank the warm ginger ale. Either that, or the scene with the vendor, or the conversation Flo and the agreeing woman now got into about where they came from, why they were going to Toronto, and Rose's morning constipation which was why she was lacking color, or the small amount of chocolate milk she had got inside her, caused her to throw up in the train toilet. All day long she was afraid people in Toronto could smell vomit on her coat.

This time Flo started the trip off by saying, "Keep an eye on her, she's never been away from home before!" to the conductor, then looking around and laughing, to show that was jokingly meant. Then she had to get off. It seemed the conductor had no more need for jokes than Rose had, and no intention of keeping an eye on anybody. He never spoke to Rose except to ask for her ticket. She had a window seat, and was soon extraordinarily happy. She felt Flo receding, West Hanratty flying away from her, her own wearying self discarded as easily as everything else. She loved the towns less and less known. A woman was standing at her back door in her nightgown, not caring if everybody on the train saw her. They were traveling south, out of the snow belt, into an earlier spring, a tenderer sort of landscape. People could grow peach trees in their backyards.

Rose collected in her mind the things she had to look for in Toronto. First, things for Flo. Special stockings for her varicose veins. A special kind of cement for sticking handles on pots. And a full set of dominoes.

For herself Rose wanted to buy hair-remover to put on her arms and legs, and if possible an arrangement of inflatable cushions, supposed to reduce your hips and thighs. She thought they probably had hair-remover in the drugstore in Hanratty, but the woman in there was a friend of Flo's and told everything. She told Flo who bought hair dye and slimming medicine and French safes. As for the cushion business, you could send away for it but there was sure to be a comment at the Post Office, and Flo knew people there as well. She also planned to buy some bangles, and an angora sweater. She had great hopes of silver bangles and powder-blue angora. She thought they could transform her, make her calm and slender and take the frizz out of her hair, dry her underarms and turn her complexion to pearl.

The money for these things, as well as the money for the trip, came from a prize Rose had won, for writing an essay called "Art and Science in the World of Tomorrow." To her surprise, Flo asked if she could read it, and while she was reading it, she remarked that they must have thought they had to give Rose the prize for swallowing the dictionary. Then she said shyly, "It's very interesting."

She would have to spend the night at Cela McKinney's. Cela McKinney was her father's cousin. She had married a hotel manager and thought she had gone up in the world. But the hotel manager came home one day and sat down on the dining room floor between two chairs and said, "I am never going to leave this house again." Nothing unusual had happened, he had just decided not to go out of the house again, and he didn't, until he died. That had made Cela McKinney odd and nervous. She locked her doors at eight o'clock. She was also very stingy. Supper was usually oatmeal porridge, with raisins. Her house was dark and narrow and smelled like a bank.

The train was filling up. At Brantford a man asked if she would mind if he sat down beside her.

"It's cooler out than you'd think," he said. He offered her part of his newspaper. She said no thanks.

Then lest he think her rude she said it really was cooler. She went on looking out the window at the spring morning. There was no snow left, down here. The trees and bushes seemed to have a paler bark than they did at home. Even the sunlight looked different. It was as different from home, here, as the coast of the Mediterranean would be, or the valleys of California.

"Filthy windows, you'd think they'd take more care," the man said. "Do you travel much by train?"

She said no.

Water was lying in the fields. He nodded at it and said there was a lot this year.

"Heavy snows."

She noticed his saying *snows*, a poetic-sounding word. Anyone at home would have said *snow*.

"I had an unusual experience the other day. I was driving out in the country. In fact I was on my way to see one of my parishioners, a lady with a heart condition—"

She looked quickly at his collar. He was wearing an ordinary shirt and tie and a dark blue suit.

"Oh, yes," he said. "I'm a United Church minister. But I don't always wear my uniform. I wear it for preaching in. I'm off duty today.

"Well as I said I was driving through the country and I saw some Canada geese down on a pond, and I took another look, and there were some swans down with them. A whole great flock of swans. What a lovely sight they were. They would be on their spring migration, I expect, heading up north. What a spectacle. I never saw anything like it."

Rose was unable to think appreciatively of the wild swans because she was afraid he was going to lead the conversation from them to Nature in general and then to God, the way a minister would feel obliged to do. But he did not, he stopped with the swans.

"A very fine sight. You would have enjoyed them."

He was between fifty and sixty years old, Rose thought. He was short, and energetic-looking, with a square ruddy face and bright waves of gray hair combed straight up from his forehead. When she realized he was not going to mention God she felt she ought to show her gratitude.

She said they must have been lovely.

"It wasn't even a regular pond, it was only some water lying in a field. It was just luck the water was lying there and they came down and I came driving by at the right time. Just luck. They come in at the east end of Lake Erie, I think. But I never was lucky enough to see them before."

She turned by degrees to the window, and he returned to his paper. She remained slightly smiling, so as not to seem rude, not to seem to be rejecting conversation altogether. The morning really was cool, and she had taken down her coat off the hook where she put it when she first got on the train, she had spread it over herself, like a lap robe. She had set her purse on the floor when the minister sat down, to give him room. He took the sections of the paper apart, shaking and rustling them in a leisurely, rather showy, way. He seemed to her the sort of person who does everything in a showy way. A ministerial way. He brushed aside the sections he didn't want at the moment. A corner of newspaper touched her leg, just at the edge of her coat.

She thought for some time that it was the paper. Then she said to herself, what if it is a hand? That was the kind of thing she could imagine. She would sometimes look at men's hands, at the fuzz on their forearms, their concentrating profiles. She would think about everything they could do. Even the stupid ones. For instance the driver-salesman who brought the bread to Flo's store. The ripeness and confidence of manner, the settled mixture of ease and alertness with which he handled the bread truck. A fold of mature belly over the belt did not displease her. Another time she had her eye on the French teacher at school. Not a Frenchman at all, really, his name was McLaren, but Rose thought teaching French had rubbed off on him, made him look like one. Quick and sallow; sharp shoulders; hooked nose and sad eyes. She saw him lapping and coiling his way through slow pleasures, a perfect autocrat of indulgences. She had a considerable longing to be somebody's object. Pounded, pleasured, reduced, exhausted.

But what if it was a hand? What if it really was a hand? She shifted slightly, moved as much as she could toward the window. Her imagination seemed to have created this reality, a reality she was not prepared for at all. She found it alarming. She was concentrating on that leg, that bit of skin with the stocking over it. She could not bring herself to look. Was there a pressure, or was there not? She shifted again. Her legs had been, and remained, tightly closed. It was. It was a hand. It was a hand's pressure.

Please don't. That was what she tried to say. She shaped the words in her mind, tried them out, then couldn't get them past her lips. Why was that? The embarrassment, was it, the fear that people might hear? People were all around them, the seats were full.

It was not only that.

She did manage to look at him, not raising her head but turning it cautiously. He had tilted his seat back and closed his eyes. There was his dark blue suit sleeve, disappearing under the newspaper. He had arranged the paper so that it overlapped Rose's coat. His hand was underneath, simply resting, as if flung out in sleep.

Now, Rose could have shifted the newspaper and removed her coat.

If he was not asleep, he would have been obliged to draw back his hand. If he was asleep, if he did not draw it back, she could have whispered, *Excuse me*, and set his hand firmly on his own knee. This solution, so obvious and foolproof, did not occur to her. And she would have to wonder, why not? The minister's hand was not, or not yet, at all welcome to her. It made her feel uncomfortable, resentful, slightly disgusted, trapped and wary. But she could not take charge of it, to reject it. She could not insist that it was there, when he seemed to be insisting that it was not. How could she declare him responsible, when he lay there so harmless and trusting, resting himself before his busy day, with such a pleased and healthy face? A man older than her father would be, if he were living, a man used to deference, an appreciator of Nature, delighter in wild swans. If she did say *Please don't* she was sure he would ignore her, as if overlooking some silliness or impoliteness on her part. She knew that as soon as she said it she would hope he had not heard.

But there was more to it than that. Curiosity. More constant, more imperious, than any lust. A lust in itself, that will make you draw back and wait, wait too long, risk almost anything, just to see what will happen. *To see what will happen.*

The hand began, over the next several miles, the most delicate, the most timid, pressures and investigations. Not asleep. Or if he was, his hand wasn't. She did feel disgust. She felt a faint, wandering nausea. She thought of flesh: lumps of flesh, pink snouts, fat tongues, blunt fingers, all on their way trotting and creeping and lolling and rubbing, looking for their comfort. She thought of cats in heat rubbing themselves along the top of board fences, yowling with their miserable complaint. It was pitiful, infantile, this itching and shoving and squeezing. Spongy tissues, inflamed membranes, tormented nerve-ends, shameful smells; humiliation.

All that was starting. His hand, that she wouldn't ever have wanted to hold, that she wouldn't have squeezed back, his stubborn patient hand was able, after all, to get the ferns to rustle and the streams to flow, to waken a sly luxuriance.

Nevertheless, she would rather not. She would still rather not. Please remove this, she said out the window. Stop it, please, she said to the stumps and barns. The hand moved up her leg past the top of her stocking to her bare skin, had moved higher, under her suspender, reached her underpants and the lower part of her belly. Her legs were still crossed, pinched together. While her legs stayed crossed she could lay claim to innocence, she had not admitted anything. She could still believe that she would stop this in a minute. Nothing was going to happen, nothing more. Her legs were never going to open.

But they were. They were. As the train crossed the Niagra Escarpment above Dundas, as they looked down at the preglacial valley, the silver-wooded rubble of little hills, as they came sliding down to the shores of Lake Ontario, she would make this slow, and silent, and definite, declaration, perhaps disappointing as much as satisfying the hand's owner. He would not lift his eyelids, his face would not alter, his fingers would not hesitate, but would go powerfully and discreetly to work. Invasion, and welcome, and sunlight flashing far and wide on the lake water; miles of bare orchards stirring round Burlington.

This was disgrace, this was beggary. But what harm in that, we say to ourselves at such moments, what harm in anything, the worse the better, as we ride the cold wave of greed, of greedy assent. A stranger's hand, or root vegetables or humble kitchen tools that people tell jokes about; the world is tumbling with innocent-seeming objects ready to declare themselves, slippery and obliging. She was careful of her breathing. She could not believe this. Victim and accomplice she was borne past Glassco's Jams and Marmalades, past the big pulsating pipes of oil refineries. They glided into suburbs where bedsheets, and towels used to wipe up intimate stains, flapped leeringly on the clotheslines, where even the children seemed to be frolicking lewdly in the schoolyards, and the very truckdrivers stopped at the railway crossings must be thrusting their thumbs gleefully into curled hands. Such cunning antics now, such popular visions. The gates and towers of the Exhibition Grounds came into view, the painted domes and pillars floated marvelously against her eyelids' rosy sky. Then flew apart in celebration. You could have had such a flock of birds, wild swans, even, wakened under one big dome together, exploding from it, taking to the sky.

She bit the edge of her tongue. Very soon the conductor passed through the train, to stir the travelers, warn them back to life.

In the darkness under the station the United Church minister, refreshed, opened his eyes and got his paper folded together, then asked if she would like some help with her coat. His gallantry was self-satisfied, dismissive. No, said Rose, with a sore tongue. He hurried out of the train ahead of her. She did not see him in the station. She never saw him again in her life. But he remained on call, so to speak, for years and years, ready to slip into place at a critical moment, without even any regard, later on, for husband or lovers. What recommended him? She could never understand it. His simplicity, his arrogance, his perversely appealing lack of handsomeness, even of ordinary grown-up masculinity? When he stood up she saw that he was shorter even than she had thought, that his face was pink and shiny, that there was something crude and pushy and childish about him.

Was he a minister, really, or was that only what he said? Flo had mentioned people who were not ministers, dressed up as if they were. Not real ministers dressed as if they were not. Or, stranger still, men who were not real ministers pretending to be real but dressed as if they were not. But that she had come as close as she had, to what could happen, was an unwelcome thing. Rose walked through Union Station feeling the little bag with the ten dollars rubbing at her, knew she would feel it all day long, rubbing its reminder against her skin.

She couldn't stop getting Flo's messages, even with that. She remembered, because she was in Union Station, that there was a girl named Mavis working here, in the Gift Shop, when Flo was working in the coffee shop. Mavis had warts on her eyelids that looked like they were going to turn into sties but they didn't, they went away. Maybe she had them removed, Flo didn't ask. She was very good-looking, without them. There was a movie star in those days she looked a lot like. The movie star's name was Frances Farmer.

Frances Farmer. Rose had never heard of her.

That was the name. And Mavis went and bought herself a big hat that dipped over one eye and a dress entirely made of lace. She went off for the weekend to Georgian Bay, to a resort up there. She booked herself in under the name of Florence Farmer. To give everybody the idea she was really the other one, Frances Farmer, but calling herself Florence because she was on holiday and didn't want to be recognized. She had a little cigarette holder that was black and mother-of-pearl. She could have been arrested, Flo said. For the *nerve*.

Rose almost went over to the Gift Shop, to see if Mavis was still there and if she could recognize her. She thought it would be an especially fine thing, to manage a transformation like that. To dare it; to get away with it, to enter on preposterous adventures in your own, but newly named, skin.

The Beggar Maid

Patrick Blatchford was in love with Rose. This had become a fixed, even furious, idea with him. For her, a continual surprise. He wanted to marry her. He waited for her after classes, moved in and walked beside her, so that anybody she was talking to would have to reckon with his presence. He would not talk, when these friends or classmates of hers were around, but he would try to catch her eye, so that he could indicate by a cold incredulous look what he thought of their conversation. Rose was flattered, but nervous. A girl named Nancy Falls, a friend of hers, mispronounced Metternich in front of him. He said to her later, "How can you be friends with people like that?"

Nancy and Rose had gone and sold their blood together, at Victoria Hospital. They each got fifteen dollars. They spent most of the money on evening shoes, tarty silver sandals. Then because they were sure the bloodletting had caused them to lose weight they had hot fudge sundaes at Boomers. Why was Rose unable to defend Nancy to Patrick?

Patrick was twenty-four years old, a graduate student, planning to be a history professor. He was tall, thin, fair, and good-looking, though he had a long pale-red birthmark, dribbling like a tear down his temple and his cheek. He apologized for it, but said it was fading, as he got older. When he was forty, it would have faded away. It was not the birthmark that canceled out his good looks, Rose thought. (Something did cancel them out, or at least diminish them, for her; she had to keep reminding herself they were there.) There was something edgy, jumpy, disconcerting, about him. His voice would break under stress —with her, it seemed he was always under stress—he knocked dishes and cups off tables, spilled drinks and bowls of peanuts, like a comedian. He was not a comedian; nothing could be further from his intentions. He came from British Columbia. His family was rich.

He arrived early to pick Rose up, when they were going to the movies. He wouldn't knock, he knew he was early. He sat on the step outside Dr. Henshawe's door. This was in the winter, it was dark out, but there was a little coach lamp beside the door.

"Oh, Rose! Come and look!" called Dr. Henshawe, in her soft, amused voice, and they looked down together from the dark window of the study. "The poor young man," said Dr. Henshawe tenderly. Dr. Henshawe was in her seventies. She was a former English professor, fastidious and lively. She had a lame leg, but a still youthfully, charmingly tilted head, with white braids wound around it.

She called Patrick poor because he was in love, and perhaps also because he was a male, doomed to push and blunder. Even from up here he looked stubborn and pitiable, determined and dependent, sitting out there in the cold.

"Guarding the door," Dr. Henshawe said. "Oh, Rose!"

Another time she said disturbingly, "Oh, dear, I'm afraid he is after the wrong girl."

Rose didn't like her saying that. She didn't like her laughing at Patrick. She didn't like Patrick sitting out on the steps that way, either. He was asking to be laughed at. He was the most vulnerable person Rose had ever known, he made himself so, didn't know anything about protecting himself. But he was also full of cruel judgments, he was full of conceit.

You are a scholar, Rose," Dr. Henshawe would say. "This will interest you." Then she would read aloud something from the paper, or, more likely, something from *Canadian Forum* or the *Atlantic Monthly*. Dr. Henshawe had at one time headed the city's school board, she was a founding member of Canada's socialist party. She still sat on committees, wrote letters to the paper, reviewed books. Her father and mother had been medical missionaries; she had been born in China. Her house was small and perfect. Polished floors, glowing rugs, Chinese vases, bowls and landscapes, black carved screens. Much that Rose could not appreciate, at the time. She could not really distinguish between the little jade animals on Dr. Henshawe's mantelpiece and the ornaments displayed in the jewelry store window, in Hanratty, though she could now distinguish between either of these and the things Flo bought from the five-and-ten.

She could not really decide how much she liked being at Dr. Henshawe's. At times she felt discouraged, sitting in the dining room with a linen napkin on her knee, eating from fine white plates on blue placemats. For one thing, there was never enough to eat, and she had taken to buying doughnuts and chocolate bars and hiding them in her room. The canary swung on its perch in the dining room window and Dr. Henshawe directed conversation. She talked about politics, about writers. She mentioned Frank Scott and Dorothy Livesay. She said Rose must read them. Rose must read this, she must read that. Rose became sullenly determined not to. She was reading Thomas Mann. She was reading Tolstoy.

Before she came to Dr. Henshawe's, Rose had never heard of the working class. She took the designation home.

"This would have to be the last part of town where they put the sewers," Flo said.

"Of course," Rose said coolly. "This is the working-class part of town."

"*Working* class?" said Flo. "Not if the ones around here can help it."

Dr. Henshawe's house had done one thing. It had destroyed the naturalness, the taken-for-granted background, of home. To go back there was to go quite literally into a crude light. Flo had put fluorescent lights in the store and the kitchen. There was also, in a corner of the kitchen, a floor lamp Flo had won at Bingo; its shade was permanently wrapped in wide strips of cellophane. What Dr. Henshawe's house and Flo's house did best, in Rose's opinion, was discredit each other. In Dr. Henshawe's charming rooms there was always for Rose the raw knowledge of home, an indigestible lump, and at home, now, her sense of order and modulation elsewhere exposed such embarrassing sad poverty, in people who never thought themselves poor. Poverty was not just wretchedness, as Dr. Henshawe seemed to think, it was not just deprivation. It meant having those ugly tube lights and being proud of them. It meant continual talk of money and malicious talk about new things people had bought and whether they were paid for. It meant pride and jealousy flaring over something like the new pair of plastic curtains, imitating lace, that Flo had bought for the front window. That as well as hanging your clothes on nails behind the door and being able to hear every sound from the bathroom. It meant decorating your walls with a number of admonitions, pious and cheerful and mildly bawdy.

THE LORD IS MY SHEPHERD
BELIEVE IN THE LORD JESUS CHRIST AND THOU SHALL BE SAVED

Why did Flo have those, when she wasn't even religious? They were what people had, common as calendars.

THIS IS MY KITCHEN AND I WILL DO AS I DARNED PLEASE
MORE THAN TWO PERSONS TO A BED IS DANGEROUS AND UNLAWFUL

Billy Pope had brought that one. What would Patrick have to say about them? What would someone who was offended by a mispronunciation of Metternich think of Billy Pope's stories?

Billy Pope worked in Tyde's Butcher Shop. What he talked about most frequently now was the D.P., the Belgian, who had come to work there, and got on Billy Pope's nerves with his impudent singing of French songs and his naive notions of getting on in this country, buying a butcher shop of his own.

"Don't you think you can come over here and get yourself ideas," Billy Pope said to the D.P. "It's *youse* workin for *us*, and don't think that'll change into *us* workin for *youse*." That shut him up, Billy Pope said.

Patrick would say from time to time that since her home was only fifty miles away he ought to come up and meet Rose's family.

"There's only my stepmother."

"It's too bad I couldn't have met your father."

Rashly, she had presented her father to Patrick as a reader of history, an amateur scholar. That was not exactly a lie, but it did not give a truthful picture of the circumstances.

"Is your stepmother your guardian?"

Rose had to say she did not know.

"Well, your father must have appointed a guardian for you in his will. Who administers his estate?"

His *estate*. Rose thought an estate was land, such as people owned in England.

Patrick thought it was rather charming of her to think that.

"No, his money and stocks and so on. What he left."

"I don't think he left any."

"Don't be silly," Patrick said.

And sometimes Dr. Henshawe would say, "Well, you are a scholar, you are not interested in that." Usually she was speaking of some event at the college; a pep rally, a football game, a dance. And usually she was right; Rose was not interested. But she was not eager to admit it. She did not seek or relish that definition of herself.

On the stairway wall hung graduation photographs of all the other girls, scholarship girls, who had lived with Dr. Henshawe. Most of them had got to be teachers, then mothers. One was a dietician, two were librarians, one was a professor of English, like Dr. Henshawe herself. Rose did not care for the look of them, for their soft-focused meekly smiling gratitude, their large teeth and maidenly rolls of hair. They seemed to be urging on her some deadly secular piety. There were no actresses among them, no brassy magazine journalists; none of them had latched on to the sort of life Rose wanted for herself. She wanted to perform in public. She thought she wanted to be an actress but she never tried to act, was afraid to go near the college drama productions. She knew she couldn't sing or dance. She would really have liked to play the harp, but she had no ear for music. She wanted to be known and envied, slim and clever. She told Dr. Henshawe that if she had been a man she would have wanted to be a foreign correspondent.

"Then you must be one," cried Dr. Henshawe alarmingly. "The future will be wide open, for women. You must concentrate on languages. You must take courses in political science. And economics. Perhaps you could get a job on the paper for the summer. I have friends there."

Rose was frightened at the idea of working on a paper, and she hated the introductory economics course; she was looking for a way of dropping it. It was dangerous to mention things to Dr. Henshawe.

She had got to live with Dr. Henshawe by accident. Another girl had been picked to move in but she got sick; she had T.B., and went instead to a sanitarium. Dr. Henshawe came up to the college office on the second day of registration to get the names of some other scholarship freshmen.

Rose had been in the office just a little while before, asking where the meeting of the scholarship students was to be held. She had lost her notice. The Bursar was giving a talk to the new scholarship students, telling them of ways to earn money and live cheaply and explaining the high standards of performance to be expected of them here, if they wanted their payments to keep coming.

Rose found out the number of the room, and started up the stairs to the first floor. A girl came up beside her and said, "Are you on your way to three-oh-twelve, too?"

They walked together, telling each other the details of their scholarships. Rose did not yet have a place to live, she was staying at the Y. She did not really have enough money to be here at all. She had a scholarship for her tuition and the county prize to buy her books and a bursary of three hundred dollars to live on; that was all.

"You'll have to get a job," the other girl said. She had a larger bursary, because she was in Science (that's where the money is, the money's all in Science, she said seriously), but she was hoping to get a job in the cafeteria. She had a room in somebody's basement. How much does your room cost? How much does a hot plate cost? Rose asked her, her head swimming with anxious calculations.

This girl wore her hair in a roll. She wore a crepe blouse, yellowed and shining from washing and ironing. Her breasts were large and sagging. She probably wore a dirty-pink hooked-up-the-side brassiere. She had a scaly patch on one cheek.

"This must be it," she said.

There was a little window in the door. They could look through at the other scholarship winners already assembled and waiting. It seemed to Rose that she saw four or five girls of the same stooped and matronly type as the girl who was beside her, and several bright-eyed, self-satisfied babyish-looking boys. It seemed to be the rule that girl scholarship winners looked about forty and boys about twelve. It was not possible, of course, that they all looked like this. It was not possible that in one glance through the windows of the door Rose could detect traces of eczema, stained underarms, dandruff, moldy deposits on the teeth and crusty flakes in the corners of the eyes. That was only what she thought. But there was a pall over them, she was not mistaken, there was a true terrible pall of eagerness and docility. How else could they have supplied so many right answers, so many pleasing answers, how else distinguished themselves and got themselves here? And Rose had done the same.

"I have to go to the john," she said.

She could see herself, working in the cafeteria. Her figure, broad enough already, broadened out still more by the green cotton uniform, her face red and her hair stringy from the heat. Dishing up stew and fried chicken for those of inferior intelligence and handsomer means. Blocked off by the steam tables, the uniform, by decent hard work that nobody need be ashamed of, by publicly proclaimed braininess and poverty. Boys could get away with that, barely. For girls it was fatal. Poverty in girls is not attractive unless combined with sweet sluttishness, stupidity. Braininess is not attractive unless combined with some signs of elegance; *class*. Was this true, and was she foolish enough to care? It was; she was.

She went back to the first floor where the halls were crowded with ordinary students who were not on scholarships, who would not be expected to get A's and be grateful and live cheap. Enviable and innocent, they milled around the registration tables in their new purple and white blazers, their purple Frosh beanies, yelling reminders to each other, confused information, nonsensical insults. She walked among them feeling bitterly superior and despondent. The skirt of her green corduroy suit kept falling back between her legs as she walked. The material was limp; she should have spent more and bought the heavier weight. She thought now that the jacket was not properly cut either, though it had looked all right at home. The whole outfit had been made by a dressmaker in Hanratty, a friend of Flo's, whose main concern had been that there should be no revelations of the figure. When Rose asked if the skirt couldn't be made tighter this woman had said, "You wouldn't want your b.t.m. to show, now would you?" and Rose hadn't wanted to say she didn't care.

Another thing the dressmaker said was, "I thought now you was through school you'd be getting a job and help out at home."

A woman walking down the hall stopped Rose.

"Aren't you one of the scholarship girls?"

It was the Registrar's secretary. Rose thought she was going to be reprimanded, for not being at the meeting, and she was going to say she felt sick. She prepared her face for this lie. But the secretary said, "Come with me, now. I've got somebody I want you to meet."

Dr. Henshawe was making a charming nuisance of herself in the office. She liked poor girls, bright girls, but they had to be fairly good-looking girls.

"I think this could be your lucky day," the secretary said, leading Rose. "If you could put a pleasanter expression on your face."

Rose hated being told that, but she smiled obediently.

Within the hour she was taken home with Dr. Henshawe, installed in the house with the Chinese screens and vases, and told she was a scholar.

She got a job working in the Library of the college, instead of in the cafeteria. Dr. Henshawe was a friend of the Head Librarian. She worked on Saturday afternoons. She worked in the stacks, putting books away. On Saturday afternoons in the fall the Library was nearly empty, because of the football games. The narrow windows were open to the leafy campus, the football field, the dry fall country. The distant songs and shouts came drifting in.

The college buildings were not old at all, but they were built to look old. They were built of stone. The Arts building had a tower, and the Library had casement windows, which might have been designed for shooting arrows through. The buildings and the books in the Library were what pleased Rose most about the place. The life that usually filled it, and that was now drained away, concentrated around the football field, letting loose those noises, seemed to her inappropriate and distracting. The cheers and songs were idiotic, if you listened to the words. What did they want to build such dignified buildings for, if they were going to sing songs like that?

She knew enough not to reveal these opinions. If anybody said to her, "It's awful you have to work Saturdays and can't get to any of the games," she would fervently agree.

Once a man grabbed her bare leg, between her sock and her skirt. It happened in the Agriculture section, down at the bottom of the stacks. Only the faculty, graduate students, and employees had access to the stacks, though someone could have hoisted himself through a ground-floor window, if he was skinny. She had seen a man crouched down looking at the books on a low shelf, further along. As she reached up to push a book into place he passed behind her. He bent and grabbed her leg, all in one smooth startling motion, and then was gone. She could feel for quite a while where his fingers had dug in. It didn't seem to her a sexual touch, it was more like a joke, though not at all a friendly one. She heard him run away, or felt him running; the metal shelves were vibrating. Then they stopped. There was no sound of him. She walked around looking between the stacks, looking into the carrels. Suppose she did see him, or bumped into him around a corner, what did she intend to do? She did not know. It was simply necessary to look for him, as in some tense childish game. She looked down at the sturdy pinkish calf of her leg. Amazing, that out of the blue somebody had wanted to blotch and punish it.

There were usually a few graduate students working in the carrels, even on Saturday afternoons. More rarely, a professor. Every carrel she looked into was empty, until she came to one in the corner. She poked her head in freely, by this time not expecting anybody. Then she had to say she was sorry.

There was a young man with a book on his lap, books on the floor, papers all around him. Rose asked him if he had seen anybody run past. He said no.

She told him what had happened. She didn't tell him because she was frightened or disgusted, as he seemed afterward to think, but just because she had to tell somebody; it was so odd. She was not prepared at all for his response. His long neck and face turned red, the flush entirely absorbing a birthmark down the side of his cheek. He was thin and fair. He stood up without any thought for the book in his lap or the papers in front of him. The book thumped on the floor. A great sheaf of papers, pushed across the desk, upset his ink bottle.

"How vile," he said.

"Grab the ink," Rose said. He leaned to catch the bottle and knocked it on to the floor. Fortunately the top was on, and it did not break.

"Did he hurt you?"

"No, not really."

"Come on upstairs. We'll report it."

"Oh, no."

"He can't get away with that. It shouldn't be allowed."

"There isn't anybody to report to," Rose said with relief. "The Librarian goes off at noon on Saturdays."

"It's disgusting," he said in a high-pitched, excitable voice. Rose was sorry now that she had told him anything, and said she had to get back to work.

"Are you really all right?"

"Oh yes."

"I'll be right here. Just call me if he comes back."

That was Patrick. If she had been trying to make him fall in love with her, there was no better way she could have chosen. He had many chivalric notions, which he pretended to mock, by saying certain words and phrases as if in quotation marks. *The fair sex*, he would say, and *damsel in distress*. Coming to his carrel with that story, Rose had turned herself into a damsel in distress. The pretended irony would not fool anybody; it was clear that he did wish to operate in a world of knights and ladies; outrages; devotions.

She continued to see him in the Library, every Saturday, and often she met him walking across the campus or in the cafeteria. He made a point of greeting her with courtesy and concern, saying, "How are you," in a way that suggested she might have suffered a further attack, or might still be recovering from the first one. He always flushed deeply when he saw her, and she thought that this was because the memory of what she had told him so embarrassed him. Later she found out it was because he was in love.

He discovered her name, and where she lived. He phoned her at Dr. Henshawe's house and asked her to go to the movies. At first when he said, "This is Patrick Blatchford speaking," Rose could not think who it was, but after a moment she recognized the high, rather aggrieved and tremulous voice. She said she would go. This was partly because Dr. Henshawe was always saying she was glad Rose did not waste her time running around with boys.

Rather soon after she started to go out with him, she said to Patrick, "Wouldn't it be funny if it was you grabbed my leg that day in the Library?"

He did not think it would be funny. He was horrified that she would think such a thing.

She said she was only joking. She said she meant that it would be a good twist in a story, maybe a Maugham story, or a Hitchcock movie. They had just been to see a Hitchcock movie.

"You know, if Hitchcock made a movie out of something like that, you could be a wild insatiable leg-grabber with one half of your personality, and the other half could be a timid scholar."

He didn't like that either.

"Is that how I seem to you, a timid scholar?" It seemed to her he deepened his voice, introduced a few growling notes, drew in his chin, as if for a joke. But he seldom joked with her; he didn't think joking was suitable when you were in love.

"I didn't say you were a timid scholar or a leg-grabber. It was just an idea."

After a while he said, "I suppose I don't seem very manly."

She was startled and irritated by such an exposure. He took such chances; had nothing ever taught him not to take such chances? But maybe he didn't, after all. He knew she would have to say something reassuring. Though she was longing not to, she longed to say judiciously, "Well, no. You don't."

But that would not actually be true. He did seem masculine to her. Because he took those chances. Only a man could be so careless and demanding.

"We come from two different worlds," she said to him, on another occasion. She felt like a character in a play, saying that. "My people are poor people. You would think the place I lived in was a dump."

Now she was the one who was being dishonest, pretending to throw herself on his mercy, for of course she did not expect him to say, oh, well, if you come from poor people and live in a dump, then I will have to withdraw my offer.

"But I'm glad," said Patrick. "I'm glad you're poor. You're so lovely. You're like the Beggar Maid."

"Who?"

"King Cophetua and the Beggar Maid. You know. The painting. Don't you know that painting?"

Patrick had a trick—no, it was not a trick, Patrick had no tricks—Patrick had a way of expressing surprise, fairly scornful surprise, when people did not know something he knew, and similar scorn, similar surprise, whenever they had bothered to know something he did not. His arrogance and humility were both oddly exaggerated. The arrogance, Rose decided in time, must come from being rich, though Patrick was never arrogant about that in itself. His sisters, when she met them, turned out to be the same way, disgusted with anybody who did not know about horses or sailing, and just as disgusted by anybody knowing about music, say, or politics. Patrick and they could do little together but radiate disgust. But wasn't Billy Pope as bad, wasn't Flo as bad, when it came to arrogance? Maybe. There was a difference, though, and the difference was that Billy Pope and Flo were not protected. Things could get at them: D.P.'s; people speaking French on the radio; changes. Patrick and his sisters behaved as if things could never get at them. Their voices, when they quarreled at the table, were astonishingly childish; their demands for food they liked, their petulance at seeing anything on the table they didn't like, were those of children. They had never had to defer and polish themselves and win favor in the world, they never would have to, and that was because they were rich.

Rose had no idea at the beginning, how rich Patrick was. Nobody believed that. Everybody believed she had been calculating and clever, and she was so far from clever, in that way, that she really did not mind if they believed it. It turned out that other girls had been trying, and had not struck, as she had, the necessary note. Older girls, sorority girls, who had never noticed her before, began to look at her with puzzlement and respect. Even Dr. Henshawe, when she saw that things were more serious than she had supposed, and settled Rose down to have a talk about it, assumed that she would have an eye on the money.

"It is no small triumph to attract the attentions of the heir to a mercantile empire," said Dr. Henshawe, being ironic and serious at the same time. "I don't despise wealth," she said. "Sometimes I wish I had some of it." (Did she really suppose she had not?) "I am sure you will learn how to put it to good uses. But what about your ambitions, Rose? What about your studies and your degree? Are you going to forget all that so soon?"

Mercantile Empire was a rather grand way of putting it. Patrick's family owned a chain of department stores in British Columbia. All Patrick had said to Rose was that his father owned some stores. When she said *two different worlds* to him she was thinking that he probably lived in some substantial house like the houses in Dr. Henshawe's neighborhood. She was thinking of the most prosperous merchants in Hanratty. She could not realize what a coup she had made because it would have been a coup for her if the butcher's son had fallen for her, or the jeweler's; people would say she had done well.

She had a look at that painting. She looked it up in an art book in the Library. She studied the Beggar Maid, meek and voluptuous, with her shy white feet. The milky surrender of her, the helplessness and gratitude. Was that how Patrick saw Rose? Was that how she could be? She would need that king, sharp and swarthy as he looked, even in his trance of passion, clever and barbaric. He could make a puddle of her, with his fierce desire. There would be no apologizing with him, none of that flinching, that lack of faith, that seemed to be revealed in all transactions with Patrick.

She could not turn Patrick down. She could not do it. It was not the amount of money but the amount of love he offered that she could not ignore; she believed that she felt sorry for him, that she had to help him out. It was as if he had come up to her in a crowd carrying a large, simple, dazzling object—a huge egg, maybe, of solid silver, something of doubtful use and punishing weight—and was offering it to her, in fact thrusting it at her, begging her to take some of the weight of it off him. If she thrust it back, how could he bear it? But that explanation left something out. It left out her own appetite, which was not for wealth but for worship. The size, the weight, the shine, of what he said was love (and she did not doubt him) had to impress her, even though she had never asked for it. It did not seem likely such an offering would come her way again. Patrick himself, though worshipful, did in some oblique way acknowledge her luck.

She had always thought this would happen, that somebody would look at her and love her totally and helplessly. At the same time she had thought that nobody would, nobody would want her at all, and up until now, nobody had. What made you wanted was nothing you did, it was something you had, and how could you ever tell whether you had it? She would look at herself in the glass and think: *wife, sweetheart.* Those mild lovely words. How could they apply to her? It was a miracle; it was a mistake. It was what she had dreamed of; it was not what she wanted.

She grew very tired, irritable, sleepless. She tried to think admiringly of Patrick. His lean, fair-skinned face was really very handsome. He must know a number of things. He graded papers, presided at examinations, he was finishing his thesis. There was a smell of pipe tobacco and rough wool about him, that she liked. He was twenty-four. No other girl she knew, who had a boyfriend, had one as old as that.

Then without warning she thought of him saying, "I suppose I don't seem very manly." She thought of him saying, "Do you love me? Do you really love me?" He would look at her in a scared and threatening way. Then when she said yes he said how lucky he was, how lucky they were, he mentioned friends of his and their girls, comparing their love affairs unfavorably to his and Rose's. Rose would shiver with irritation and misery. She was sick of herself as much as him, she was sick of the picture they made at this moment, walking across a snowy downtown park, her bare hand snuggled in Patrick's, in his pocket. Some outrageous and cruel things were being shouted, inside her. She had to do something, to keep them from getting out. She started tickling and teasing him.

Outside Dr. Henshawe's back door, in the snow, she kissed him, tried to make him open his mouth, she did scandalous things to him. When he kissed her his lips were soft; his tongue was shy; he collapsed over rather than held her, she could not find any force in him.

"You're lovely. You have lovely skin. Such fair eyebrows. You're so delicate."

She was pleased to hear that, anybody would be. But she said warningly, "I'm not so delicate, really. I'm quite large."

"You don't know how I love you. There's a book I have called *The White Goddess.* Every time I look at the title it reminds me of you."

She wriggled away from him. She bent down and got a handful of snow from the drift by the steps and clapped it on his head.

"My White God."

He shook the snow out. She scooped up some more and threw it at him. He didn't laugh, he was surprised and alarmed. She brushed the snow off his eyebrows and licked it off his ears. She was laughing, though she felt desperate rather than merry. She didn't know what made her do this.

"Dr. *Hen*-shawe," Patrick hissed at her. The tender poetic voice he used for rhapsodizing about her could entirely disappear, could change to remonstrance, exasperation, with no steps at all between.

"Dr. Henshawe will hear you!"

"Dr. Henshawe says you are an honorable young man," Rose said dreamily. "I think she's in love with you." It was true; Dr. Henshawe had said that. And it was true that he was. He couldn't bear the way Rose was talking. She blew at the snow in his hair. "Why don't you go in and deflower her? I'm sure she's a virgin. That's her window. Why don't you?" She rubbed his hair, then slipped her hand inside his overcoat and rubbed the front of his pants. "You're hard!" she said triumphantly. "Oh, Patrick! You've got a hard-on for Dr. Henshawe!" She had never said anything like this before, never come near behaving like this.

"Shut up!" said Patrick, tormented. But she couldn't. She raised her head and in a loud whisper pretended to call toward an upstairs window, "Dr. Henshawe! Come and see what Patrick's got for you!" Her bullying hand went for his fly.

To stop her, to keep her quiet, Patrick had to struggle with her. He got a hand over her mouth, with the other hand beat her away from his zipper. The big loose sleeves of his overcoat beat at her like floppy wings. As soon as he started to fight she was relieved—that was what she wanted from him, some sort of action. But she had to keep resisting, until he really proved himself stronger. She was afraid he might not be able to.

But he was. He forced her down, down, to her knees, face down in the snow. He pulled her arms back and rubbed her face in the snow. Then he let her go, and almost spoiled it.

"Are you all right? Are you? I'm sorry. Rose?"

She staggered up and shoved her snowy face into his. He backed off.

"Kiss me! Kiss the snow! I love you!"

"Do you?" he said plaintively, and brushed the snow from a corner of her mouth and kissed her, with understandable bewilderment. "Do you?"

Then the light came on, flooding them and the trampled snow, and Dr. Henshawe was calling over their heads.

"Rose! Rose!"

She called in a patient, encouraging voice, as if Rose was lost in a fog nearby, and needed directing home.

Do you love him, Rose?" said Dr. Henshawe. "No, think about it. Do you?" Her voice was full of doubt and seriousness. Rose took a deep breath and answered as if filled with calm emotion, "Yes, I do."

"Well, then."

In the middle of the night Rose woke up and ate chocolate bars. She craved sweets. Often in class or in the middle of a movie she started thinking about fudge cupcakes, brownies, some kind of cake Dr. Henshawe bought at the European Bakery; it was filled with dollops of rich bitter chocolate, that ran out on the plate. Whenever she tried to think about herself and Patrick, whenever she made up her mind to decide what she really felt, these cravings intervened.

She was putting on weight, and had developed a nest of pimples between her eyebrows.

Her bedroom was cold, being over the garage, with windows on three sides. Otherwise it was pleasant. Over the bed hung framed photographs of Greek skies and ruins, taken by Dr. Henshawe herself on her Mediterranean trip.

She was writing an essay on Yeats's plays. In one of the plays a young bride is lured away by the fairies from her sensible unbearable marriage.

"Come away, O human child . . ." Rose read, and her eyes filled up with tears for herself, as if she was that shy elusive virgin, too fine for the bewildered peasants who have entrapped her. In actual fact she was the peasant, shocking high-minded Patrick, but he did not look for escape.

She took down one of those Greek photographs and defaced the wallpaper, writing the start of a poem which had come to her while she ate chocolate bars in bed and the wind from Gibbons Park banged at the garage walls.

> Heedless in my dark womb
> I bear a madman's child . . .

She never wrote any more of it, and wondered sometimes if she had meant headless. She never tried to rub it out, either.

Patrick shared an apartment with two other graduate students. He lived plainly, did not own a car or belong to a fraternity. His clothes had an ordinary academic shabbiness. His friends were the sons of teachers and ministers. He said his father had all but disowned him, for becoming an intellectual. He said he would never go into business.

They came back to the apartment in the early afternoon when they knew both the other students would be out. The apartment was cold. They undressed quickly and got into Patrick's bed. Now was the time. They clung together, shivering and giggling. Rose was doing the giggling. She felt a need to be continually playful. She was terrified that they would not manage it, that there was a great humiliation in store, a great exposure of their poor deceits and stratagems. But the deceits and stratagems were only hers. Patrick was never a fraud; he managed, in spite of gigantic embarrassment, apologies; he passed through some amazed pantings and flounderings, to peace. Rose was no help, presenting instead of an honest passivity much twisting and fluttering eagerness, unpracticed counterfeit of passion. She was pleased when it was accomplished; she did not have to counterfeit that. They had done what others did, they had done what lovers did. She thought of celebration. What occurred to her was something delicious to eat, a sundae at Boomers, apple pie with hot cinnamon sauce. She was not at all prepared for Patrick's idea, which was to stay where they were and try again.

When pleasure presented itself, the fifth or sixth time they were together, she was thrown out of gear entirely, her passionate carrying-on was silenced.

Patrick said, "What's the matter?"

"Nothing!" Rose said, turning herself radiant and attentive once more. But she kept forgetting, the new developments interfered, and she had finally to give in to that struggle, more or less ignoring Patrick. When she could take note of him again she overwhelmed him with gratitude; she was really grateful now, and she wanted to be forgiven, though she could not say so, for all her pretended gratitude, her patronizing, her doubts.

Why should she doubt so much, she thought, lying comfortably in the bed while Patrick went to make some instant coffee. Might it not be possible, to feel as she pretended? If this sexual surprise was possible, wasn't anything? Patrick was not much help; his chivalry and self-abasement, next door to his scoldings, did discourage her. But wasn't the real fault hers? Her conviction that anyone who could fall in love with her must be hopelessly lacking, must finally be revealed as a fool? So she took note of anything that was foolish about Patrick, even though she thought she was looking for things that were masterful, admirable. At this moment, in his bed, in his room, surrounded by his books and clothes, his shoe brushes and typewriter, some tacked-up cartoons—she sat up in bed to look at them, and they really were quite funny, he must allow things to be funny when she was not here—she could see him as a likable, intelligent, even humorous person; no hero; no fool. Perhaps they could be ordinary. If only, when he came back in, he would not start thanking and fondling and worshiping her. She didn't like worship, really; it was only the idea of it she liked. On the other hand, she didn't like it when he started to correct and criticize her. There was much he planned to change.

Patrick loved her. What did he love? Not her accent, which he was trying hard to alter, though she was often mutinous and unreasonable, declaring in the face of all evidence that she did not have a country accent, everybody talked the way she did. Not her jittery sexual boldness (his relief at her virginity matched hers at his competence). She could make him flinch at a vulgar word, a drawling tone. All the time, moving and speaking, she was destroying herself for him, yet he looked right through her, through all the distractions she was creating, and loved some obedient image that she herself could not see. And his hopes were high. Her accent could be eliminated, her friends could be discredited and removed, her vulgarity could be discouraged.

What about all the rest of her? Energy, laziness, vanity, discontent, ambition? She concealed all that. He had no idea. For all her doubts about him, she never wanted him to fall out of love with her.

They made two trips.

They went to British Columbia, on the train, during the Easter holidays. His parents sent Patrick money for his ticket. He paid for Rose, using up what he had in the bank and borrowing from one of his roommates. He told her not to reveal to his parents that she had not paid for her own ticket. She saw that he meant to conceal that she was poor. He knew nothing about women's clothes, or he would not have thought that possible. Though she had done the best she could. She had borrowed Dr. Henshawe's raincoat for the coastal weather. It was a bit long, but otherwise all right, due to Dr. Henshawe's classically youthful tastes. She had sold more blood and bought a fuzzy angora sweater, peach-colored, which was extremely messy and looked like a small-town girl's idea of dressing up. She always realized things like that as soon as a purchase was made, not before.

Patrick's parents lived on Vancouver Island, near Sidney. About half an acre of clipped green lawn—green in the middle of winter; March seemed like the middle of winter to Rose—sloped down to a stone wall and a narrow pebbly beach and salt water. The house was half stone, half stucco-and-timber. It was built in the Tudor style, and others. The windows of the living room, the dining room, the den, all faced the sea, and because of the strong winds that sometimes blew onshore, they were made of thick glass, plate glass Rose supposed, like the windows of the automobile showroom in Hanratty. The seaward wall of the dining room was all windows, curving out in a gentle bay; you looked through the thick curved glass as through the bottom of a bottle. The sideboard too had a curving, gleaming belly, and seemed as big as a boat. Size was noticeable everywhere and particularly thickness. Thickness of towels and rugs and handles of knives and forks, and silences. There was a terrible amount of luxury and unease. After a day or so there Rose became so discouraged that her wrists and ankles felt weak. Picking up her knife and fork was a chore; cutting and chewing the perfect roast beef was almost beyond her; she got short of breath climbing the stairs. She had never known before how some places could choke you off, choke off your very life. She had not known this in spite of a number of very unfriendly places she had been in.

The first morning, Patrick's mother took her for a walk on the grounds, pointing out the greenhouse, the cottage where "the couple" lived: a charming, ivied, shuttered cottage, bigger than Dr. Henshawe's house. The couple, the servants, were more gentle-spoken, more discreet and dignified, than anyone Rose could think of in Hanratty, and indeed they were superior in these ways to Patrick's family.

Patrick's mother showed her the rose garden, the kitchen garden. There were many low stone walls.

"Patrick built them," said his mother. She explained anything with an indifference that bordered on distaste. "He built all these walls."

Rose's voice came out full of false assurance, eager and inappropriately enthusiastic.

"He must be a true Scot," she said. Patrick was a Scot, in spite of his name. The Blatchfords had come from Glasgow. "Weren't the best stonemasons always Scotsmen?" (She had learned quite recently not to say "Scotch.") "Maybe he had stonemason ancestors."

She cringed afterward, thinking of these efforts, the pretense of ease and gaiety, as cheap and imitative as her clothes.

"No," said Patrick's mother. "No. I don't think they were stonemasons." Something like fog went out from her: affront, disapproval, dismay. Rose thought that perhaps she had been offended by the suggestion that her husband's family might have worked with their hands. When she got to know her better—or had observed her longer; it was impossible to get to know her—she understood that Patrick's mother disliked anything fanciful, speculative, abstract, in conversation. She would also, of course, dislike Rose's chatty tone. Any interest beyond the factual consideration of the matter at hand—food, weather, invitations, furniture, servants—seemed to her sloppy, ill-bred, and dangerous. It was all right to say, "This is a warm day," but not, "This day reminds me of when we used to—" She hated people being *reminded*.

She was the only child of one of the early lumber barons of Vancouver Island. She had been born in a vanished northern settlement. But whenever Patrick tried to get her to talk about the past, whenever he asked her for the simplest sort of information—what steamers went up the coast, what year was the settlement abandoned, what was the route of the first logging railway—she would say irritably, "I don't know. How would I know about that?" This irritation was the strongest note that ever got into her words.

Neither did Patrick's father care for this concern about the past. Many things, most things, about Patrick, seemed to strike him as bad signs.

"What do you want to know all that for?" he shouted down the table. He was a short square-shouldered man, red-faced, astonishingly belligerent. Patrick looked like his mother, who was tall, fair, and elegant in the most muted way possible, as if her clothes, her makeup, her style, were chosen with an ideal neutrality in mind.

"Because I am interested in history," said Patrick in an angry, pompous, but nervously breaking voice.

"Because-I-am-interested-in-history," said his sister Marion in an immediate parody, break and all. "History!"

The sisters Joan and Marion were younger than Patrick, older than Rose. Unlike Patrick they showed no nervousness, no cracks in self-satisfaction. At an earlier meal they had questioned Rose.

"Do you ride?"

"No."

"Do you sail?"

"No."

"Play tennis? Play golf? Play badminton?"

No. No. No.

"Perhaps she is an intellectual genius, like Patrick," the father said. And Patrick, to Rose's horror and embarrassment, began to shout at the table in general an account of her scholarships and prizes. What did he hope for? Was he so witless as to think such bragging would subdue them, would bring out anything but further scorn? Against Patrick, against his shouting boasts, his contempt for sports and television, his so-called intellectual interests, the family seemed united. But this alliance was only temporary. The father's dislike of his daughters was minor only in comparison with his dislike of Patrick. He railed at them too, when he could spare a moment; he jeered at the amount of time they spent at their games, complained about the cost of their equipment,. their boats, their horses. And they wrangled with each other, on obscure questions of scores and borrowings and damages. All complained to the mother about the food, which was plentiful and delicious. The mother spoke as little as possible to anyone and to tell the truth Rose did not blame her. She had never imagined so much true malevolence collected in one place. Billy Pope was a bigot and a grumbler, Flo was capricious, unjust, and gossipy, her father, when he was alive, had been capable of cold judgments and unremitting disapproval; but compared to Patrick's family, all Rose's own people seemed jovial and content.

"Are they always like this?" she said to Patrick. "Is it me? They don't like me."

"They don't like you because I chose you," said Patrick with some satisfaction.

They lay on the stony beach after dark, in their raincoats, hugged and kissed and uncomfortably, unsuccessfully, attempted more. Rose got seaweed stains on Dr. Henshawe's coat. Patrick said, "You see why I need you? I need you so much!"

She took him to Hanratty. It was just as bad as she had thought it would be. Flo had gone to great trouble, and cooked a meal of scalloped potatoes, turnips, big country sausages which were a special present from Billy Pope, from the butcher shop. Patrick detested coarse-textured food, and made no pretense of eating it. The table was spread with a plastic cloth, they ate under the tube of fluorescent light. The centerpiece was new and especially for the occasion. A plastic swan, lime green in color, with slits in the wings, in which were stuck folded, colored paper napkins. Billy Pope, reminded to take one, grunted, refused. Otherwise he was on dismally good behavior. Word had reached him, word had reached both of them, of Rose's triumph. It had come from their superiors in Hanratty; otherwise they could not have believed it. Customers in the butcher shop—formidable ladies, the dentist's wife, the veterinarian's wife—had said to Billy Pope that they heard Rose had picked herself up a millionaire. Rose knew Billy Pope would go back to work tomorrow with stories of the millionaire, or millionaire's son, and that all these stories would focus on his— Billy Pope's—forthright and unintimidated behavior in the situation.

"We just set him down and give him some sausages, don't make no difference to us what he comes from!"

She knew Flo would have her comments too, that Patrick's nervousness would not escape her, that she would be able to mimic his voice and his flapping hands that had knocked over the ketchup bottle. But at present they both sat hunched over the table in miserable eclipse. Rose tried to start some conversation, talking brightly, unnaturally, rather as if she was an interviewer trying to draw out a couple of simple local people. She felt ashamed on more levels than she could count. She was ashamed of the food and the swan and the plastic tablecloth; ashamed for Patrick, the gloomy snob, who made a startled grimace when Flo passed him the toothpick-holder; ashamed for Flo with her timidity and hypocrisy and pretensions; most of all ashamed for herself. She didn't even have any way that she could talk, and sound natural. With Patrick there, she couldn't slip back into an accent closer to Flo's, Billy Pope's and Hanratty's. That accent jarred on her ears now, anyway. It seemed to involve not just a different pronunciation but a whole different approach to talking. Talking was shouting; the words were separated and emphasized so that people could bombard each other with them. And the things people said were like lines from the most hackneyed rural comedy. *Wal if a feller took a notion to*, they said. They really said that. Seeing them through Patrick's eyes, hearing them through his ears, Rose too had to be amazed.

She was trying to get them to talk about local history, some things she thought Patrick might be interested in. Presently Flo did begin to talk, she could only be held in so long, whatever her misgivings. The conversation took another line from anything Rose had intended.

"The line I lived on when I was just young," Flo said, "it was the worst place ever created for suiciding."

"A line is a concession road. In the township," Rose said to Patrick. She had doubts about what was coming, and rightly so, for then Patrick got to hear about a man who cut his own throat, *his own throat*, from ear to ear, a man who shot himself the first time and didn't do enough damage, so he loaded up and fired again and managed it, another man who hanged himself using a chain, the kind of chain you hook on a tractor with, so it was a wonder his head was not torn off.

Tore off, Flo said.

She went on to a woman who, though not a suicide, had been dead in her house a week before she was found, and that was in the summer. She asked Patrick to imagine it. All this happened, said Flo, within five miles of where she herself was born. She was presenting credentials, not trying to horrify Patrick, at least not more than was acceptable, in a social way; she did not mean to disconcert him. How could he understand that?

"You were right," said Patrick, as they left Hanratty on the bus. "It is a dump. You must be glad to get away."

Rose felt immediately that he should not have said that.

"Of course that's not your real mother," Patrick said. "Your real parents can't have been like that." Rose did not like his saying that either, though it was what she believed, herself. She saw that he was trying to provide for her a more genteel background, perhaps something like the homes of his poor friends: a few books about, a tea tray, and mended linen, worn good taste; proud, tired, educated people. What a coward he was, she thought angrily, but she knew that she herself was the coward, not knowing any way to be comfortable with her own people or the kitchen or any of it. Years later she would learn how to use it, she would be able to amuse or intimidate right-thinking people at dinner parties with glimpses of her early home. At the moment she felt confusion, misery.

Nevertheless her loyalty was starting. Now that she was sure of getting away, a layer of loyalty and protectiveness was hardening around every memory she had, around the store and the town, the flat, somewhat scrubby, unremarkable countryside. She would oppose this secretly to Patrick's views of mountains and ocean, his stone and timbered mansion. Her allegiances were far more proud and stubborn than his.

But it turned out he was not leaving anything behind.

Patrick gave her a diamond ring and announced that he was giving up being a historian for her sake. He was going into his father's business.

She said she thought he hated his father's business. He said that he could not afford to take such an attitude now that he would have a wife to support.

It seemed that Patrick's desire to marry, even to marry Rose, had been taken by his father as a sign of sanity. Great streaks of bounty were mixed in with all the ill will in that family. His father at once offered a job in one of the stores, offered to buy them a house. Patrick was as incapable of turning down this offer as Rose was of turning down Patrick's, and his reasons were as little mercenary as hers.

"Will we have a house like your parents?" Rose said. She really thought it might be necessary to start off in that style.

"Well, maybe not at first. Not quite so—"

"I don't want a house like that! I don't want to live like that!"

"We'll live however you like. We'll have whatever kind of house you like."

Provided it's not a dump, she thought nastily.

Girls she hardly knew stopped and asked to see her ring, admired it, wished her happiness. When she went back to Hanratty for a weekend, alone this time, thank God, she met the dentist's wife on the main street.

"Oh, Rose, isn't it wonderful! When are you coming back again? We're going to give a tea for you, the ladies in town all want to give a tea for you!"

This woman had never spoken to Rose, never given any sign before of knowing who she was. Paths were opening now, barriers were softening. And Rose—oh, this was the worst, this was the shame of it— Rose, instead of cutting the dentist's wife, was blushing and skittishly flashing her diamond and saying yes, that would be a lovely idea. When people said how happy she must be she did think herself happy. It was as simple as that. She dimpled and sparkled and turned herself into a fiancée with no trouble at all. Where will you live, people said and she said, Oh, in British Columbia! That added more magic to the tale. Is it really beautiful there, they said, is it never winter?

"Oh, yes!" cried Rose. "Oh, no!"

She woke up early, got up and dressed and let herself out of the side door of Dr. Henshawe's garage. It was too early for the buses to be running. She walked through the city to Patrick's apartment. She walked across the park. Around the South African War Memorial a pair of greyhounds were leaping and playing, an old woman standing by, holding their leashes. The sun was just up, shining on their pale hides. The grass was wet. Daffodils and narcissus in bloom.

Patrick came to the door, tousled, frowning sleepily, in his gray and maroon striped pajamas.

"Rose! What's the matter?"

She couldn't say anything. He pulled her into the apartment. She put her arms around him and hid her face against his chest and in a stagey voice said, "Please Patrick. Please let me not marry you."

"Are you sick? What's the matter?"

"Please let me not marry you," she said again, with even less conviction.

"You're crazy."

She didn't blame him for thinking so. Her voice sounded so unnatural, wheedling, silly. As soon as he opened the door and she faced the fact of him, his sleepy eyes, his pajamas, she saw that what she had come to do was enormous, impossible. She would have to explain everything to him, and of course she could not do it. She could not make him see her necessity. She could not find any tone of voice, any expression of the face, that would serve her.

"Are you upset?" said Patrick. "What's happened?"

"Nothing."

"How did you get here anyway?"

"Walked."

She had been fighting back a need to go to the bathroom. It seemed that if she went to the bathroom she would destroy some of the strength of her case. But she had to. She freed herself. She said, "Wait a minute, I'm going to the john."

When she came out Patrick had the electric kettle going, was measuring out instant coffee. He looked decent and bewildered.

"I'm not really awake," he said. "Now. Sit down. First of all, are you premenstrual?"

"No." But she realized with dismay that she was, and that he might be able to figure it out, because they had been worried last month.

"Well, if you're not premenstrual, and nothing's happened to upset you, then what is all this about?"

"I don't want to get married," she said, backing away from the cruelty of *I don't want to marry you.*

"When did you come to this decision?"

"Long ago. This morning."

They were talking in whispers. Rose looked at the clock. It was a little after seven.

"When do the others get up?"

"About eight."

"Is there milk for the coffee?" She went to the refrigerator.

"Quiet with the door," said Patrick, too late.

"I'm sorry," she said, in her strange silly voice.

"We went for a walk last night and everything was fine. You come this morning and tell me you don't want to get married. *Why* don't you want to get married?"

"I just don't. I don't want to be married."

"What else do you want to do?"

"I don't know."

Patrick kept staring at her sternly, drinking his coffee. He who used to plead with her *do you love me, do you really*, did not bring the subject up now.

"Well I know."

"What?"

"I know who's been talking to you."

"Nobody has been talking to me."

"Oh, no. Well, I bet. Dr. Henshawe has."

"No."

"Some people don't have a very high opinion of her. They think she has an influence on girls. She doesn't like the girls who live with her to have boyfriends. Does she? You even told me that. She doesn't like them to be normal."

"That's not it."

"What did she say to you, Rose?"

"She didn't say anything." Rose began to cry.

"Are you sure?"

"Oh, Patrick, listen, please, I can't marry you, please, I don't know why, I can't, please, I'm sorry, believe me, I can't," Rose babbled at him, weeping, and Patrick saying, "Ssh! You'll wake them up!" lifted or dragged her out of the kitchen chair and took her to his room, where she sat on the bed. He shut the door. She held her arms across her stomach, and rocked back and forth.

"What is it, Rose? What's the matter? Are you sick!"

"It's just so hard to tell you!"

"Tell me what?"

"What I just did tell you!"

"I mean have you found out you have T.B. or something?"

"No!"

"Is there something in your family you haven't told me about? Insanity?" said Patrick encouragingly.

"No!" Rose rocked and wept.

"So what is it?"

"I don't love you!" she said. "I don't love you. I don't love you." She fell on the bed and put her head in the pillow. "I'm so sorry. I'm so sorry. I can't help it."

After a moment or two Patrick said, "Well. If you don't love me you don't love me. I'm not forcing you to." His voice sounded strained and spiteful, against the reasonableness of what he was saying. "I just wonder," he said, "if you know what you do want. I don't think you do. I don't think you have any idea what you want. You're just in a state."

"I don't have to know what I want to know what I don't want!" Rose said, turning over. This released her. "I never loved you."

"Ssh. You'll wake them. We have to stop."

"I never loved you. I never wanted to. It was a mistake."

"All right. All right. You made your point."

"Why am I supposed to love you? Why do you act as if there was something wrong with me if I didn't? You despise me. You despise my family and my background and you think you are doing me a *great favor*—"

"I fell in love with you," Patrick said. "I don't despise you. Oh, Rose. I worship you."

"You're a sissy," Rose said. "You're a prude." She jumped off the bed with great pleasure as she said this. She felt full of energy. More was coming. Terrible things were coming.

"You don't even know how to make love right. I always wanted to get out of this from the very first. I felt sorry for you. You won't look where you're going, you're always knocking things over, just because you can't be bothered, you can't be bothered noticing anything, you're wrapped up in yourself, and you're always bragging, it's so stupid, you don't even know how to brag right, if you really want to impress people you'll never do it, the way you do it all they do is laugh at you!"

Patrick sat on the bed and looked up at her, his face open to whatever she would say. She wanted to beat and beat him, to say worse and worse, uglier and crueller, things. She took a breath, drew in air, to stop the things she felt rising in her from getting out.

"I don't want to see you, ever!" she said viciously. But at the door she turned and said in a normal and regretful voice, "Good-bye."

Patrick wrote her a note: "I don't understand what happened the other day and I want to talk to you about it. But I think we should wait for two weeks and not see or talk to each other and find out how we feel at the end of that time."

Rose had forgotten all about giving him back his ring. When she came out of his apartment building that morning she was still wearing it. She couldn't go back, and it seemed too valuable to send through the mail. She continued to wear it, mostly because she did not want to have to tell Dr. Henshawe what had happened. She was relieved to get Patrick's note. She thought that she could give him back the ring then.

She thought about what Patrick had said about Dr. Henshawe. No doubt there was some truth in that, else why should she be so reluctant to tell Dr. Henshawe she had broken her engagement, so unwilling to face her sensible approval, her restrained, relieved congratulations?

She told Dr. Henshawe that she was not seeing Patrick while she studied for her exams. Rose could see that even that pleased her.

She told no one that her situation had changed. It was not just Dr. Henshawe she didn't want knowing. She didn't like giving up being envied; the experience was so new to her.

She tried to think what to do next. She could not stay on at Dr. Henshawe's. It seemed clear that if she escaped from Patrick, she must escape from Dr. Henshawe too. And she did not want to stay on at the college, with people knowing about her broken engagement, with the girls who now congratulated her saying they had known all along it was a fluke, her getting Patrick. She would have to get a job.

The Head Librarian had offered her a job for the summer but that was perhaps at Dr. Henshawe's suggestion. Once she moved out, the offer might not hold. She knew that instead of studying for her exams she ought to be downtown, applying for work as a filing clerk at the insurance offices, applying at Bell Telephone, at the department stores. The idea frightened her. She kept on studying. That was the one thing she really knew how to do. She was a scholarship student after all.

On Saturday afternoon, when she was working at the Library, she saw Patrick. She did not see him by accident. She went down to the bottom floor, trying not to make a noise on the spiraling metal staircase. There was a place in the stacks where she could stand, almost in darkness, and see into his carrel. She did that. She couldn't see his face. She saw his long pink neck and the old plaid shirt he wore on Saturdays. His long neck. His bony shoulders. She was no longer irritated by him, no longer frightened by him; she was free. She could look at him as she would look at anybody. She could appreciate him. He had behaved well. He had not tried to rouse her pity, he had not bullied her, he had not molested her with pitiful telephone calls and letters. He had not come and sat on Dr. Henshawe's doorstep. He was an honorable person, and he would never know how she acknowledged that, how she was grateful for it. The things she had said to him made her ashamed now. And they were not even true. Not all of them. He did know how to make love. She was so moved, made so gentle and wistful, by the sight of him, that she wanted to give him something, some surprising bounty, she wished to undo his unhappiness.

Then she had a compelling picture of herself. She was running softly into Patrick's carrel, she was throwing her arms around him from behind, she was giving everything back to him. Would he take it from her, would he still want it? She saw them laughing and crying, explaining, forgiving. *I love you. I do love you, it's all right, I was terrible, I didn't mean it, I was just crazy, I love you, it's all right.* This was a violent temptation for her; it was barely resistable. She had an impulse to hurl herself. Whether it was off a cliff or into a warm bed of welcoming grass and flowers, she really could not tell.

It was not resistable, after all. She did it.

When Rose afterward reviewed and talked about this moment in her life—for she went through a period, like most people nowadays, of talking freely about her most private decisions, to friends and lovers and party acquaintances whom she might never see again, while they did the same—she said that comradely compassion had overcome her, she was not proof against the sight of a bare bent neck. Then she went further into it, and said greed, greed. She said she had run to him and clung to him and overcome his suspicions and kissed and cried and reinstated herself simply because she did not know how to do without his love and his promise to look after her; she was frightened of the world and she had not been able to think up any other plan for herself. When she was seeing life in economic terms, or was with people who did, she said that only middle-class people had choices anyway, that if she had had the price of a train ticket to Toronto her life would have been different.

Nonsense, she might say later, never mind that, it was really vanity, it was vanity pure and simple, to resurrect him, to bring him back his happiness. To see if she could do that. She could not resist such a test of power. She explained then that she had paid for it. She said that she and Patrick had been married ten years, and that during that time the scenes of the first breakup and reconciliation had been periodically repeated, with her saying again all the things she had said the first time, and the things she had held back, and many other things which occurred to her. She hopes she did not tell people (but thinks she did) that she used to beat her head against the bedpost, that she smashed a gravy boat through a dining-room window; that she was so frightened, so sickened by what she had done that she lay in bed, shivering, and begged and begged for his forgiveness. Which he granted. Sometimes she flew at him; sometimes he beat her. The next morning they would get up early and make a special breakfast, they would sit eating bacon and eggs and drinking filtered coffee, worn out, bewildered, treating each other with shamefaced kindness.

What do you think triggers the reaction? they would say.

Do you think we ought to take a holiday? A holiday together? Holidays alone?

A waste, a sham, those efforts, as it turned out. But they worked for the moment. Calmed down, they would say that most people probably went through the same things like this, in a marriage, and indeed they seemed to know mostly people who did. They could not separate until enough damage had been done, until nearly mortal damage had been done, to keep them apart. And until Rose could get a job and make her own money, so perhaps there was a very ordinary reason after all.

What she never said to anybody, never confided, was that she sometimes thought it had not been pity or greed or cowardice or vanity but something quite different, like a vision of happiness. In view of everything else she had told she could hardly tell that. It seems very odd; she can't justify it. She doesn't mean that they had perfectly ordinary, bearable times in their marriage, long busy stretches of wallpapering and vacationing and meals and shopping and worrying about a child's illness, but that sometimes, without reason or warning, happiness, the possibility of happiness, would surprise them. Then it was as if they were in different though identical-seeming skins, as if there existed a radiantly kind and innocent Rose and Patrick, hardly ever visible, in the shadow of their usual selves. Perhaps it was that Patrick she saw when she was free of him, invisible to him, looking into his carrel. Perhaps it was. She should have left him there.

She knew that was how she had seen him; she knows it, because it happened again. She was in Toronto Airport, in the middle of the night. This was about nine years after she and Patrick were divorced. She had become fairly well-known by this time, her face was familiar to many people in this country. She did a television program on which she interviewed politicians, actors, writers, *personalities*, and many ordinary people who were angry about something the government or the police or a union had done to them. Sometimes she talked to people who had seen strange sights. UFO's, or sea monsters, or who had unusual accomplishments or collections, or kept up some obsolete custom.

She was alone. No one was meeting her. She had just come in on a delayed flight from Yellowknife. She was tired and bedraggled. She saw Patrick standing with his back to her, at a coffee bar. He wore a raincoat. He was heavier than he had been, but she knew him at once. And she had the same feeling that this was a person she was bound to, that by a certain magical, yet possible trick, they could find and trust each other, and that to begin this all that she had to do was go up and touch him on the shoulder, surprise him with his happiness.

She did not do this, of course, but she did stop. She was standing still when he turned around, heading for one of the little plastic tables and curved seats grouped in front of the coffee bar. All his skinniness and academic shabbiness, his look of prim authoritarianism, was gone. He had smoothed out, filled out, into such a modish and agreeable, responsible, slightly complacent-looking man. His birthmark had faded. She thought how haggard and dreary she must look, in her rumpled trenchcoat, her long, graying hair fallen forward around her face, old mascara smudged under her eyes.

He made a face at her. It was a truly hateful, savagely warning, face; infantile, self-indulgent, yet calculated; it was a timed explosion of disgust and loathing. It was hard to believe. But she saw it.

Sometimes when Rose was talking to someone in front of the television cameras she would sense the desire in them to make a face. She would sense it in all sorts of people, in skillful politicians and witty liberal bishops and honored humanitarians, in housewives who had witnessed natural disasters and in workmen who had performed heroic rescues or been cheated out of disability pensions. They were longing to sabotage themselves, to make a face or say a dirty word. Was this the face they all wanted to make? To show somebody, to show everybody? They wouldn't do it, though; they wouldn't get the chance. Special circumstances were required. A lurid unreal place, the middle of the night, a staggering unhinging weariness, the sudden, hallucinatory appearance of your true enemy.

She hurried away then, down the long varicolored corridor, shaking. She had seen Patrick; Patrick had seen her; he had made that face. But she was not really able to understand how she could be an enemy. How could anybody hate Rose so much, at the very moment when she was ready to come forward with her good will, her smiling confession of exhaustion, her air of diffident faith in civilized overtures?

Oh, Patrick could. Patrick could.

Mischief

Rose fell in love with Clifford at a party which Clifford and Jocelyn gave and Patrick and Rose attended. They had been married about three years at this time, Clifford and Jocelyn a year or so longer.

Clifford and Jocelyn lived out past West Vancouver, in one of those summer cottages, haphazardly winterized, that used to line the short curving streets between the lower highway and the sea. The party was in March, on a rainy night. Rose was nervous about going to it. She felt almost sick as they drove through West Vancouver, watched the neon lights weeping in the puddles on the road, listened to the condemning tick of the windshield wipers. She would often afterward look back and see herself sitting beside Patrick, in her low-cut black blouse and black velvet skirt which she hoped would turn out to be the right thing to wear; she was wishing they were just going to the movies. She had no idea that her life was going to be altered.

Patrick was nervous too, although he would not have admitted it. Social life was a puzzling, often disagreeable business for them both. They had arrived in Vancouver knowing nobody. They followed leads. Rose was not sure whether they really longed for friends, or simply believed they ought to have them. They dressed up and went out to visit people, or tidied up the living room and waited for the people who had been invited to visit them. In some cases they established steady visiting patterns. They had some drinks, during those evenings, and around eleven or eleven-thirty—which hardly ever came soon enough—Rose went out to the kitchen and made coffee and something to eat. The things she made to eat were usually squares of toast, with a slice of tomato on top, then a square of cheese, then a bit of bacon, the whole thing broiled and held together with a toothpick. She could not manage to think of anything else.

It was easier for them to become friends with people Patrick liked than with people Rose liked because Rose was very adaptable, in fact deceitful, and Patrick was hardly adaptable at all. But in this case, the case of Jocelyn and Clifford, the friends were Rose's. Or Jocelyn was. Jocelyn and Rose had known enough not to try to establish couple-visiting. Patrick disliked Clifford without knowing him because Clifford was a violinist; no doubt Clifford disliked Patrick because Patrick worked in a branch of his family's department store. In those days the barriers between people were still strong and reliable; between arty people and business people; between men and women.

Rose did not know any of Jocelyn's friends, but understood they were musicians and journalists and lecturers at the University and even a woman writer who had had a play performed on the radio. She expected them to be intelligent, witty, and easily contemptuous. It seemed to her that all the time she and Patrick were sitting in the living rooms, visiting or being visited, really clever and funny people, who had a right to despise them, were conducting irregular lives and parties elsewhere. Now came the chance to be with those people, but her stomach rejected it, her hands were sweating.

Jocelyn and Rose had met in the maternity ward of the North Vancouver General Hospital. The first thing Rose saw, on being taken back to the ward after having Anna, was Jocelyn sitting up in bed reading the *Journals of André Gide*. Rose knew the book by its colors, having noticed it on the drugstore stands. Gide was on the list of writers she meant to work through. At that time she read only great writers.

The immediately startling and comforting thing to Rose, about Jocelyn, was how much Jocelyn looked like a student, how little she had let herself be affected by the maternity ward. Jocelyn had long black braids, a heavy pale face, thick glasses, no trace of prettiness, and an air of comfortable concentration.

A woman in the bed beside Jocelyn was describing the arrangement of her kitchen cupboards. She would forget to tell where she kept something—rice, say, or brown sugar—and then she would have to start all over again, making sure her audience was with her by saying "Remember on the right hand highest shelf next the stove, that's where I keep the packages of soup but not the canned soup, I keep the canned soup underneath the counter in with the canned goods, well, right next to that—"

Other women tried to interrupt, to tell how they kept things, but they were not successful, or not for long. Jocelyn sat reading, and twiddling the end of a braid between her fingers, as if she was in a library, at college, as if she was researching for a paper, and this world of other women had never closed down on her at all. Rose wished she could manage as well.

She was still dazed from the birth. Whenever she closed her eyes she saw an eclipse, a big black ball with a ring of fire. That was the baby's head, ringed with pain, the instant before she pushed it out. Across this image, in disturbing waves, went the talking woman's kitchen shelves, dipping under their glaring weight of cans and packages. But she could open her eyes and see Jocelyn, black and white, braids falling over her hospital nightgown. Jocelyn was the only person she saw who looked calm and serious enough to match the occasion.

Soon Jocelyn got out of bed, showing long white unshaved legs and a stomach still stretched by pregnancy. She put on a striped bathrobe. Instead of a cord, she tied a man's necktie around her waist. She slapped across the hospital linoleum in her bare feet. A nurse came running, warned her to put on slippers.

"I don't own any slippers."

"Do you own shoes?" said the nurse rather nastily.

"Oh, yes. I own shoes."

Jocelyn went back to the little metal cabinet beside her bed and took out a pair of large, dirty, run-over moccasins. She went off making as sloppy and insolent a noise as before.

Rose was longing to know her.

The next day Rose had her own book out to read. It was *The Last Puritan*, by George Santayana, but unfortunately it was a library copy; the title on the cover was rubbed and dim, so it was impossible that

Jocelyn should admire Rose's reading material as Rose had admired hers. Rose didn't know how she could get to talk to her.

The woman who had explained about her cupboards was talking about how she used her vacuum cleaner. She said it was very important to use all the attachments because they each had a purpose and after all you had paid for them. Many people didn't use them. She described how she vacuumed her living-room drapes. Another woman said she had tried to do that but the material kept getting bunched up. The authoritative woman said that was because she hadn't been doing it properly.

Rose caught Jocelyn's eye around the corner of her book.

"I hope you polish your stove knobs," she said quietly.

"I certainly do," said Jocelyn.

"Do you polish them every day?"

"I used to polish them twice a day but now that I have the new baby I just don't know if I'll get around to it."

"Do you use that special stove-knob polish?"

"I certainly do. And I use the special stove-knob cloths that come in that special package."

"That's good. Some people don't."

"Some people will use anything."

"Old dishrags."

"Old snotrags."

"Old snot."

After this their friendship bloomed in a hurry. It was one of those luxuriant intimacies that spring up in institutions; in schools, at camp, in prison. They walked in the halls, disobeying the nurses. They annoyed and mystified the other women. They became hysterical as schoolgirls, from the things they read aloud to each other. They did not read Gide or Santayana but the copies of *True Love* and *Personal Romances* which they had found in the waiting room.

"It says here you can buy false calves," Rose read. "I don't see how you'd hide them, though. I guess you strap them on your legs. Or maybe they just sit inside your stockings but wouldn't you think they'd show?"

"On your legs?" said Jocelyn. "You strap them on your legs? Oh, false calves! False calves! I thought you were talking about false *calves*! False baby cows!"

Anything like that could set them off.

"False baby cows!"

"False tits, false bums, false baby cows!"

"What will they think of next!"

The vacuum-cleaning woman said they were always butting in and spoiling other people's conversations and she didn't see what was so funny about dirty language. She said if they didn't stop the way they carried on they would sour their milk.

"I've been wondering if maybe mine *is* sour," Jocelyn said. "It's an awfully disgusting color."

"What color?" Rose asked.

"Well. Sort of blue."

"Good God, maybe it's ink!"

The vacuum-cleaning woman said she was going to tell the nurse they were swearing. She said she was no prude, but. She asked if they were fit to be mothers. How was Jocelyn going to manage to wash diapers, when anybody could see she never washed her dressing gown?

Jocelyn said she planned to use moss, she was an Indian.

"I can believe it," the woman said.

After this Jocelyn and Rose prefaced many remarks with: *I'm no prude, but.*

"I'm no prude but would you look at this pudding!"

"I'm no prude but it feels like this kid has a full set of teeth."

The nurse said, wasn't it time for them to grow up?

Walking in the halls, Jocelyn told Rose that she was twenty-five, that her baby was to be called Adam, that she had a two-year-old boy at home, named Jerome, that her husband's name was Clifford and that he played the violin for a living. He played in the Vancouver Symphony. They were poor. Jocelyn came from Massachusetts and had gone to Wellesley College. Her father was a psychiatrist and her mother was a pediatrician. Rose told Jocelyn that she came from a small town in Ontario and that Patrick came from Vancouver Island and that his parents did not approve of the marriage.

"In the town I come from," Rose said, exaggerating, "everybody says yez. What'll yez have? How're yez doin?"

"Yez?"

"Youse. It's the plural of you."

"Oh. Like Brooklyn. And James Joyce. Who does Patrick work for?"

"His family's store. His family has a department store."

"So aren't you rich now? Aren't you too rich to be in the ward?"

"We just spent all our money on a house Patrick wanted."

"Didn't you want it?"

"Not so much as he did."

That was something Rose had never said before.

They plunged into more random revelations.

Jocelyn hated her mother. Her mother had made her sleep in a room with white organdy curtains and had encouraged her to collect ducks. By the time she was thirteen Jocelyn had probably the largest collection in the world of rubber ducks, ceramic ducks, wooden ducks, pictures of ducks, embroidered ducks. She had also written what she described as a hideously precocious story called "The Marvelous Great Adventures of Oliver the Grand Duck," which her mother actually got printed and distributed to friends and relatives at Christmas time.

"She is the sort of person who just covers everything with a kind of rotten smarminess. She sort of oozes over everything. She never talks in a normal voice, never. She's coy. She's just so filthy coy. Naturally she's a great success as a pediatrician. She has these rotten coy little names for all the parts of your body."

Rose, who would have been delighted with organdy curtains, perceived the fine lines, the ways of giving offense, that existed in Jocelyn's world. It seemed a much less crude and provisional world than her own. She doubted if she could tell Jocelyn about Hanratty but she began to try. She delivered Flo and the store in broad strokes. She played up the poverty. She didn't really have to. The true facts of her childhood were exotic enough to Jocelyn, and of all things, enviable.

"It seems more real," Jocelyn said. "I know that's a romantic notion."

They talked of their youthful ambitions. (They really believed their youth to be past.) Rose said she had wanted to be an actress though she was too much of a coward ever to walk on a stage. Jocelyn had wanted to be a writer but was shamed out of it by memories of the Grand Duck.

"Then I met Clifford," she said. "When I saw what real talent was, I knew that I would probably just be fooling around, trying to write, and I'd be better off nurturing him, or whatever the hell it is I do for him. He is really gifted. Sometimes he's a squalid sort of person. He gets away with it because he is really gifted."

"I think *that* is a romantic notion," Rose said firmly and jealously. "That gifted people ought to get away with things."

"Do you? But great artists always have."

"Not women."

"But women usually aren't great artists, not in the same way."

These were the ideas of most well-educated, thoughtful, even unconventional or politically radical young women of the time. One of the reasons Rose did not share them was that she had not been well educated. Jocelyn said to her, much later in their friendship, that one of the reasons she found it so interesting to talk to Rose, from the start, was that Rose had ideas but was uneducated. Rose was surprised at this, and mentioned the college she had attended in Western Ontario. Then she saw by an embarrassed withdrawal or regret, a sudden lack of frankness in Jocelyn's face—very unusual with her—that that was exactly what Jocelyn had meant.

After the difference of opinion about artists, and about men and women artists, Rose took a good look at Clifford when he came visiting in the evening. She thought him wan, self-indulgent, and neurotic-looking. Further discoveries concerning the tact, the effort, the sheer physical energy Jocelyn expended on this marriage (it was she who fixed the leaky taps and dug up the clogged drains) made Rose certain that Jocelyn was wasting herself, she was mistaken. She had a feeling that Jocelyn did not see much point in marriage with Patrick, either.

At first the party was easier than Rose had expected. She had been afraid that she would be too dressed-up; she would have liked to wear her toreador pants but Patrick would never have stood for it. But only a few of the girls were in slacks. The rest wore stockings, earrings, outfits much like her own. As at any gathering of young women at that time, three or four were noticeably pregnant. And most of the men were in suits and shirts and ties, like Patrick. Rose was relieved. Not only did she want Patrick to fit into the party; she wanted him to accept the people there, to be convinced they were not all freaks. When Patrick was a student he had taken her to concerts and plays and did not seem overly suspicious of the people who participated in them; indeed he rather favored these things, because they were detested by his family, and at that time—the time he chose Rose—he was having a brief rebellion against his family. Once he and Rose had gone to Toronto and sat in the Chinese temple room at the Museum, looking at the frescoes. Patrick told her how they were brought in small pieces from Shansi province; he seemed quite proud of his knowledge, and at the same time disarmingly, uncharacteristically humble, admitting he had got it all on a tour. It was since he had gone to work that he had developed harsh opinions and delivered wholesale condemnations. Modern Art was a Hoax. Avant-garde plays were filthy. Patrick had a special, mincing, spitting way of saying avant-garde, making the words seem disgustingly pretentious. And so they were, Rose thought. In a way, she could see what he meant. She could see too many sides of things; Patrick did not have that problem.

Except for some great periodic fights she was very docile with Patrick, she tried to keep in favor. It was not easy to do so. Even before they were married he had a habit of delivering reproving lectures, in response to a simple question or observation. Sometimes in those days she would ask him a question in the hope that he would show off some superior knowledge that she could admire him for, but she was usually sorry she had asked, the answer was so long and had such a scolding tone, and the knowledge wouldn't be so superior, either. She did want to admire him, and respect him; it seemed that was a leap she was always on the edge of taking.

Later she thought that she did respect Patrick, but not in the way he wanted to be respected, and she did love him, not in the way he wanted to be loved. She didn't know it then. She thought she knew something about him, she thought she knew that he didn't really want to be whatever he was zealously making himself into. That arrogance might be called respect; that high-handedness, love. It didn't do anything to make him happy.

A few men wore jeans and turtlenecks or sweatshirts. Clifford was one of them, all in black. It was the time of the beatniks in San Francisco. Jocelyn had called Rose up on the phone and read her *Howl*. Clifford's skin looked very tanned, against the black, his hair was long for the time and almost as light a color as unbleached cotton; his eyes too were very light in color, a bright gray-blue. He looked small and catlike to Rose, rather effeminate; she hoped Patrick wouldn't be too put off by him.

There was beer to drink, and a wine punch. Jocelyn, who was a splendid cook, was stirring a pot of jambalaya. Rose make a trip to the bathroom to remove herself from Patrick, who seemed to want to stick close to her (she thought he was being a watchdog; she forgot that he might be shy). When she came out he had moved on. She drank three cups of punch in quick succession and was introduced to the woman who had written the play. To Rose's surprise this woman was one of the drabbest, least confident-looking people in the room.

"I liked your play," Rose told her. As a matter of fact she had found it mystifying, and Patrick had thought it was revolting. It seemed to be about a woman who ate her own children. Rose knew that was symbolic, but couldn't quite figure out what it was symbolic of.

"Oh, but the production was terrible!" the woman said. In her embarrassment, her excitement and eagerness to talk about her play, she sprayed Rose with punch. "They made it so literal. I was afraid it would just come across as gruesome and I meant it to be delicate, I meant it to be so different from the way they made it." She started telling Rose everything that had gone wrong, the miscasting, the chopping of the most important—the *crucial*—lines. Rose felt flattered, listening to these details, and tried inconspicuously to wipe away the spray.

"But you did see what I meant?" the woman said.

"Oh, yes!"

Clifford poured Rose another cup of punch and smiled at her.

"Rose, you look delicious."

Delicious seemed an odd word for Clifford to use. Perhaps he was drunk. Or perhaps, hating parties altogether as Jocelyn said he did, he had taken on a role; he was the sort of man who told a girl she looked delicious. He might be adept at disguises, as Rose thought she herself was getting to be. She went on talking to the writer and a man who taught English Literature of the Seventeenth Century. She too might have been poor and clever, radical and irreverent, for all anybody could tell.

A man and a girl were embracing passionately in the narrow hall. Whenever anybody wanted to get through, this couple had to separate, but they continued looking at each other, and did not even close their mouths. The sight of those wet open mouths made Rose shiver. She had never been embraced like that in her life, never had her mouth opened like that. Patrick thought French-kissing was disgusting.

A little bald man named Cyril had stationed himself outside the bathroom door, and was kissing any girl who came out, saying, "Welcome, sweetheart, so glad you could come, so glad you went."

"Cyril is awful," the woman writer said. "Cyril thinks he has to try to act like a poet. He can't think of anything to do but hang around the john and upset people. He thinks he's outrageous."

"Is he a poet?" Rose said.

The lecturer in English Literature said, "He told me he had burned all his poems."

"How flamboyant of him," Rose said. She was delighted with herself for saying this, and with them for laughing.

The lecturer began to think of Tom Swifties.

"I can never think of any of those things," said the writer mournfully, "I care too much about language."

Loud voices were coming from the living room. Rose recognized Patrick's voice, soaring over and subduing everyone else's. She opened her mouth to say something, anything, to cover him up—she knew some disaster was on the way—but just then a tall, curly-haired, elated-looking man came through the hall, pushing the passionate couple unceremoniously apart, holding up his hands for attention.

"Listen to this," he said to the whole kitchen. "There's this guy in the living room you wouldn't believe him. Listen."

There must have been a conversation about Indians going on in the living room. Now Patrick had taken it over.

"Take them away," said Patrick. "Take them away from their parents as soon as they're born and put them in a civilized environment and educate them and they will turn out just as good as whites any day." No doubt he thought he was expressing liberal views. If they thought this was amazing, they should have got him on the execution of the Rosenbergs or the trial of Alger Hiss or the necessity for nuclear testing.

Some girl said mildly, "Well, you know, there is their own culture."

"Their culture is done for," said Patrick. "Kaput." This was a word he was using a good deal right now. He could use some words, clichés, editorial phrases—*massive reappraisal* was one of them—with such relish and numbing authority that you would think he was their originator, or at least that the very fact of his using them gave them weight and luster.

"They want to be civilized," he said. "The smarter ones do."

"Well, perhaps they don't consider they're exactly uncivilized," said the girl with an icy demureness that was lost on Patrick.

"Some people need a push."

The self-congratulatory tones, the ripe admonishment, caused the man in the kitchen to throw up his hands, and wag his head in delight and disbelief. "This has got to be a Socred politician."

As a matter of fact Patrick did vote Social Credit.

"Yes, well, like it or not," he was saying, "they have to be dragged kicking and screaming into the twentieth century."

"Kicking and screaming?" someone repeated.

"Kicking and screaming into the twentieth century," said Patrick, who never minded saying anything again.

"What an interesting expression. So human as well."

Wouldn't he understand now, that he was being cornered, being baited and laughed at? But Patrick, being cornered, could only grow more thunderous. Rose could not listen any longer. She headed for the back passage, which was full of all the boots, coats, bottles, tubs, toys, that Jocelyn and Clifford had pitched out of the way for the party. Thank God it was empty of people. She went out of the back door and stood burning and shivering in the cool wet night. Her feelings were as confused as anybody's can get. She was humiliated, she was ashamed of Patrick. But she knew that it was his style that most humiliated her, and that made her suspect something corrupt and frivolous in herself. She was angry at those other people who were cleverer, or at least far quicker, than he was. She wanted to think badly of them. What did they care about Indians, really? Given a chance to behave decently to an Indian, Patrick might just come out ahead of them. This was a long shot, but she had to believe it. Patrick was a good person. His opinions were not good, but he was. The core of Patrick, Rose believed, was simple, pure and trustworthy. But how was she to get at it, to reassure herself, much less reveal it to others?

She heard the back door close and was afraid that Jocelyn had come out looking for her. Jocelyn was not someone who could believe in Patrick's core. She thought him stiff-necked, thick-skulled, and essentially silly.

It was not Jocelyn. It was Clifford. Rose didn't want to have to say anything to him. Slightly drunk as she was, woebegone, wet-faced from the rain, she looked at him without welcome. But he put his arms around her and rocked her.

"Oh Rose. Rose baby. Never mind. Rose."

So this was Clifford.

For five minutes or so they were kissing, murmuring, shivering, pressing, touching. They returned to the party by the front door. Cyril was there. He said, "Hey, wow, where have you two been?"

"Walking in the rain," said Clifford coolly. The same light possibly hostile voice in which he had told Rose she looked delicious. The Patrick-baiting had stopped. Conversation had become looser, drunker, more irresponsible. Jocelyn was serving jambalaya. She went to the bathroom to dry her hair and put lipstick on her rubbed-bare mouth. She was transformed, invulnerable. The first person she met coming out was Patrick. She had a wish to make him happy. She didn't care now what he had said, or would say.

"I don't think we've met, sir," she said, in the tiny flirtatious voice she used with him sometimes, when they were feeling easy together. "But you may kiss my hand."

"For crying out loud," said Patrick heartily, and he did squeeze her and kiss her, with a loud smacking noise, on the cheek. He always smacked when he kissed. And his elbows always managed to dig in somewhere and hurt her.

"Enjoying yourself?" Rose said.

"Not bad, not bad."

During the rest of the evening, of course, she played the game of watching Clifford while pretending not to watch him, and it seemed to her he was doing the same, and their eyes met, a few times, without expression, sending a perfectly clear message that rocked her on her feet. She saw him quite differently now. His body that had seemed small and tame now appeared to her light and slippery and full of energy; he was like a lynx or a bobcat. He had his tan from skiing. He went up Seymour Mountain and skied. An expensive hobby, but one which Jocelyn felt could not be denied him, because of the problems he had with his image. His masculine image, as a violinist, in this society. So Jocelyn said. Jocelyn had told Rose all about Clifford's background: the arthritic father, the small grocery store in a town in upstate New York, the poor tough neighborhood. She had talked about his problems as a child; the inappropriate talent, the grudging parents, the jeering schoolmates. His childhood left him bitter, Jocelyn said. But Rose no longer believed that Jocelyn had the last word on Clifford.

The party was on a Friday night. The phone rang the next morning, when Patrick and Anna were at the table eating eggs.

"How are you?" said Clifford.

"Fine."

"I wanted to phone you. I thought you might think I was just drunk or something. I wasn't."

"Oh, no."

"I've thought about you all night. I thought about you before, too."

"Yes." The kitchen was dazzling. The whole scene in front of her, of Patrick and Anna at the table, the coffee pot with dribbles down the side, the jar of marmalade, was exploding with joy and possibility and danger. Rose's mouth was so dry she could hardly talk.

"It's a lovely day," she said. "Patrick and Anna and I might go up the mountain."

"Patrick's home?"

"Yes."

"Oh God. That was dumb of me. I forgot nobody else works Saturdays. I'm over here at a rehearsal."

"Yes."

"Can you pretend it's somebody else? Pretend it's Jocelyn."

"Sure."

"I love you, Rose," said Clifford, and hung up.

"Who was that?" said Patrick.

"Jocelyn."

"Does she have to call when I'm home?"

"She forgot. Clifford's at a rehearsal so she forgot other people aren't working." Rose delighted in saying Clifford's name. Deceitfulness, concealment, seemed to come marvelously easy to her; that might almost be a pleasure in itself.

"I didn't realize they'd have to work Saturdays," she said, to keep on the subject. "They must work terribly long hours."

"They don't work any longer hours than normal people, it's just strung out differently. He doesn't look capable of much work."

"He's supposed to be quite good. As a violinist."

"He looks like a jerk."

"Do you think so?"

"Don't you?"

"I guess I never considered him, really."

Jocelyn phoned on Monday and said she didn't know why she gave parties, she was still wading through the mess.

"Didn't Clifford help clean it up?"

"You are joking. I hardly saw him all weekend. He rehearsed Saturday and played yesterday. He says parties are my idea, I can deal with the aftermath. It's true. I get these fits of gregariousness, a party is the only cure. Patrick was interesting."

"Very."

"He's a stunning type, really, isn't he?"

"There are lots and lots like him. You just don't get to meet them."

"Woe is me."

This was just like any other conversation with Jocelyn. Their conversations, their friendship, could go on in the same way. Rose did not feel bound by any loyalty to Jocelyn because she had divided Clifford. There was the Clifford Jocelyn knew, the same one she had always presented to Rose; there was also the Clifford Rose knew, now. She thought Jocelyn could be mistaken about him. For instance, when she said his childhood had left him bitter. What Jocelyn called bitterness seemed to Rose something more complex and more ordinary; just the weariness, suppleness, deviousness, meanness, common to a class. Common to Clifford's class, and Rose's. Jocelyn had been insulated in some ways, left stern and innocent. In some ways she was like Patrick.

From now on Rose did see Clifford and herself as being one sort of people, and Jocelyn and Patrick, though they seemed so different, and so disliked each other, as being another. They were whole and predictable. They took the lives they were leading absolutely seriously. Compared to them, both Clifford and Rose were shifty pieces of business.

If Jocelyn fell in love with a married man, what would she do? Before she even touched his hand, she would probably call a conference. Clifford would be invited, and the man himself, and the man's wife, and very likely Jocelyn's psychiatrist. (In spite of her rejection of her family Jocelyn believed that going to a psychiatrist was something everybody should do at developing or adjusting stages of life and she went herself, once a week.) Jocelyn would consider the implications; she would look things in the face. Never try to sneak her pleasure. She had never learned to sneak things. That was why it was unlikely that she would ever fall in love with another man. She was not greedy. And Patrick was not greedy either now, at least not for love.

If loving Patrick was recognizing something good, and guileless, at the bottom of him, being in love with Clifford was something else altogether. Rose did not have to believe that Clifford was good, and certainly she knew he was not guileless. No revelation of his duplicity or heartlessness, toward people other than herself, could have mattered to her. What was she in love with, then, what did she want of him? She wanted tricks, a glittering secret, tender celebrations of lust, a regular conflagration of adultery. All this after five minutes in the rain.

Six months or so after that party Rose lay awake all night. Patrick slept beside her in their stone and cedar house in a suburb called Capilano Heights, on the side of Grouse Mountain. The next night it was arranged that Clifford would sleep beside her, in Powell River, where he was playing with the touring orchestra. She could not believe that this would really happen. That is, she placed all her faith in the event, but could not fit it into the order of things that she knew.

During all these months Clifford and Rose had never gone to bed together. They had not made love anywhere else, either. This was the situation: Jocelyn and Clifford did not own a car. Patrick and Rose owned a car, but Rose did not drive it. Clifford's work did have the advantage of irregular hours, but how was he to get to see Rose? Could he ride the bus across the Lions Gate Bridge, then walk up her suburban street in broad daylight, past the neighbors' picture windows? Could Rose hire a baby-sitter, pretend she was going to see the dentist, take the bus over to town, meet Clifford in a restaurant, go with him to a hotel room? But they didn't know which hotel to go to; they were afraid that without luggage they would be turned out on the street, or reported to the Vice Squad, made to sit in the Police Station while Jocelyn and Patrick were summoned to come and get them. Also, they didn't have enough money.

Rose had gone over to Vancouver, though, using the dentist excuse, and they had sat in a café, side by side in a back booth, kissing and fondling, right out in public in a place frequented by Clifford's students and fellow musicians; what a risk to take. On the bus going home Rose looked down her dress at the sweat blooming between her breasts and could have fainted at the splendor of herself, as well as at the thought of the risk undertaken. Another time, a very hot August afternoon, she waited in an alley behind the theater where Clifford was rehearsing, lurked in the shadows then grappled with him deliriously, unsatisfactorily. They saw a door open, and slipped inside. There were boxes stacked all around. They were looking for some nesting spot when a man spoke to them.

"Can I do anything for you?"

They had entered the back storeroom of a shoe store. The man's voice was icy, terrifying. The Vice Squad. The Police Station. Rose's dress was undone to the waist.

Once they met in a park, where Rose often took Anna, and pushed her on the swings. They held hands on a bench, under cover of Rose's wide cotton skirt. They laced their fingers together and squeezed painfully. Then Anna surprised them, coming up behind the bench and shouting, "Boo! I caught you!" Clifford turned disastrously pale. On the way home Rose said to Anna, "That was funny when you jumped out behind the bench. I thought you were still on the swing."

"I know," said Anna.

"What did you mean, you'd caught us?"

"I *caught* you," said Anna, and giggled, in what seemed to Rose a disturbingly pert and knowledgeable way.

"Would you like a Fudgsicle? I would!" Rose said gaily, with thoughts of blackmail and bargains, Anna dredging this up for *her* psychiatrist in twenty years' time. The episode made her feel shaky and sick and she wondered if it had given Clifford a distaste for her. It had, but only temporarily.

As soon as it was light she got out of bed and went to look at the day, to see if it would be good for flying. The sky was clear; no sign of the fog that often grounded planes at this time of year. Nobody but Clifford knew she was going to Powell River. They had been planning this for six weeks, ever since they knew he was going on tour. Patrick thought she was going to Victoria, where she had a friend whom she had known at college. She had pretended, during the past few weeks, to have been in touch with this friend again. She had said she would be back tomorrow night. Today was Saturday. Patrick was at home to look after Anna.

She went into the dining room to check the money she had saved from Family Allowance checks. It was in the bottom of the silver muffin dish. Thirteen dollars. She meant to add that to what Patrick gave her to get to Victoria. Patrick always gave her money when she asked, but he wanted to know how much and what for. Once when they were out walking she wanted to go into a drugstore; she asked him for money and he said, with no more than customary sternness, "What for?" and Rose began to cry, because she had been going to buy vaginal jelly. She might just as well have laughed, and would have, now. Since she had fallen in love with Clifford, she never quarreled with Patrick.

She figured out again the money she would need. The plane ticket, the money for the airport bus, from Vancouver, and for the bus or maybe it would have to be a taxi into Powell River, something left over for food and coffee. Clifford would pay for the hotel. The thought filled her with sexual comfort, submissiveness, though she knew Jerome needed new glasses, Adam needed rubber boots. She thought of that neutral, smooth, generous bed, which already existed, was waiting for them. Long ago when she was a young girl (she was now twenty-three) she had often thought of bland rented beds and locked doors, with such luxuriant hopes, and now she did again, though for a time in between, before and after she was married, the thought of anything connected with sex irritated her, rather in the way Modern Art irritated Patrick.

She walked around the house softly, planning her day as a series of actions. Take a bath, oil and powder herself, put her diaphragm and jelly in her purse. Remember the money. Mascara, face cream, lipstick. She stood at the top of the two steps leading down into the living room. The walls of the living room were moss green, the fireplace was white, the curtains and slipcovers had a silky pattern of gray and green and yellow leaves on a white background. On the mantel were two Wedgwood vases, white with a circlet of green leaves. Patrick was very fond of these vases. Sometimes when he came home from work he went straight into the living room and shifted them around a bit on the mantel, thinking their symmetrical position had been disturbed.

"Has anybody been fooling around with these vases?"

"Well of course. As soon as you leave for work I rush in and juggle them around."

"I meant Anna. You don't let her touch them, do you?"

Patrick didn't like to hear her refer to the vases in any joking way. He thought she didn't appreciate the house. He didn't know, but maybe could guess what she had said to Jocelyn, the first time Jocelyn came here, and they were standing where Rose stood now, looking down at the living room.

"The department store heir's dream of elegance."

At this treachery even Jocelyn looked abashed. It was not exactly true. Patrick dreamed of getting much more elegant. And it was not true in the implication that it had all been Patrick's choice, and that Rose had always held aloof from it. It had been Patrick's choice, but there were a lot of things she had liked at one time. She used to climb up and polish the glass drops of the dining-room chandelier, using a cloth dipped in water and baking soda. She liked the chandelier; its drops had a blue or lilac cast. But people she admired would not have chandeliers in their dining rooms. It was unlikely that they would have dining rooms. If they did, they would have thin white candles stuck

into the branches of a black metal candleholder, made in Scandinavia.
Or else they would have heavy candles in wine bottles, loaded with
drippings of colored wax. The people she admired were inevitably
poorer than she was. It seemed a bad joke on her, after being poor all
her life in a place where poverty was never anything to be proud of,
that now she had to feel apologetic and embarrassed about the opposite condition—with someone like Jocelyn, for instance, who could say
middle-class prosperity so viciously and despisingly.

But if she hadn't been exposed to other people, if she hadn't
learned from Jocelyn, would she still have liked the house? No. She
must have been souring on it, anyway. When people came to visit for
the first time Patrick always took them on a tour, pointing out the
chandelier, the powder room with concealed lighting, by the front
door, the walk-in closets and the louvered doors opening on to the
patio. He was proud of this house, as eager to call attention to its
small distinctions, as if he, not Rose, had grown up poor. Rose had
been uneasy about these tours from the start, and tagged along in silence, or made deprecating remarks which Patrick did not like. After a
while she stayed in the kitchen, but she could still hear Patrick's voice
and she knew beforehand everything he would say. She knew that he
would pull the dining-room curtains and point to the small illumi-
nated fountain—Neptune with a fig leaf—he had put in the garden,
and then he would say, "Now there is our answer to the suburban
swimming-pool mania!"

After she bathed she reached for a bottle of what she thought was
baby oil, to pour over her body. The clear liquid ran down over her
breasts and belly, stinging and burning. She looked at the label and
saw that this was not baby oil at all, it was nail polish remover. She
scrubbed it off, splashed herself with cold water, towelled desperately,
thinking of ruined skin, the hospital; grafts, scars, punishment.

Anna was scratching sleepily but urgently at the bathroom door.
Rose had locked it, for this preparation, though she didn't usually lock
it when she took a bath. She let Anna in.

"Your front is all red," Anna said, as she hoisted herself on to the
toilet. Rose found the baby oil and tried to cool herself with it. She
used too much, and got oily spots on her new brassiere.

She had thought Clifford might write to her while he was touring, but he did not. He called her from Prince George, and was businesslike.

"When do you get into Powell River?"

"Four o'clock."

"Okay, take the bus or whatever they have into town. Have you ever been there?"

"No."

"Neither have I. I only know the name of our hotel. You can't wait there."

"How about the bus depot? Every town has a bus depot."

"Okay, the bus depot. I'll pick you up there probably about five o'clock, and we can get you into some other hotel. I hope to God there's more than one. Okay then."

He was pretending to the other members of the orchestra that he was spending the night with friends in Powell River.

"I could go and hear you play," Rose said. "Couldn't I?"

"Well. Sure."

"I'd be very inconspicuous. I'd sit at the back. I'll disguise myself as an old lady. I love to hear you play."

"Okay."

"You don't mind?"

"No."

"Clifford?"

"Yes?"

"You still want me to come?"

"Oh, Rose."

"I know. It's just the way you sound."

"I'm in the hotel lobby. They're waiting for me. I'm supposed to be talking to Jocelyn."

"Okay. I know. I'll come."

"Powell River. The bus depot. Five o'clock."

This was different from their usual telephone conversations. Usually they were plaintive and silly; or else they worked each other up so that they could not talk at all.

"Heavy breathing there."

"I know."

"We'll have to talk about something else."

"What else is there?"

"Is it foggy where you are too?"

"Yes. Is it foggy where you are too?"

"Yes. Can you hear the foghorn?"

"Yes."

"Isn't it a horrible sound?"

"I don't mind it, really. I sort of like it."

"Jocelyn doesn't. You know how she describes it? She says it's the sound of a cosmic boredom."

They had at first avoided speaking of Jocelyn and Patrick at all. Then they spoke of them in a crisp practical way, as if they were adults, parents, to be outwitted. Now they could mention them almost tenderly, admiringly, as if they were their children.

There was no bus depot in Powell River. Rose got into the airport limousine with four other passengers, all men, and told the driver she wanted to go to the bus depot.

"You know where that is?"

"No," she said. Already she felt them all watching her.

"Did you want to catch a bus?"

"No."

"Just wanted to go to the bus depot?"

"I planned to meet somebody there."

"I didn't even know there was a bus depot here," said one of the passengers.

"There isn't, that I know of," said the driver. "Now there is a bus, it goes down to Vancouver in the morning and it comes back at night, and it stops at the old men's home. The old loggers' home. That's where it stops. All I can do is take you there. Is that all right?"

Rose said it would be fine. Then she felt she had to go on explaining.

"My friend and I just arranged to meet there because we couldn't think where else. We don't know Powell River at all and we just thought, every town has a bus depot!"

She was thinking that she shouldn't have said *my friend*, she should have said *my husband*. They were going to ask her what she and her friend were doing here if neither of them knew the town.

"My friend is playing in the orchestra that's giving a concert here tonight. She plays the violin."

All looked away from her, as if that was what a lie deserved. She was trying to remember if there was a female violinist. What if they should ask her name?

The driver let her off in front of a long two-story wooden building with peeling paint.

"I guess you could go in the sunporch, there at the end. That's where the bus picks them up, anyway."

In the sunporch there was a pool table. Nobody was playing. Some old men were playing checkers; others watched. Rose thought of explaining herself to them but decided not to; they seemed mercifully uninterested. She was worn out by her explanations in the limousine.

It was ten past four by the sunporch clock. She thought she could put in the time till five by walking around the town.

As soon as she went outside she noticed a bad smell, and became worried, thinking it might come from herself. She got out the stick cologne she had bought in the Vancouver airport—spending money she could not afford—and rubbed it on her wrists and neck. The smell persisted, and at last she realized it came from the pulp mills. The town was difficult to walk around in because the streets were so steep, and in many places there was no sidewalk. There was no place to loiter. She thought people stared at her, recognizing a stranger. Some men in a car yelled at her. She saw her own reflection in store windows and understood that she looked as if she wanted to be stared at and yelled at. She was wearing black velvet toreador pants, a tight-fitting high-necked black sweater and a beige jacket which she slung over her shoulder, though there was a chilly wind. She who had once chosen full skirts and soft colors, babyish angora sweaters, scalloped necklines, had now taken to wearing dramatic sexually advertising clothes. The new underwear she had on at this moment was black lace and pink nylon. In the waiting room at the Vancouver airport she had done her eyes with heavy mascara, black eyeliner, and silver eyeshadow; her lipstick was almost white. All this was a fashion of those years and so looked less bizarre than it would seem later, but it was alarming enough. The assurance with which she carried such a disguise fluctuated considerably. She would not have dared parade it in front of Patrick or Jocelyn. When she went to see Jocelyn she always wore her baggiest slacks and sweaters. Nevertheless when she opened the door Jocelyn would say, "Hello, Sexy," in a tone of friendly scorn. Jocelyn herself had become spectacularly unkempt. She dressed exclusively in old clothes of Clifford's. Old pants that didn't quite zip up on her because her stomach had never flattened out after Adam, and frayed white shirts Clifford had once worn for performances. Apparently Jocelyn thought the whole business of keeping your figure and wearing makeup and trying to look in any way seductive was sourly amusing, beneath contempt; it was like vacuuming the curtains. She said that Clifford felt the same way. Clifford, reported Jocelyn, was attracted by the very absence of female artifice and trappings; he liked unshaved legs and hairy armpits and natural smells. Rose wondered if Clifford had really said this, and why. Out of pity, or comradeliness; or as a joke?

Rose found a public library and went in and looked at the titles of the books, but she could not pay attention. There was a fairly incapacitating though not unpleasant buzzing throughout her head and body. At twenty to five she was back in the sunporch, waiting.

She was still waiting at ten past six. She had counted the money in her purse. A dollar and sixty-three cents. She could not go to a hotel. She did not think they would let her stay in the sunporch all night. There was nothing at all that she could do except pray that Clifford might still arrive. She did not believe he would. The schedule had been changed; he had been summoned home because one of the children was sick; he had broken his wrist and couldn't play the violin; Powell River was not a real place at all but a bad-smelling mirage where guilty travelers were trapped for punishment. She wasn't really surprised. She had made the jump that wasn't to be made, and this was how she had landed.

Before the old men went in to supper she asked them if they knew of a concert being given that night in the high school auditorium. They answered grudgingly, no.

"Never heard of them giving no concerts here."

She said that her husband was playing in the orchestra, it was on tour from Vancouver, she had flown up to meet him; she was supposed to meet him here.

Here?

"Maybe got lost," said one of the old men in what seemed to her a spiteful, knowing way. "Maybe your husband got lost, heh? Husbands always getting lost!"

It was nearly dark out. This was October, and farther north than Vancouver. She tried to think what to do. The only thing that occurred to her was to pretend to pass out, then claim loss of memory. Would Patrick ever believe that? She would have to say she had no idea what she was doing in Powell River. She would have to say she didn't remember anything she had said in the limousine, didn't know anything about the orchestra. She would have to convince policemen and doctors, be written about in the newspapers. Oh, where was Clifford, why had he abandoned her, could there have been an accident on the road? She thought she should destroy the piece of paper in her purse, on which she had written his instructions. She thought that she had better get rid of her diaphragm as well.

She was going through her purse when a van parked outside. She thought it must be a police van; she thought the old men must have phoned up and reported her as a suspicious character.

Clifford got out and came running up the sunporch steps. It took her a moment to recognize him.

They had beer and hamburgers in one of the hotels, a different hotel from the one where the orchestra was staying. Rose's hands were shaking so that she slopped the beer. There had been a rehearsal he hadn't counted on, Clifford said. Then he had been about half an hour looking for the bus depot.

"I guess it wasn't such a bright idea, the bus depot."

Her hand was lying on the table. He wiped the beer off with a napkin, then put his own hand over hers. She thought of this often, afterward.

"We better get you checked in here."

"Don't we check in together?"

"Better if it's just you."

"Ever since I got here," Rose said, "it has been so peculiar. It has been so sinister. I felt everybody knew." She started telling him, in what she hoped was an entertaining way, about the limousine driver, the other passengers, the old men in the Loggers' Home. "It was such a relief when you showed up, such a terrible relief. That's why I'm shaking." She told him about her plan to fake amnesia and the realization that she had better throw her diaphragm away. He laughed, but without delight, she thought. It seemed to her that when she spoke of the diaphragm his lips tightened, in reproof or distaste.

"But it's lovely now," she said hastily. This was the longest conversation they had ever had, face to face.

"It was just your guilt feelings," he said. "Which are natural."

He stroked her hand. She tried to rub her finger on his pulse, as they used to do. He let go.

Half an hour later, she was saying, "Is it all right if I still go to the concert?"

"Do you still want to?"

"What else is there to do?"

She shrugged as she said this. Her eyelids were lowered, her lips full and brooding. She was doing some sort of imitation, of Barbara Stanwyck perhaps, in similar circumstances. She didn't intend to do an imitation, of course. She was trying to find some way to be so enticing, so aloof and enticing, that she would make him change his mind.

"The thing is, I have to get the van back. I have to pick up the other guys."

"I can walk. Tell me where it is."

"Uphill from here, I'm afraid."

"That won't hurt me."

"Rose. It's much better this way, Rose. It really is."

"If you say so." She couldn't manage another shrug. She still thought there must be some way to turn things around and start again. Start again; set right whatever she had said or done wrong; make none of this true. She had already made the mistake of asking what she had said or done wrong and he had said, nothing. Nothing. She had nothing to do with it, he said. It was being away from home for a month that had made him see everything differently. Jocelyn. The children. The damage.

"It's only mischief," he said.

He had got his hair cut shorter than she had ever seen it. His tan had faded. Indeed, indeed, he looked as if he had shed a skin, and it was the skin that had hankered after hers. He was again the pale, and rather irritable, but dutiful, young husband she had observed paying visits to Jocelyn in the maternity ward.

"What is?"

"What we're doing. It's not some big necessary thing. It's ordinary mischief."

"You called me from Prince George." Barbara Stanwyck had vanished, Rose heard herself begin to whine.

"I know I did." He spoke like a nagged husband.

"Did you feel like this then?"

"Yes and no. We'd made all the plans. Wouldn't it have been worse if I'd told you on the phone?"

"What do you mean, mischief?"

"Oh, Rose."

"What do you mean?"

"You know what I mean. If we went ahead with this, what good do you think it would do anybody? Rose? Really?"

"Us," Rose said. "It would do us good."

"No it wouldn't. It would end up in one big mess."

"Just once."

"No."

"You said just once. You said we would have a memory instead of a dream."

"Jesus. I said a lot of puke."

He had said her tongue was like a little warm-blooded snake, a pretty snake, and her nipples like berries. He would not care to be reminded.

Overture to Russlan and Ludmilla: Glinka
Serenade for Strings: Tchaikovsky
Beethoven's Sixth Symphony, the Pastoral: First Movement
The Moldau: Smetana
William Tell Overture: Rossini

She could not hear any of this music for a long time without a specific attack of shame, that was like a whole wall crumbling in on her, rubble choking her.

Just before Clifford left on tour, Jocelyn had phoned Rose and said that her baby-sitter could not come. It was the day she went to see her psychiatrist. Rose offered to come and look after Adam and Jerome. She had done this before. She made the long trip on three buses, taking Anna with her.

Jocelyn's house was heated by an oil stove in the kitchen, and an enormous stone fireplace in the small living room. The oil stove was covered with spill marks; orange peel and coffee grounds and charred wood and ashes tumbled out of the fireplace. There was no basement and no clothes dryer. The weather was rainy, and the ceiling-racks and stand-up racks were draped with damp graying sheets and diapers, hardening towels. There was no washing machine either. Jocelyn had washed those sheets in the bathtub.

"No washer or dryer but she's going to a psychiatrist," said Patrick, to whom Rose sometimes disloyally reported what she knew he would like to hear.

"She must be crazy," Rose said. She made him laugh.

But Patrick didn't like her going to baby-sit.

"You're certainly at her beck and call," he said. "It's a wonder you don't go and scrub her floors for her."

As a matter of fact, Rose did.

When Jocelyn was there, the disorder of the house had a certain willed and impressive quality. When she was gone, it became unbearable. Rose would go to work with a knife, scraping at ancient crusts of Pablum on the kitchen chairs, scouring the coffee pot, wiping the floor. She did spare some time for investigation. She went into the bedroom—she had to watch out for Jerome, a precocious and irritating child—and looked at Clifford's socks and underwear, all crumpled in with Jocelyn's old nursing brassieres and torn garter belts. She looked to see if he had a record on the turntable, wondering if it would be something that would make him think of her.

Telemann. Not likely. But she played it, to hear what he had been hearing. She drank coffee from what she believed to be his dirty breakfast cup. She covered the casserole of Spanish rice from which he had taken his supper the night before. She sought out traces of his presence (he didn't use an electric razor, he used old-fashioned shaving soap in a wooden bowl), but she believed that his life in that house, Jocelyn's house, was all pretense, and waiting, like her own life in Patrick's house.

When Jocelyn came home Rose felt she ought to apologize for the cleaning she had done, and Jocelyn, really wanting to talk about her fight with the psychiatrist who reminded her of her mother, agreed that it certainly was a cowardly mania, this thing Rose had about housecleaning, and she had better go to a psych herself, if she ever wanted to get rid of it. She was joking; but going home on the bus, with Anna cranky and no preparations made for Patrick's supper, Rose did wonder why she always seemed to be on the wrong end of things, disapproved of by her own neighbors because she didn't pay enough attention to housework, and reproved by Jocelyn for being insufficiently tolerant of the natural chaos and refuse of life. She thought of love, to reconcile herself. She was loved, not in a dutiful, husbandly way but crazily, adulterously, as Jocelyn and her neighbors were not. She used that to reconcile herself to all sorts of things: to Patrick, for instance, turning over in bed with an indulgent little clucking noise that meant she was absolved of all her failings for the moment, they were to make love.

The sane and decent things Clifford had said cut no ice with Rose at all. She saw that he had betrayed her. Sanity and decency were never what she had asked of him. She watched him, in the auditorium of the Powell River High School. She watched him playing his violin, with a somber and attentive expression she had once seen directed toward herself. She did not see how she could do without him.

In the middle of the night she phoned him, from her hotel to his.

"Please talk to me."

"That's okay," said Clifford, after a moment's silence. "That's okay, Joss."

He must have a roommate, whom the phone might have wakened. He was pretending to talk to Jocelyn. Or else he was so sleepy he really thought she was Jocelyn.

"Clifford, it's me."

"That's okay," Clifford said. "Take it easy. Go to sleep."

He hung up the phone.

Jocelyn and Clifford are living in Toronto. They are not poor anymore. Clifford is successful. His name is seen on record jackets, heard on the radio. His face and more frequently his hands have appeared on television as he labors at his violin. Jocelyn has dieted and become slender, has had her hair cut and styled; it is parted in the middle and curves away from her face, with a wing of pure white rising from each temple.

They live in a large brick house on the edge of a ravine. There are bird-feeders in the backyard. They have installed a sauna. Clifford spends a good deal of time sitting there. He thinks that will keep him from becoming arthritic, like his father. Arthritis is his greatest fear.

Rose used to go to see them sometimes. She was living in the country, by herself. She taught at a community college and liked to have a place to stay overnight when she came in to Toronto. They seemed glad to have her. They said she was their oldest friend.

One time when Rose was visiting them Jocelyn told a story about Adam. Adam had an apartment in the basement of the house. Jerome lived downtown, with his girl friend. Adam brought his girls here.

"I was reading in the den," said Jocelyn, "when Clifford was out. I heard this girl, down in Adam's apartment, saying *no, no!* The noise from his apartment comes straight up into the den. We warned him about that, we thought he'd be embarrassed—"

"I didn't think he'd be embarrassed," said Clifford.

"But he just said, we should put on the record player. So, I kept hearing the poor unknown girl bleating and protesting, and I didn't know what to do. I thought these situations are really new, there are no precedents, are you supposed to stop your son from raping some girl if that's what he's doing, right under your nose or at least under your feet? I went downstairs eventually and I started getting all the family skis out of the closet that backs on his bedroom, I stayed there slamming those skis around, thinking I'd say I was going to polish them. It was July. Adam never said anything to me. I wish he'd move out."

Rose told about how much money Patrick had and how he had married a sensible woman even richer than he was, who had made a dazzling living room with mirrors and pale velvet and a wire sculpture like blasted bird cages. Patrick did not mind Modern Art anymore.

"Of course it isn't the same," said Rose to Jocelyn, "it isn't the same house. I wonder what she has done with the Wedgwood vases."

"Maybe she has a campy laundry room. She keeps the bleach in one and the detergent in the other."

"They sit perfectly symmetrically on the shelf."

But Rose had her old, old, twinge of guilt.

"Just the same, I like Patrick."

Jocelyn said, "Why?"

"He's nicer than most people."

"Silly rot," said Jocelyn. "And I bet he doesn't like you."

"That's right," Rose said. She started to tell them about her trip down on the bus. It was one of the times when she was not driving her car, because too many things were wrong with it and she could not afford to get it fixed.

"The man in the seat across from me was telling me about how he used to drive big trucks. He said we never seen trucks in this country like they got in the States." She put on her country accent. "In the Yewnited States they got these special roads what they call turnpikes, and only trucks is allowed to go on them. They get serviced on these roads from one end of the country to the other and so most people never sees them at all. They're so big the cab is half the size of a bus and they got a driver in there and an assistant driver and another driver and another assistant driver havin a sleep. Toilet and kitchen and beds and all. They go eighty, ninety miles an hour, because there is never no speed limit on them turnpikes."

"You are getting very weird," said Clifford. "Living up there."

"Never mind the trucks," Jocelyn said. "Never mind the old mythology. Clifford wants to leave me again."

They settled down to drinking and talking about what Clifford and Jocelyn should do. This was not an unfamiliar conversation. What does Clifford really want? Does he really want not to be married to Jocelyn or does he want something unattainable? Is he going through a middle-age crisis?

"Don't be so banal," Clifford said to Rose. She was the one who said middle-age crisis. "I've been going through this ever since I was twenty-five. I've wanted out ever since I got in."

"That is new, for Clifford to say that," said Jocelyn. She went out to the kitchen to get some cheese and grapes. "For him to actually come out and say that," she yelled from the kitchen. Rose avoided looking at Clifford, not because they had any secrets but because it seemed a courtesy to Jocelyn not to look at each other while she was out of the room.

"What is happening now," said Jocelyn, coming back with a platter of cheese and grapes in one hand and a bottle of gin in the other, "is that Clifford is wide open. He used to bitch and stew and some other bilge would come out that had nothing to do with the real problem. Now he just comes out with it. The great blazing truth. It's a total illumination."

Rose had a bit of difficulty catching the tone. She felt as if living in the country had made her slow. Was Jocelyn's talk a parody, was she being sarcastic? No. She was not.

"But then I go and deflate the truth for you," said Clifford, grinning. He was drinking beer from the bottle. He thought beer was better for him than gin. "It's absolutely true I've wanted out ever since I got in. And it's also true that I wanted in, and I wanted to stay in. I wanted to be married to you and I want to be married to you and I couldn't stand being married to you and I can't stand being married to you. It's a static contradiction."

"It sounds like hell," Rose said.

"I didn't say that. I am just making the point that it is no middle-age crisis."

"Well, maybe that was oversimplifying," said Rose. Nevertheless, she said firmly, in the sensible, down-to-earth, countrified style she was adopting for the moment, all they were hearing about was Clifford. What did Clifford really want, what did Clifford need? Did he need a studio, did he need a holiday, did he need to go to Europe by himself? What made him think, she said, that Jocelyn could be endlessly concerned about his welfare? Jocelyn was not his mother.

"And it's your fault," she said to Jocelyn, "for not telling him to put up or shut up. Never mind what he really wants. Get out or shut up. That's all you need to say to him. Shut up or get out," she said to Clifford with mock gruffness. "Excuse me for being so unsubtle. Or frankly hostile."

She didn't run any risk at all by sounding hostile, and she knew it. She would run a risk by being genteel and indifferent. The way she was talking now was a proof that she was their true friend and took them seriously. And so she did, up to a point.

"She's right, you fucking son-of-a-bitch," said Jocelyn experimentally. "Shut up or get out."

When Jocelyn called Rose on the phone, years ago, to read her the

poem *Howl*, she was not able, in spite of her usual boldness of speech,
to say the word *fuck*. She tried to force herself, then she said, "Oh, it's
stupid, but I can't say it. I'm going to have to say eff. You'll know
what I mean when I say eff?"

"But she said it's your fault," said Clifford. "You want to be the
mother. You want to be the grownup. You want to be long-suffering."

"Balls," said Jocelyn. "Oh, maybe. Maybe, yes. Maybe I do."

"I bet at school you were always latching on to those kids with the
problems," said Clifford with his tender grin. "Those poor kids, the
ones with acne or awful clothes or speech impediments. I bet you just
persecuted those poor kids with friendliness."

Jocelyn picked up the cheese knife and waved it at him.

"You be careful. You haven't got acne or a speech impediment.
You are sickeningly good-looking. And talented. And lucky."

"I have nearly insuperable problems coming to terms with the adult
male role," said Clifford priggishly. "The psych says so."

"I don't believe you. Psychs never say anything like nearly insuperable. And they don't use that jargon. And they don't make those
judgments. I don't believe you, Clifford."

"Well, I don't really go to the psych at all. I go to the dirty movies
down on Yonge."

Clifford went off to sit in the sauna.

Rose watched him leave the room. He was wearing jeans, and a T-
shirt that said *Just passin thru*. His waist and hips were as narrow as a
twelve-year-old's. His gray hair was cut in a very short brush cut,
showing his skull. Was this the way musicians wore their hair nowadays, when politicians and accountants were bushy and bearded, or
was it Clifford's own perversity? His tan looked like pancake makeup,
though it was probably all real. There was something theatrical about
him altogether, tight and glittery and taunting. Something obscene
about his skinniness and sweet, hard smile.

"Is he well?" she said to Jocelyn. "He's terribly thin."

"He wants to look like that. He eats yogurt and black bread."

"You can never split up," Rose said, "because your house is too
beautiful." She stretched out on the hooked rug. The living room had
white walls, thick white curtains, old pine furniture, large bright
paintings, hooked rugs. On a low round table at her elbow was a bowl
of polished stones for people to pick up and hold and run through

their fingers. The stones came from Vancouver beaches, from Sandy Cove and English Bay and Kitsilano and Ambleside and Dundarave. Jerome and Adam had collected them a long time ago.

Jocelyn and Clifford left British Columbia soon after Clifford returned from his provincial tour. They went to Montreal, then to Halifax, then to Toronto. They seemed hardly to remember Vancouver. Once they tried to think of the name of the street where they had lived and it was Rose who had to supply it for them. When Rose lived in Capilano Heights she used to spend a lot of time remembering the parts of Ontario where she had lived, being faithful, in a way, to that earlier landscape. Now that she was living in Ontario she put the same sort of effort into remembering things about Vancouver, puzzling to get details straight, that were in themselves quite ordinary. For instance, she tried to remember just where you waited for the Pacific Stage bus, when you were going from North Vancouver to West Vancouver. She pictured herself getting on that old green bus around one o'clock, say, on a spring day. Going to baby-sit for Jocelyn. Anna with her, in her yellow slicker and rainhat. Cold rain. The long, swampy stretch of land as you went into West Vancouver. Where the shopping centers and high-rises are now. She could see the streets, the houses, the old Safeway, St. Mawes Hotel, the thick closing-in of the woods, the place where you got off the bus at the little store. Black Cat cigarettes sign. Cedar dampness as you walked in through the woods to Jocelyn's house. Deadness of early afternoon. Nap time. Young women drinking coffee looking out of rainy windows. Retired couples walking dogs. Pad of feet on the thick mold. Crocuses, early daffodils, the cold bulbs blooming. That profound difference of the air close to the sea, the inescapable dripping vegetation, the stillness. Anna pulling on her hand, Jocelyn's brown wooden cottage ahead. Such a rich weight of apprehension, complications descending as she neared that house.

Other things she was not so keen on remembering.

She had wept on the plane, behind her sunglasses, all the way from Powell River. She wept, sitting in the waiting room at the Vancouver airport. She was not able to stop weeping and go home to Patrick. A plainclothes policeman sat down beside her, opened his jacket to show her his badge, asked if there was anything he could do for her. Some-one must have summoned him. Terrified at being so conspicuous, she fled to the Ladies'. She didn't think to comfort herself with a drink, didn't think of looking for the bar. She never went to bars then. She didn't take a tranquilizer, didn't have any, didn't know about them. Maybe there weren't such things.

The suffering. What was it? It was all a waste, it reflected no credit. An entirely dishonorable grief. All mashed pride and ridiculed fantasy. It was as if she had taken a hammer and deliberately smashed her big toe. That's what she thinks sometimes. At other times she thinks it was necessary, it was the start of wrecks and changes, the start of being where she is now instead of in Patrick's house. Life making a gigantic fuss, as usual, for a small effect.

Patrick could not speak when she told him. He had no lecture pre-pared. He didn't speak for a long time but followed her around the house while she kept justifying herself, complaining. It was as if he wanted her to go on talking, though he couldn't credit what she was saying, because it would be much worse if she stopped.

She didn't tell him the whole truth. She said that she had "had an affair" with Clifford, and by the telling gave herself a dim secondhand sort of comfort, which was pierced, presently, but not really destroyed, by Patrick's look and silence. It seemed ill-timed, unfair of him, to show such a bare face, such an inappropriate undigestible chunk of grief.

Then the phone rang, and she thought it would be Clifford, ex-periencing a change of heart. It was not Clifford, it was a man she had met at Jocelyn's party. He said he was directing a radio play, and he needed a country girl. He remembered her accent.

Not Clifford.

She would rather not think of any of this. She prefers to see through metal window-frames of dripping cedars and salmonberry bushes and the proliferating mortal greenery of the rain forest some small views of lost daily life. Anna's yellow slicker. The smoke from Jocelyn's foul fire.

Do you want to see the junk I've been buying?" said Jocelyn, and took Rose upstairs. She showed her an embroidered skirt and a deep-red satin blouse. A daffodil-colored silk pajama suit. A long shapeless rough-woven dress from Ireland.

"I'm spending a fortune. What I would once have thought was a fortune. It took me so long. It took us both so long, just to be able to spend money. We could not bring ourselves to do it. We despised people who had color television. And you know something—color television is great! We sit around now and say, what would we like? Maybe one of those little toaster-ovens for the cottage? Maybe I'd like a hair blower? All those things everybody else has known about for years but we thought we were too good for. You know what we are, we say to each other? We're Consumers! And it's Okay!

"And not just paintings and records and books. We always knew they were okay. Color TV! Hair dryers! Waffle irons!"

"Remote-control birdcages!" Rose cried cheerfully.

"That's the idea."

"Heated towels."

"Heated towel racks, dummy! They're lovely."

"Electric carving knives, electric toothbrushes, electric toothpicks."

"Some of those things are not as bad as they sound. Really they're not."

Another time when Rose came down Jocelyn and Clifford had a party. When everyone had gone home the three of them, Jocelyn and Clifford and Rose, sat around on the living-room floor, all fairly drunk, and very comfortable. The party had gone well. Rose was feeling a remote and wistful lust; a memory lust, maybe. Jocelyn said she didn't want to go to bed.

"What can we do?" said Rose. "We shouldn't drink anymore."

"We could make love," Clifford said.

Jocelyn and Rose said, "Really?" at exactly the same time. Then they linked their little fingers and said, "Smoke goes up the chimney."

Following which, Clifford removed their clothes. They didn't shiver, it was warm in front of the fire. Clifford kept switching his attention nicely from one to the other. He got out of his own clothes as well. Rose felt curious, disbelieving, hardly willing, slightly aroused and, at some level she was too sluggish to reach for, appalled and sad. Though Clifford paid preliminary homage to them both, she was the one he finally made love to, rather quickly on the nubbly hooked rug.

Jocelyn seemed to hover above them making comforting noises of assent.

The next morning Rose had to go out before Jocelyn and Clifford were awake. She had to go downtown on the subway. She found she was looking at men with that speculative hunger, that cold and hurtful need, which for a while she had been free of. She began to get very angry. She was angry at Clifford and Jocelyn. She felt that they had made a fool of her, cheated her, shown her a glaring lack, that otherwise she would not have been aware of. She resolved never to see them again and to write them a letter in which she would comment on their selfishness, obtuseness, and moral degeneracy. By the time she had the letter written to her own satisfaction, in her head, she was back in the country again and had calmed down. She decided not to write it. Sometime later she decided to go on being friends with Clifford and Jocelyn, because she needed such friends occasionally, at that stage of her life.

Providence

Rose had a dream about Anna. This was after she had gone away and left Anna behind. She dreamed she met Anna walking up Gonzales Hill. She knew she was coming from school. She went up to speak to her but Anna walked past not speaking. No wonder. She was covered with clay that seemed to have leaves or branches in it, so that the effect was of dead garlands. Decoration; ruination. And the clay or mud was not dry, it was still dripping off her, so that she looked crude and sad, a botched heavy-headed idol.

"Do you want to come with me, do you want to stay with Daddy?" Rose had said to her, but Anna had refused to answer, saying instead, "I don't want you to go." Rose had got a job at a radio station in a town in the Kootenay mountains.

Anna was lying in the four-poster bed where Patrick and Rose used to sleep, where Patrick now slept alone. Rose slept in the den.

Anna would go to sleep in that bed, then Patrick would carry her to her own bed. Neither Patrick nor Rose knew when this stopped being occasional, and became essential. Everything in the house was out of kilter. Rose was packing her trunk. She did it in the daytime when Patrick and Anna were not around. She and Patrick spent the evenings in different parts of the house. Once she went into the dining room and found him putting fresh Scotch tape on the snapshots in the album. She was angry at him for doing this. She saw a snapshot of herself, pushing Anna on a swing in the park; herself smirking in a bikini; true lies.

"It wasn't any better then," she said. "Not really." She meant that she had always been planning, at the back of her mind, to do what she was doing now. Even on her wedding day she had known this time would come, and that if it didn't she might as well be dead. The betrayal was hers.

"I know that," said Patrick angrily.

But of course it had been better, because she hadn't started to try to make the break come, she had forgotten for long stretches that it would have to come. Even to say she had been planning to break, had started to break, was wrong, because she had done nothing deliberately, nothing at all intelligently, it had happened as painfully and ruinously as possible with all sorts of shilly-shallying and reconciling and berating, and right now she felt as if she was walking a swinging bridge and could only keep her eyes on the slats ahead, never look down or around.

"Which do you want?" she said softly to Anna. Instead of answering, Anna called out for Patrick. When he came she sat up and pulled them both down on the bed, one on each side of her. She held on to them, and began to sob and shake. A violently dramatic child, sometimes, a bare blade.

"You don't have to," she said. "You don't have fights anymore."

Patrick looked across at Rose without accusation. His customary look for years, even when they were making love, had been accusing, but he felt such pain on Anna's account that all accusation was wiped out. Rose had to get up and go out, leaving him to comfort Anna, because she was afraid a great, deceptive rush of feeling for him was on the way.

It was true, they did not have fights anymore. She had scars on her wrists and her body, which she had made (not quite in the most dangerous places) with a razor blade. Once in the kitchen of this house Patrick had tried to choke her. Once she had run outside and knelt in her nightgown, tearing up handfuls of grass. Yet for Anna this bloody fabric her parents had made, of mistakes and mismatches, that anybody could see ought to be torn up and thrown away, was still the true web of life, of father and mother, of beginning and shelter. What fraud, thought Rose, what fraud for everybody. We come from unions which don't have in them anything like what we think we deserve.

She wrote to Tom, to tell him what she was going to do. Tom was a teacher at the University of Calgary. Rose was a little bit in love with him (so she said to friends who knew about the affair: *a little bit in love*). She had met him here a year ago—he was the brother of a woman she sometimes acted with in radio plays—and since then she had stayed with him once in Victoria. They wrote long letters to each other. He was a courtly man, a historian, he wrote witty and delicately amorous letters. She had been a little afraid that when she announced that she was leaving Patrick, Tom would write less often, or more guardedly, in case she might be hoping for too much from him. *Getting ideas.* But he did not, he was not so vulgar or so cowardly; he trusted her.

She said to her friends that leaving Patrick had nothing to do with Tom and that she would probably not see Tom any more often than she had before. She believed that, but she had chosen between the job in the mountain town and one on Vancouver Island because she liked the idea of being closer to Calgary.

In the morning Anna was cheerful, she said it was all right. She said she wanted to stay. She wanted to stay in her school, with her friends. She turned halfway down the walk to wave and shriek at her parents.

"Have a happy divorce!"

Rose had thought that once she got out of Patrick's house she would live in a bare room, some place stained and shabby. She would not care, she would not bother making a setting for herself, she disliked all that. The apartment which she found—the upstairs of a brown brick house halfway up the mountainside—was stained and shabby, but she immediately set to work to fix it up. The red-and-gold wallpaper (these places, she was to discover, were often tricked out with someone's idea of elegant wallpaper) had been hastily put on, and was ripping and curling away from the baseboard. She bought some paste and pasted it down. She bought hanging plants and coaxed them not to die. She put up amusing posters in the bathroom. She paid insulting prices for an Indian bedspread, baskets and pottery and painted mugs, in the only shop in town where such things were to be found. She painted the kitchen blue and white, trying to get the colors of willow-pattern china. The landlord promised to pay for the paint but didn't. She bought blue candles, some incense, a great bunch of dried gold leaves and grass. What she had, when all this was finished, was a place which belonged quite recognizably to a woman, living alone, probably no longer young, who was connected, or hoped to be connected, with a college or the arts. Just as the house she had lived in before, Patrick's house, belonged recognizably to a successful business or professional man with inherited money and standards.

The town in the mountains seemed remote from everything. But Rose liked it, partly because of that. When you come back to living in a town after having lived in cities you have the idea that everything is comprehensible and easy there, almost as if some people have got together and said, "Let's play Town." You think that nobody could die there.

Tom wrote that he must come to see her. In October (she had hardly expected it would be so soon) there was an opportunity, a conference in Vancouver. He planned to leave the conference a day early, and to pretend to have taken an extra day there, so that he could have two days free. But he phoned from Vancouver that he could not come. He had an infected tooth, he was in bad pain, he was to have emergency dental surgery on the very day he had planned to spend with Rose. So he was to get the extra day after all, he said, did she think it was a judgment on him? He said he was taking a Calvinistic view of things, and was groggy with pain and pills.

Rose's friend Dorothy asked did she believe him? It had not occurred to Rose not to.

"I don't think he'd do that," she said, and Dorothy said quite cheerfully, even negligently, "Oh, they'll do anything."

Dorothy was the only other woman at the station; she did a homemakers' program twice a week, and went around giving talks to women's groups; she was much in demand as mistress of ceremonies at prize-giving dinners for young people's organizations; that sort of thing. She and Rose had struck up a friendship based mostly on their more-or-less single condition and their venturesome natures. Dorothy had a lover in Seattle, and she did not trust him.

"They'll do anything," Dorothy said. They were having coffee in the Hole-in-One, a little coffee-and-doughnut shop next to the radio station. Dorothy began telling Rose a story about an affair she had had with the owner of the station who was an old man now and spent most of his time in California. He had given her a necklace for Christmas that he said was jade. He said he had bought it in Vancouver. She went to have the clasp fixed and asked proudly how much the necklace was worth. She was told it was not jade at all, the jeweler explained how to tell, holding it up to the light. A few days later the owner's wife came into the office showing off an identical necklace; she too had been told the jade story. While Dorothy was telling her this, Rose was looking at Dorothy's ash-blonde wig, which was glossy and luxuriant and not for a moment believable, and her face, whose chipped and battered look the wig and her turquoise eye shadow emphasized. In a city she would have looked whorish; here people thought she was outlandish, but glamorous, a representative of some legendary fashionable world.

"That was the last time I trusted a man," Dorothy said. "At the same time as me he was laying a girl who worked in here—married girl, a waitress—and his *grandchildren's baby-sitter.* How do you like that?"

At Christmas Rose went back to Patrick's house. She had not seen Tom yet, but he had sent her a fringed, embroidered, dark blue shawl, bought during a conference holiday in Mexico, in early December, to which he had taken his wife (after all he had promised her, Rose said to Dorothy). Anna had stretched out in three months. She loved to suck her stomach in and stick her ribs out, looking like a child of famine. She was high-spirited, acrobatic, full of antics and riddles. Walking to the store with her mother—for Rose was again doing the shopping, the cooking, sometimes was desperate with fear that her job and her apartment and Tom did not exist outside of her imagination—she said, "I always forget when I'm at school."

"Forget what?"

"I always forget you're not at home and then I remember. It's only Mrs. Kreber." Mrs. Kreber was the housekeeper Patrick had hired.

Rose decided to take her away. Patrick did not say no, he said that maybe it was best. But he could not stay in the house while Rose was packing Anna's things.

Anna said later on she had not known she was coming to live with Rose, she had thought she was coming for a visit. Rose believed she had to say and think something like this, so she would not be guilty of any decision.

The train into the mountains was slowed by a great fall of snow.

The water froze. The train stood a long time in the little stations, wrapped in clouds of steam as the pipes were thawed. They got into their outdoor clothes and ran along the platform. Rose said, "I'll have to buy you a winter coat. I'll have to buy you some warm boots." In the dark coastal winters rubber boots and hooded raincoats were enough. Anna must have understood then that she was staying, but she said nothing.

At night while Anna slept Rose looked out at the shocking depth and glitter of the snow. The train crept along slowly, fearful of avalanches. Rose was not alarmed, she liked the idea of their being shut up in this dark cubicle, under the rough train blankets, borne through such implacable landscape. She always felt that the progress of trains, however perilous, was safe and proper. She felt that planes, on the other hand, might at any moment be appalled by what they were doing, and sink through the air without a whisper of protest.

She sent Anna to school, in her new winter clothes. It was all right, Anna did not shrink or suffer as an outsider. Within a week there were children coming home with her, she was going to the houses of other children. Rose went out to meet her, in the early winter dark, along the streets with their high walls of snow. In the fall a bear had come down the mountain, entered the town. News of it came over the radio. *An unusual visitor, a black bear, is strolling along Fulton Street. You are advised to keep your children indoors.* Rose knew that a bear was not likely to walk into town in the winter, but she was worried just the same. Also she was afraid of cars, with the streets so narrow and the corners hard to see around. Sometimes Anna would have gone home another way, and Rose would go all the way to the other child's house and find her not there. Then she would run, run all the way home along the hilly streets and up the long stairs, her heart pounding from the exercise and from fear, which she tried to hide when she found Anna there.

Her heart would pound also from hauling the laundry, the groceries. The Laundromat, the supermarket, the liquor store, were all at the bottom of the hill. She was busy all the time. She always had urgent plans for the next hour. Pick up the resoled shoes, wash and tint her hair, mend Anna's coat for school tomorrow. Besides her job, which was hard enough, she was doing the same things she had always done, and doing them under harder circumstances. There was a surprising amount of comfort in these chores.

Two things she bought for Anna: the goldfish, and the television set. Cats or dogs were not permitted in the apartment, only birds or fish. One day in January, the second week Anna was there, Rose walked down the hill to meet her, after school, to take her to Woolworth's to buy the fish. She looked at Anna's face and thought it was dirty, then saw that it was stained with tears.

"Today I heard somebody calling Jeremy," Anna said, "and I thought Jeremy was here." Jeremy was a little boy she had often played with at home.

Rose mentioned the fish.

"My stomach hurts."

"Are you hungry maybe? I wouldn't mind a cup of coffee. What would you like?"

It was a terrible day. They were walking through the park, a shortcut to downtown. There had been a thaw, then a freeze, so that there was ice everywhere, with water or slush on top of it. The sun was shining, but it was the kind of winter sunshine that only makes your eyes hurt, and your clothes too heavy, and emphasizes all disorder and difficulty, such as the difficulty now, in trying to walk on the ice. All around were teenagers just out of school, and their noise, their whooping and sliding, the way a boy and girl sat on a bench on the ice, kissing ostentatiously, made Rose feel even more discouraged.

Anna had chocolate milk. The teenagers had accompanied them into the restaurant. It was an old-fashioned place with the high-backed booths of the forties, and an orange-haired owner-cook whom everyone called Dree; it was the shabby reality that people recognized nostalgically in movies, and, best of all, nobody there had any idea that it was anything to be nostalgic about. Dree was probably saving to fix it up. But today Rose thought of those restaurants it reminded her of, where she had gone after school, and thought that she had after all been very unhappy in them.

"You don't love Daddy," said Anna. "I know you don't."

"Well, I like him," Rose said. "We just can't live together, that's all."

Like most things you are advised to say, this rang false, and Anna said, "You don't like him. You're just lying." She was beginning to sound more competent, and seemed to be looking forward to getting the better of her mother.

"Aren't you?"

Rose was in fact just on the verge of saying no, she did not like him. If that's what you want, you can have it, she felt like saying. Anna did want it, but could she stand it? How do you ever judge what children can stand? And actually the words *love, don't love, like, don't like,* even *hate,* had no meaning for Rose where Patrick was concerned.

"My stomach still hurts," said Anna with some satisfaction, and pushed the chocolate milk away. But she caught the danger signals, she did not want this to go any further. "When are we getting the fish?" she said, as if Rose had been stalling.

They bought an orange fish, a blue spotted fish, a black fish with a velvety-looking body and horrible bulging eyes, all of which they carried home in a plastic bag. They bought a fishbowl, colored pebbles, a green plastic plant. Both of them were restored by the inside of Woolworth's, the flashing fish and the singing birds and the bright pink and green lingerie and the gilt-framed mirrors and the kitchen plastic and a large lobster of cold red rubber.

On the television set Anna liked to watch *Family Court,* a program about teenagers needing abortions, and ladies picked up for shoplifting, and fathers showing up after long years away to reclaim their lost children who liked their stepfathers better. Another program she liked was called *The Brady Bunch.* The Brady Bunch was a family of six beautiful, busy, comically misunderstood or misunderstanding children, with a pretty blonde mother, a handsome dark father, a cheerful housekeeper. The Brady Bunch came on at six o'clock, and Anna wanted to eat supper watching it. Rose allowed this because she often wanted to work through Anna's suppertime. She began putting things in bowls, so that Anna could manage more easily. She stopped making suppers of meat and potatoes and vegetables, because she had to throw so much out. She made chili instead, or scrambled eggs, bacon and tomato sandwiches, wieners wrapped in biscuit dough. Sometimes Anna wanted cereal, and Rose let her have it. But then she would think there was something disastrously wrong, when she saw Anna in front of the television set eating Captain Crunch, at the very hour when families everywhere were gathered at kitchen or dining-room tables, preparing to eat and quarrel and amuse and torment each other. She got a chicken, she made a thick golden soup with vegetables and barley. Anna wanted Captain Crunch instead. She said the soup had a funny taste. It's *lovely* soup, cried Rose, you've hardly tasted it, Anna, please *try* it.

"For my sake," it's a wonder she didn't say. She was relieved, on the whole, when Anna said calmly, "No."

At eight o'clock she began to hound Anna into her bath, into bed. It was only when all this was accomplished—when she had brought the final glass of chocolate milk, mopped up the bathroom, picked up the papers, crayons, felt cutouts, scissors, dirty socks, Chinese checkers, also the blanket in which Anna wrapped herself to watch television, because the apartment was cold, made Anna's lunch for the next day, turned off her light over her protest—that Rose could settle down with a drink, or a cup of coffee laced with rum, and give herself over to satisfaction, appreciation. She would turn off the lights and sit by the high front window looking out over this mountain town she had hardly known existed a year ago, and she would think what a miracle it was that this had happened, that she had come all this way and was working, she had Anna, she was paying for Anna's life and her own. She could feel the weight of Anna in the apartment then just as naturally as she had felt her weight in her body, and without having to go and look at her she could see with stunning, fearful pleasure the fair hair and fair skin and glistening eyebrows, the profile along which, if you looked closely, you could see the tiny almost invisible hairs rise, catching the light. For the first time in her life she understood domesticity, knew the meaning of shelter, and labored to manage it.

"What made you want out of marriage?" said Dorothy. She had been married too, a long time ago.

Rose didn't know what to mention first. The scars on her wrist? The choking in the kitchen, the grubbing at the grass? All beside the point.

"I was just bored," said Dorothy. "It just bored the hell out of me, to tell you the honest truth."

She was half drunk. Rose started to laugh and Dorothy said, "What in hell are you laughing at?"

"It's just a relief to hear somebody say that. Instead of talking about how you didn't communicate."

"Well, we didn't communicate, either. No, the fact was I was out of my mind over somebody else. I was having an affair with a guy who worked for a newspaper. A journalist. Well, he went off to England, the journalist did, and he wrote me a letter over the Atlantic saying he really truly loved me. He wrote me that letter because he was over the Atlantic, and I was here, but I didn't have sense enough to know that. Do you know what I did? I left my husband—well, that was no loss— and I borrowed money, fifteen hundred dollars I borrowed from the *bank*. And I flew to England after him. I phoned his paper, they said he'd gone to Turkey. I sat in the hotel waiting for him to come back. Oh, what a time. I never went out of the hotel. If I went to get a massage or have my hair done I told them where to page me. I kept pestering them fifty times a day. Isn't there a letter? Wasn't there a phone call? Jesus, Jesus, Jesus."

"Did he ever come back?"

"I phoned again, they told me he'd gone to Kenya. I had started getting the shakes. I saw I had to get hold of myself so I did, in the nick of time. I flew home. I started paying back the bloody bank."

Dorothy drank vodka, unmixed, from a water tumbler.

"Oh, two or three years later I met him, where was it. It was in an airport. No, it was in a department store. I'm sorry I missed you when you came to England, he said. I said, oh, that's all right, I managed to have a good time anyway. I was still paying it back. I should've told him he was a shit."

At work Rose read commercials and the weather forecasts, answered letters, answered the telephone, typed up the news, did the voices in Sunday skits written by a local minister, and planned to do interviews. She wanted to do a story on the town's early settlers; she went and talked to an old blind man who lived above a feed store. He told her that in the old days apples and cherries had been tied to the boughs of pine and cedar trees, pictures taken of them and sent to England. That brought the English immigrants, convinced they were coming to a land where the orchards were already in bloom. When she got back to the station with this story everybody laughed; they had heard it so often before.

She wasn't forgetting Tom. He wrote; she wrote. Without this connection to a man, she might have seen herself as an uncertain and pathetic person; that connection held her new life in place. For a while it looked as if luck was with them. A conference was set up in Calgary, on radio in rural life, or something of that sort, and the station was sending Rose. All without the least connivance on her part. She and Tom were jubilant and silly on the phone. She asked one of the young teachers across the hall if she would move in and look after Anna. The girl was glad to agree to do it; the other teacher's boyfriend had moved in, and they were temporarily crowded. Rose went back to the shop where she had bought the bedspread and the pots; she bought a caftan-nightgown sort of robe with a pattern of birds on it, in jewel colors. It made her think of the Emperor's nightingale. She put a fresh rinse on her hair. She was to go sixty miles by bus, then catch a plane. She would exchange an hour of terror for the extra time in Calgary. People at the station enjoyed scaring her, telling her how the little planes rose almost straight up out of the mountain airport, then bucked and shivered their way over the Rockies. She did think it would not be right to die that way, to crash in the mountains going to see Tom. She thought this, in spite of the fever she was in to go. It seemed too frivolous an errand to die on. It seemed like treachery, to take such a risk; not treachery to Anna and certainly not to Patrick but perhaps to herself. But just because the journey was frivolously undertaken, because it was not entirely real, she believed she would not die.

She was in such high spirits she played Chinese checkers all the time with Anna. She played Sorry, or any game Anna wanted. The night before she was to leave—she had arranged for a taxi to pick her up, at half past five in the morning—they were playing Chinese checkers, and Anna said, "Oh, I can't see with these *blue* ones," and drooped over the board, about to cry, which she never did, in a game. Rose touched her forehead and led her, complaining, to bed. Her temperature was a hundred and two. It was too late to phone Tom at his office and of course Rose couldn't phone him at home. She did phone the taxi, and the airport, to cancel. Even if Anna seemed better in the morning, she wouldn't be able to go. She went over and told the girl who had been going to stay with Anna, then phoned the man who was arranging the conference, in Calgary. "Oh God, yes," he said. "Kids!" In the morning, with Anna wrapped in her blanket, watching cartoons, she phoned Tom in his office. "You're here, you're here!" he said. "Where are you?"

Then she had to tell him.

Anna coughed, her fever went up and down. Rose tried to get the heat up, fiddled with the thermostat, drained the radiators, phoned the landlord's office and left a message. He didn't phone back. She phoned him at home at seven o'clock the next morning, told him her child had bronchitis (which she may have believed at the time, but it was not true), told him she would give him one hour to get her some heat or she would phone the newspaper, she would denounce him over the radio, she would sue him, she would find the proper channels. He came at once, with a put-upon face (a poor man trying to make ends meet bedeviled by hysterical women), he did something to the thermostat in the hall, and the radiators started to get hot. The teachers told Rose that he had the hall thermostat fixed to control the heat and that he had never given in to protests before. She felt proud, she felt like a fierce slum mother who had screamed and sworn and carried on, for her child's sake. She forgot that slum mothers are seldom fierce, being too tired and bewildered. It was her middle-class certainties, her expectations of justice, that had given her such energy, such a high-handed style of abuse; that had scared him.

After two days she had to go back to work. Anna had improved, but Rose was worried all the time. She could not swallow a cup of coffee, for the chunk of anxiety in her throat. Anna was all right, she took her cough medicine, she sat up in bed, crayoning. When her mother came home she had a story to tell her. It was about some princesses.

There was a white princess who dressed all in bride clothes and wore pearls. Swans and lambs and polar bears were her pets, and she had lilies and narcissus in her garden. She ate mashed potatoes, vanilla ice cream, shredded coconut and meringue off the top of pies. A pink princess grew roses and ate strawberries, kept flamingoes (Anna described them, could not think of the name) on a leash. The blue princess subsisted on grapes and ink. The brown princess though drably dressed feasted better than anybody; she had roast beef and gravy and chocolate cake with chocolate icing, also chocolate ice cream with chocolate fudge sauce. What was there in her garden?

"Rude things," said Anna. "All over the ground."

This time Tom and Rose did not refer so openly to their disappointment. They had begun to hold back a little, maybe to suspect that they were unlucky for each other. They wrote tenderly, carefully, amusingly, and almost as if the last failure had not happened.

In March he phoned to tell her that his wife and children were going to England. He was going to join them there, but later, ten days later. So there will be ten days, cried Rose, blotting out the long absence to come (he was to stay in England until the end of the summer). It turned out not to be ten days, not quite, because he was obliged to go to Madison, Wisconsin, on the way to England. But you must come here first, Rose said, swallowing this disappointment, how long can you stay, can you stay a week? She pictured them eating long sunny breakfasts. She saw herself in the Emperor's nightingale outfit. She would have filtered coffee (she must buy a filter pot) and that good bitter marmalade in the stone jar. She didn't give any thought to her morning chores at the station.

He said he didn't know about that, his mother was coming to help Pamela and the children get off, and he couldn't just pack up and leave her. It would really be so much better, he said, if she could come to Calgary.

Then he became very happy and said they would go to Banff. They would take three or four days' holiday, could she manage that, how about a long weekend? She said wasn't Banff difficult for him, he might run into someone he knew. He said no, no, it would be all right. She wasn't quite so happy as he was because she hadn't altogether liked being in the hotel with him, in Victoria. He had gone down to the lobby to get a paper, and phoned their room, to see if she knew enough not to answer. She knew enough, but the maneuver depressed her. Nevertheless she said fine, wonderful, and they got calendars at each end of the phone, so that they could figure out which days. They could take in a weekend, she had a weekend coming to her. And she could probably manage Friday as well, and at least part of Monday. Dorothy could do the absolutely necessary things for her. Dorothy owed her some working time. Rose had covered for her, when she was fogged in, in Seattle; she had spent an hour on the air reading household hints and recipes she never believed would work.

She had nearly two weeks to make the arrangements. She spoke to the teacher again and the teacher said she could come. She bought a sweater. She hoped she would not be expected to learn to ski, in that time. There must be walks they could take. She thought they would spend most of their time eating and drinking and talking and making love. Thoughts of this latter exercise troubled her a bit. Their talk on the phone was decorous, almost shy, but their letters, now that they were sure of meeting, were filled with inflammatory promises. These were what Rose loved reading and writing, but she could not remember Tom as clearly as she wanted to. She could remember what he looked like, that he was not very tall, and spare, with gray waving hair and a long, clever face, but she could not remember any little, maddening things about him, any tone or smell. The thing she could remember too well was that their time in Victoria had not been completely successful; she could remember something between a curse and an apology, the slippery edge of failure. This made her especially eager to try again, to succeed.

She was to leave Friday, early in the morning, taking the same bus and plane she had planned to take before.

Tuesday morning it began to snow. She did not pay much attention. It was wet, pretty snow, coming straight down in big flakes. She wondered if it would be snowing in Banff. She hoped so, she liked the idea of lying in bed and watching it. It snowed more or less steadily for two days, and late Thursday afternoon when she went to pick up her ticket at the travel agency they told her the airport had been closed. She did not show or even feel any worry; she was a bit relieved, that she would not have to fly. How about trains, she said, but of course the train didn't go to Calgary, it went down to Spokane. She knew that already. Then the bus, she said. They phoned to make sure the highways were open and the buses were running. During that conversation her heart began to pound a bit, but it was all right, everything was all right, the bus was running. It won't be much fun, they said, it leaves here at half past twelve, that's twelve midnight, and it gets into Calgary around 2 P.M. the next day.

"That's all right."

"You must really want to get to Calgary," the grubby young man said. This was a most ramshackle informal travel agency, set up in a hotel lobby outside the door of the beer parlor.

"It's Banff, actually," she said brazenly. "And I do."

"Going to do some skiing?"

"Maybe." She was convinced he guessed everything. She didn't know then how commonplace such illicit jaunts were; she thought the aura of sin was dancing round her like half-visible flames on a gas burner.

She went home thinking she would be better off, really, sitting on the bus, getting closer and closer to Tom, than lying in bed unable to sleep. She would just have to ask the teacher to move in tonight.

The teacher was waiting for her, playing Chinese checkers with Anna. "Oh, I don't know how to tell you," she said, "I'm so awfully sorry, but something's happened."

She said her sister had had a miscarriage and was in need of her help. Her sister lived in Vancouver.

"My boyfriend is driving me down tomorrow if we can get through."

This was the first Rose had heard of any boyfriend, and she immediately suspected the whole story. Some flying chance the girl was off on; she too had smelled love and hope. Somebody's husband, maybe, or some boy her own age. Rose looked at her once-acned face now rosy with shame and excitement and knew she would never budge her. The teacher went on to embroider her story with talk of her sister's two little children; both boys, and they had been just longing for a girl.

Rose started phoning, to get somebody else. She phoned students, wives of the men she worked with, who might be able to give her names; she phoned Dorothy who hated children. It was no use. She followed leads that people had given her, though she realized these were probably worthless, given only to get rid of her. She was ashamed of her persistence. At last Anna said, "I could stay here by myself."

"Don't be silly."

"I did before. When I was sick and you had to go to work."

"How would you like," said Rose, and felt a true sudden pleasure at so easy and reckless a solution, "how would you like to come to Banff?"

They packed in a great rush. Fortunately Rose had been to the Laundromat the night before. She did not allow herself to think about what Anna would do in Banff, about who would pay for the extra room, about whether Anna would in fact agree to having a separate room. She threw in coloring books and storybooks and messy kits of do-it-yourself decorations, anything she thought might do for amusement. Anna was excited by the turn of events, not dismayed at the thought of the bus ride. Rose remembered to call ahead of time for the taxi to pick them up at midnight.

They almost got stuck driving down to the bus depot. Rose thought what a good idea it had been to call the taxi half an hour ahead of time, for what was usually a five-minute drive. The bus depot was an old service station, a dreary place. She left Anna on a bench with the luggage and went to buy their tickets. When she came back Anna was drooped over the suitcase, having given way to sleepiness as soon as her mother's back was turned.

"You can sleep on the bus."

Anna straightened up, denied being tired. Rose hoped it would be warm on the bus. Perhaps she should have brought a blanket, to wrap around Anna. She had thought of it, but they had enough to carry already, with the shopping bag full of Anna's books and amusements; it was too much to think of arriving in Calgary straggle-haired, cranky and constipated, with crayons spilling from the bag and a trailing blanket as well. She had decided not to.

There were just a few other passengers waiting. A young couple in jeans, looking cold and undernourished. A poor, respectable old woman wearing her winter hat; an Indian grandmother with a baby. A man lying on one of the benches looked sick or drunk. Rose hoped he was just in the bus depot getting warm, not waiting for the bus, because he looked as if he might throw up. Or if he was getting on the bus, she hoped he would throw up now, not later. She thought she had better take Anna to the washroom here. However unpleasant it was, it was probably better than what they had on the bus. Anna was wandering around looking at the cigarette machines, candy machines, drink and sandwich machines. Rose wondered if she should buy some sandwiches, some watery hot chocolate. Once into the mountains, she might wish she had.

Suddenly she thought that she had forgotten to phone Tom, to tell him to meet the bus not the plane. She would do it when they stopped for breakfast.

Attention all passengers waiting for the bus to Cranbrook, Radium Hot Springs, Golden, Calgary. Your bus has been canceled. Bus due to leave here at twelve-thirty has been canceled.

Rose went up to the wicket and said what is this, what happened, tell me, is the highway closed? Yawning, the man told her, "It's closed past Cranbrook. Open from here to Cranbrook but closed past that. And closed west of here to Grand Forks so the bus won't even get here tonight."

Calmly, Rose asked, what were the other buses she could take?

"What do you mean, other buses?"

"Well, isn't there a bus to Spokane? I could get from there to Calgary."

Unwillingly he pulled out his schedules. Then they both remembered that if the highway was closed between here and Grand Forks, that was no good, no bus would be coming through. Rose thought of the train to Spokane, then the bus to Calgary. She could never do it, it would be impossible with Anna. Nevertheless she asked about trains, had he heard anything about the trains?

"Heard they're running twelve hours late."

She kept standing at the wicket, as if some solution was owing to her, would have to appear.

"I can't do anything more for you here, lady."

She turned away and saw Anna at the pay phones, fiddling with the coin return boxes. Sometimes she found a dime that way.

Anna came walking over, not running, but walking quickly, in an unnaturally sedate and agitated way. "Come here," she said, "come here." She pulled Rose, numb as she was, over to one of the pay phones. She dipped the coin box toward her. It was full of silver. Full. She began scraping it into her hand. Quarters, nickels, dimes. More and more. She filled her pockets. It looked as if the box was refilling every time she closed it, as it might in a dream or a fairy tale. Finally she did empty it, she picked out the last dime. She looked up at Rose with a pale, tired, blazing face.

"Don't say anything," she commanded.

Rose told her that they were not going on the bus after all. She phoned for the same taxi, to take them home. Anna accepted the change in plans without interest. Rose noticed that she settled herself very carefully into the taxi, so that the coins would not clink in her pockets.

In the apartment Rose made herself a drink. Without taking off her boots or her coat Anna started spreading the money out on the kitchen table and separating it into piles to be counted.

"I can't believe this," she said. "I can't be-*lieve* it." She was using a strange adult voice, a voice of true astonishment masked by social astonishment, as if the only way she could control and deal with the event was to dramatize it in this way.

"It must be from a long distance call," said Rose. "The money didn't go through. I suppose it all belongs to the phone company."

"But we can't give it back, can we?" said Anna, guilty and triumphant, and Rose said no.

"It's crazy," Rose said. She meant the idea of the money belonging to the phone company. She was tired and mixed-up but beginning to feel temporarily and absurdly lighthearted. She could see showers of coins coming down on them, or snowstorms; what carelessness there was everywhere, what elegant caprice.

They tried to count it, but kept getting confused. They played with it instead, dropping coins ostentatiously through their fingers. That was a giddy time late at night in the rented kitchen on the mountainside. Bounty where you'd never look for it; streaks of loss and luck. One of the few times, one of the few hours, when Rose could truly say she was not at the mercy of past or future, or love, or anybody. She hoped it was the same for Anna.

Tom wrote her a long letter, a loving, humorous letter, mentioning fate. A grieved, relieved renunciation, before he set off for England. Rose didn't have any address for him, there, or she might have written asking him to give them another chance. That was her nature.

This last snow of the winter was quickly gone, causing some flooding in the valleys. Patrick wrote that he would drive up in June, when school was out, and take Anna back with him for the summer. He said he wanted to start the divorce, because he had met a girl he wanted to marry. Her name was Elizabeth. He said she was a fine and stable person.

And did Rose not think, said Patrick, that it might be better for Anna to be settled in her old home next year, in the home she had always known, to be back at her old school with her old friends (Jeremy kept asking about her) rather than traipsing around with Rose in her new independent existence? Might it not be true—and here Rose thought she heard the voice of the stable girl friend—that she was using Anna to give herself some stability, rather than face up to the consequences of the path she had chosen? Of course, he said, Anna must be given her choice.

Rose wanted to reply that she was making a home for Anna here, but she could not do that, truthfully. She no longer wanted to stay. The charm, the transparency, of this town was gone for her. The pay was poor. She would never be able to afford anything but this cheap apartment. She might never get a better job, or another lover. She was thinking of going east, going to Toronto, trying to get a job there, with a radio or television station, perhaps even some acting jobs. She wanted to take Anna with her, set them up again in some temporary shelter. It was just as Patrick said. She wanted to come home to Anna, to fill her life with Anna. She didn't think Anna would choose that life. Poor, picturesque, gypsying childhoods are not much favored by children, though they will claim to value them, for all sorts of reasons, later on.

The spotted fish died first, then the orange one. Neither Anna nor Rose suggested another trip to Woolworth's, so that the black one could have company. It didn't look as if it wanted company. Swollen, bug-eyed, baleful and at ease, it commanded the whole fishbowl for its own.

Anna made Rose promise not to flush it down the toilet after she was gone. Rose promised, and before she left for Toronto she walked over to Dorothy's house, carrying the fishbowl, to make her this unwelcome present. Dorothy accepted it decently, said she would name it after the man in Seattle, and congratulated Rose on leaving.

Anna went to live with Patrick and Elizabeth. She began to take drama and ballet lessons. Elizabeth believed that children should have accomplishments, and keep busy. They gave her the four-poster bed. Elizabeth made a canopy and coverlet for it, and she made Anna a nightdress and cap to match.

They got Anna a kitten, and they sent Rose a picture of her sitting with the kitten on the bed, looking demure and satisfied in the midst of all that flowered cloth.

Simon's Luck

Rose gets lonely in new places; she wishes she had invitations. She goes out and walks the streets and looks in the lighted windows at all the Saturday-night parties, the Sunday-night family suppers. It's no good telling herself she wouldn't be long inside there, chattering and getting drunk, or spooning up the gravy, before she'd wish she was walking the streets. She thinks she could take on any hospitality. She could go to parties in rooms hung with posters, lit by lamps with Coca-Cola shades, everything crumbly and askew; or else in warm professional rooms with lots of books, and brass rubbings, and maybe a skull or two; even in the recreation rooms she can just see the tops of, through the basement windows: rows of beer steins, hunting horns, drinking horns, guns. She could go and sit on Lurex-threaded sofas under hangings of black velvet displaying mountains, galleons, polar bears executed in brushed wool. She would like very much to be dishing up a costly *cabinet de diplomate* out of a cut-glass bowl in a rich dining room with a big gleaming belly of sideboard behind her, and a dim picture of horses feeding, cows feeding, sheep feeding, on badly painted purple grass. Or she could do as well with batter pudding in the eating nook of a kitchen in a little stucco house by the bus stop, plaster pears and peaches decorating the wall, ivy curling out of little brass pots. Rose is an actress; she can fit in anywhere.

She does get asked to parties. About two years ago, she was at a party in a high-rise apartment building in Kingston. The windows looked out on Lake Ontario and Wolfe Island. Rose didn't live in Kingston. She lived up-country; she had been teaching drama for two years at a community college. Some people were surprised that she would do this. They did not know how little money an actress might make; they thought that being well-known automatically meant being well-off.

She had driven down to Kingston just for this party, a fact which slightly shamed her. She had not met the hostess before. She had known the host last year, when he was teaching at the community college and living with another girl.

The hostess, whose name was Shelley, took Rose into the bedroom to put down her coat. Shelley was a thin, solemn-looking girl, a true blonde, with nearly white eyebrows, hair long and thick and straight as if cut from a block of wood. It seemed that she took her waif style seriously. Her voice was low and mournful, making Rose's own voice, her greeting of a moment ago, sound altogether too sprightly in her own ears.

In a basket at the foot of the bed a tortoiseshell cat was suckling four tiny, blind kittens.

"That's Tasha," the hostess said. "We can look at her kittens but we can't touch them, else she wouldn't feed them anymore."

She knelt down by the basket, crooning, talking to the mother cat with an intense devotion that Rose thought affected. The shawl around her shoulders was black, rimmed with jet beads. Some beads were crooked, some were missing. It was a genuine old shawl, not an imitation. Her limp, slightly yellowed, eyelet-embroidered dress was genuine too, though probably a petticoat in the first place. Such clothes took looking for.

On the other side of the spool bed was a large mirror, hung suspiciously high, and tilted. Rose tried to get a look at herself when the girl was bent over the basket. It is very hard to look in the mirror when there is another, and particularly a younger, woman in the room. Rose was wearing a flowered cotton dress, a long dress with a tucked bodice and puffed sleeves, which was too short in the waist and too tight in the bust to be comfortable. There was something wrongly youthful or theatrical about it; perhaps she was not slim enough to wear that style. Her reddish-brown hair was dyed at home. Lines ran both ways under her eyes, trapping little diamonds of darkened skin.

Rose knew by now that when she found people affected, as she did this girl, and their rooms coyly decorated, their manner of living irritating (that mirror, the patchwork quilt, the Japanese erotic drawings over the bed, the African music coming from the living room), it was usually because she, Rose, hadn't received and was afraid she wouldn't receive the attention she wanted, hadn't penetrated the party, felt that she might be doomed to hang around on the fringes of things, making judgments.

She felt better in the living room, where there were some people she knew, and some faces as old as her own. She drank quickly at first, and before long was using the newborn kittens as a springboard for her own story. She said that something dreadful had happened to her cat that very day.

"And the worst of it is," she said, "I never liked my cat much. It wasn't my idea to have a cat. It was his. He followed me home one day and insisted on being taken in. He was just like some big sneering hulk of an unemployable, set on convincing me I owed him a living. Well, he always had a fondness for the clothes dryer. He liked to jump in when it was warm, as soon as I'd taken the clothes out. Usually I just have one load but today I had two, and when I reached in to take the second load out, I thought I felt something. I thought, what do I have that's fur?"

People moaned or laughed, in a sympathetically horrified way. Rose looked around at them appealingly. She felt much better. The living room, with its lake view, its careful decor (a jukebox, barbershop mirrors, turn-of-the-century advertisements—*Smoke, for your throat's sake*—old silk lampshades, farmhouse bowls and jugs, primitive masks and sculptures), no longer seemed so hostile. She took another drink of her gin and knew there was a limited time coming now when she would feel light and welcome as a hummingbird, convinced that many people in the room were witty and many were kind, and some were both together.

"Oh, *no*, I thought. But it was. It was. Death in the dryer."

"A warning to all pleasure seekers," said a little sharp-faced man at her elbow, a man she had known slightly for years. He taught in the English department of the university, where the host taught now, and the hostess was a graduate student.

"That's terrible," said the hostess, with her cold, fixed look of sensitivity. Those who had laughed looked a bit abashed, as if they thought they might have seemed heartless. "Your cat. That's terrible. How could you come tonight?"

As a matter of fact the incident had not happened today at all; it had happened last week. Rose wondered if the girl meant to put her at a disadvantage. She said sincerely and regretfully that she hadn't been very fond of the cat and that had made it seem worse, somehow. That's what she was trying to explain, she said.

"I felt as if maybe it was my fault. Maybe if I'd been fonder, it wouldn't have happened."

"Of course it wouldn't," said the man beside her. "It was warmth he was seeking in the dryer. It was love. Ah, Rose!"

"Now you won't be able to fuck the cat anymore," said a tall boy Rose hadn't noticed before. He seemed to have sprung up, right in front of her. "Fuck the dog, fuck the cat, I don't know what you do, Rose."

She was searching for his name. She had recognized him as a student, or former student.

"David," she said. "Hello, David." She was so pleased at coming up with the name that she was slow in registering what he had said.

"Fuck the dog, fuck the cat," he repeated, swaying over her.

"I beg your pardon," Rose said, and put on a quizzical, indulgent, charming expression. The people around her were finding it as hard to adjust to what the boy said as she was. The mood of sociability, sympathy, expectation of goodwill was not easy to halt; it rolled on in spite of signs that there was plenty here it wasn't going to be able to absorb. Almost everyone was still smiling, as if the boy was telling an anecdote or playing a part, the point of which would be made clear in a moment. The hostess cast down her eyes and slipped away.

"Beg yours," said the boy in a very ugly tone. "Up yours, Rose." He was white and brittle-looking, desperately drunk. He had probably been brought up in a gentle home, where people talked about answering Nature's call and blessed each other for sneezing.

A short, strong man with black curly hair took hold of the boy's arm just below the shoulder.

"Move it along," he said, almost maternally. He spoke with a muddled European accent, mostly French, Rose thought, though she was not good about accents. She did tend to think, in spite of knowing better, that such accents spring from a richer and more complicated masculinity than the masculinity to be found in North America and in places like Hanratty, where she had grown up. Such an accent promised masculinity tinged with suffering, tenderness, and guile.

The host appeared in a velvet jumpsuit and took hold of the other arm, more or less symbolically, at the same time kissing Rose's cheek, because he hadn't seen her when she came in. "Must talk to you," he murmured, meaning he hoped he wouldn't have to, because there was so much tricky territory; the girl he had lived with last year, for one thing, and a night he had spent with Rose toward the end of term, when there had been a lot of drinking and bragging and lamenting about faithlessness, as well as some curiously insulting though pleasurable sex. He was looking very brushed and tended, thinner but softened, with his flowing hair and suit of bottle-green velvet. Only three years younger than Rose, but look at him. He had shed a wife, a family, a house, a discouraging future, set himself up with new clothes and new furniture and a succession of student mistresses. Men can do it.

"My, my," Rose said and leaned against the wall. "What was that all about?"

The man beside her, who had smiled all the time and looked into his glass, said, "Ah, the sensitive youth of our time! Their grace of language, their depth of feeling! We must bow before them."

The man with the black curly hair came back, didn't say a word, but handed Rose a fresh drink and took her glass.

The host came back too.

"Rose baby. I don't know how he got in. I said no bloody students. There's got to be some place safe from them."

"He was in one of my classes last year," Rose said. That really was all she could remember. She supposed they were thinking there must be more to it.

"Did he want to be an actor?" said the man beside her. "I'll bet he did. Remember the good old days when they all wanted to be lawyers and engineers and business executives? They tell me that's coming back. I hope so. I devoutly hope so. Rose, I bet you listened to his problems. You must never do that. I bet that's what you did."

"Oh, I suppose."

"They come along looking for a parent-substitute. It's banal as can be. They trail around worshiping you and bothering you and then bam! It's parent-substitute rejecting time!"

Rose drank, and leaned against the wall, and heard them take up the theme of what students expected nowadays, how they broke down your door to tell you about their abortions, their suicide attempts, their creativity crises, their weight problems. Always using the same words: personhood, values, rejection.

"I'm not rejecting you, you silly bugger, I'm flunking you!" said the little sharp man, recalling a triumphant confrontation he had had with one such student. They laughed at that and at the young woman who said, "God, the difference when I was at university! You wouldn't have mentioned an abortion in a professor's office any more than you would have shit on the floor. *Shat* on the floor."

Rose was laughing too, but felt smashed, under the skin. It would be better, in a way, if there were something behind this such as they suspected. If she had slept with that boy. If she had promised him something, if she had betrayed him, humiliated him. She could not remember anything. He had sprung out of the floor to accuse her. She must have done something, and she could not remember it. She could not remember anything to do with her students; that was the truth. She was solicitous and charming, all warmth and acceptance; she listened and advised; then she could not get their names straight. She could not remember a thing she had said to them.

A woman touched her arm. "Wake up," she said, in a tone of sly intimacy that made Rose think she must know her. Another student? But no, the woman introduced herself.

"I'm doing a paper on female suicide," she said. "I mean the suicide of female artists." She said she had seen Rose on television and was longing to talk to her. She mentioned Diane Arbus, Virginia Woolf, Sylvia Plath, Anne Sexton, Christiane Pflug. She was well informed. She looked like a prime candidate herself, Rose thought: emaciated, bloodless, obsessed. Rose said she was hungry, and the woman followed her out to the kitchen.

"And too many actresses to count—" the woman said. "Margaret Sullavan—"

"I'm just a teacher now."

"Oh, nonsense. I'm sure you are an actress to the marrow of your bones."

The hostess had made bread: glazed and braided and decorated loaves. Rose wondered at the pains taken here. The bread, the pâté, the hanging plants, the kittens, all on behalf of a most precarious and temporary domesticity. She wished, she often wished, that she could take such pains, that she could make ceremonies, impose herself, make bread.

She noticed a group of younger members of the faculty—she would have thought them students, except for what the host had said about students not being let in—who were sitting on the counters and standing in front of the sink. They were talking in low, serious voices. One of them looked at her. She smiled. Her smile was not returned. A couple of others looked at her, and went on talking. She was sure they were talking about her, about what had happened in the living room. She urged the woman to try some bread and pâté. Presumably that would keep her quiet, so that Rose could overhear what was being said.

"I never eat at parties."

The woman's manner toward her was turning dark and vaguely accusing. Rose had learned that this was a department wife. Perhaps it had been a political move, inviting her. And promising her Rose; had that been part of the move?

"Are you always so hungry?" the woman said. "Are you never ill?"

"I am when there's something this good to eat," Rose said. She was only trying to set an example, and could hardly chew or swallow, in her anxiety to hear what was being said of her. "No, I'm not often ill," she said. It surprised her to realize that was true. She used to get sick with colds and flu and cramps and headaches; those definite ailments had now disappeared, simmered down into a low, steady hum of uneasiness, fatigue, apprehension.

Fucked-up jealous establishment.

Rose heard that, or thought she heard it. They were giving her quick, despising looks. Or so she thought; she could not look directly at them. *Establishment.* That was Rose. Was it? Was that Rose? Was that Rose who had taken a teaching job because she wasn't getting enough acting jobs to support herself, was granted the teaching job because of her experience on stage and television, but had to accept a cut in pay because she lacked degrees? She wanted to go over and tell them that. She wanted to state her case. The years of work, the exhaustion, the traveling, the high school auditoriums, the nerves, the boredom, the never knowing where your next pay was coming from. She wanted to plead with them, so they would forgive her and love her and take her on their side. It was their side she wanted to be on, not the side of the people in the living room who had taken up her cause. But that was a choice made because of fear, not on principle. She feared them. She feared their hardhearted virtue, their cool despising faces, their secrets, their laughter, their obscenities.

She thought of Anna, her own daughter. Anna was seventeen. She had long fair hair and wore a fine gold chain around her throat. It was so fine you had to look closely to make sure it was a chain, not just a glinting of her smooth bright skin. She was not like these young people but she was equally remote. She practiced ballet and rode her horse every day, but she didn't plan to ride in competitions or be a ballerina. Why not?

"Because it would be silly."

Something about Anna's style, the fine chain, her silences, made Rose think of her grandmother, Patrick's mother. But then, she thought, Anna might not be so silent, so fastidious, so unforthcoming, with anybody but her mother.

The man with the black curly hair stood in the kitchen doorway giving her an impudent and ironic look.

"Do you know who that is?" Rose said to the suicide woman. "The man who took the drunk away?"

"That's Simon. I don't think the boy was drunk, I think he's on drugs."

"What does he do?"

"Well, I expect he's a student of sorts."

"No," said Rose. "That man—Simon?"

"Oh, Simon. He's in the classics department. I don't think he's always been a teacher."

"Like me," Rose said, and turned the smile she had tried on the young people on Simon. Tired and adrift and witless as she was, she was beginning to feel familiar twinges, tidal promises.

If he smiles back, things will start to be all right.

He did smile, and the suicide woman spoke sharply.

"Look, do you come to a party just to meet men?"

When Simon was fourteen, he and his older sister and another boy, a friend of theirs, were hidden in a freight car, traveling from occupied to unoccupied France. They were on their way to Lyons, where they would be looked after, redirected to safe places, by members of an organization that was trying to save Jewish children. Simon and his sister had already been sent out of Poland, at the beginning of the war, to stay with French relatives. Now they had to be sent away again.

The freight car stopped. The train was standing still, at night somewhere out in the country. They could hear French and German voices. There was some commotion in the cars ahead. They heard the doors grinding open, heard and felt the boots striking on the bare floors of those cars. An inspection of the train. They lay down under some sacks, but did not even try to cover their faces; they thought there was no hope. The voices were getting closer and they heard the boots on the gravel beside the track. Then the train began to move. It moved so slowly that they did not notice for a moment or so, and even then thought it was just a shunting of the cars. They expected it to stop, so that the inspection could continue. But the train kept moving. It moved a little faster, then faster; it picked up its ordinary speed, which was nothing very great. They were moving, they were free of the inspection, they were being carried away. Simon never knew what had happened. The danger was past.

Simon said that when he realized they were safe he suddenly felt that they would get through, that nothing could happen to them now, that they were particularly blessed and lucky. He took what happened for a lucky sign.

Rose asked him, had he ever seen his friend and his sister again?

"No. Never. Not after Lyons."

"So, it was lucky only for you."

Simon laughed. They were in bed, in Rose's bed in an old house, on the outskirts of a crossroads village; they had driven there straight from the party. It was April, the wind was cold, and Rose's house was chilly. The furnace was inadequate. Simon put a hand to the wallpaper behind the bed, made her feel the draft.

"What it needs is some insulation."

"I know. It's awful. And you should see my fuel bills."

Simon said she should get a wood stove. He told her about various kinds of firewood. Maple, he said, was a lovely wood to burn. Then he held forth on different kinds of insulation. Styrofoam, Micafil, fiberglass. He got out of bed and padded around naked, looking at the walls of her house. Rose shouted after him.

"Now I remember. It was a grant."

"What? I can't hear you."

She got out of bed and wrapped herself in a blanket. Standing at the top of the stairs, she said, "That boy came to me with an application for a grant. He wanted to be a playwright. I just this minute remembered."

"What boy?" said Simon. "Oh."

"But I recommended him. I know I did." The truth was she recommended everybody. If she could not see their merits, she believed it might just be a case of their having merits she was unable to see.

"He must not have got it. So he thought I shafted him."

"Well, suppose you had," said Simon, peering down the cellarway. "That would be your right."

"I know. I'm a coward about that lot. I hate their disapproval. They are so virtuous."

"They are not virtuous at all," said Simon. "I'm going to put my shoes on and look at your furnace. You probably need the filters cleaned. That is just their style. They are not much to be feared, they are just as stupid as anybody. They want a chunk of the power. Naturally."

"But would you get such venomous"—Rose had to stop and start the word again—"such *venomousness*, simply from ambition?"

"What else?" said Simon, climbing the stairs. He made a grab for the blanket, wrapped himself up with her, pecked her nose. "Enough of that Rose. Have you no shame? I'm a poor fellow come to look at your furnace. Your basement furnace. Sorry to bump into you like this, ma'am." She already knew a few of his characters. This was The Humble Workman. Some others were The Old Philosopher, who bowed low to her, Japanese style, as he came out of the bathroom, murmuring *memento mori, memento mori*; and, when appropriate, The Mad Satyr, nuzzling and leaping, making triumphant smacking noises against her navel.

At the crossroads store she bought real coffee instead of instant, real cream, bacon, frozen broccoli, a hunk of local cheese, canned crabmeat, the best-looking tomatoes they had, mushrooms, long-grained rice. Cigarettes as well. She was in that state of happiness which seems perfectly natural and unthreatened. If asked, she would have said it was because of the weather—the day was bright, in spite of the harsh wind—as much as because of Simon.

"You must've brought home company," said the woman who kept the store. She spoke with no surprise or malice or censure, just a comradely sort of envy.

"When I wasn't expecting it." Rose dumped more groceries on the counter. "What a lot of bother they are. Not to mention expense. Look at that bacon. And cream."

"I could stand a bit of it," the woman said.

Simon cooked a remarkable supper from the resources provided, while Rose did nothing much but stand around watching, and change the sheets.

"Country life," she said. "It's changed, or I'd forgotten. I came here with some ideas about how I would live. I thought I would go for long walks on deserted country roads. And the first time I did, I heard a car coming tearing along on the gravel behind me. I got well off. Then I heard shots. I was terrified. I hid in the bushes and a car came roaring past, weaving all over the road—and they were shooting out of the windows. I cut back through the fields and told the woman at the store I thought we should call the police. She said oh, yes, weekends the boys get a case of beer in the car and they go out shooting groundhogs. Then she said, what were you doing up that road anyway? I could see she thought going for walks by yourself was a lot more suspicious than shooting groundhogs. There were lots of things like that. I don't think I'd stay, but the job's here and the rent's cheap. Not that she isn't nice, the woman in the store. She tells fortunes. Cards and teacups."

Simon said that he had been sent from Lyons to work on a farm in the mountains of Provence. The people there lived and farmed very much as in the Middle Ages. They could not read or write or speak French. When they got sick they waited either to die or to get better. They had never seen a doctor, though a veterinarian came once a year to inspect the cows. Simon ran a pitchfork into his foot, the wound became infected, he was feverish and had the greatest difficulty in persuading them to send for the veterinarian, who was then in the next village. At last they did, and the veterinarian came and gave Simon a shot with a great horse needle, and he got better. The household was bewildered and amused to see such measures taken on behalf of human life.

He said that while he was getting better he taught them to play cards. He taught the mother and the children; the father and the grandfather were too slow and unwilling, and the grandmother was kept shut up in a cage in the barn, fed scraps twice a day.

"Is that true? Is it possible?"

They were at the stage of spreading things out for each other: pleasures, stories, jokes, confessions.

"Country life!" said Simon. "But here it is not so bad. This house could be made very comfortable. You should have a garden."

"That was another idea I had, I tried to have a garden. Nothing did very well. I was looking forward to the cabbages, I think cabbages are beautiful, but some worm got into them. It ate up the leaves till they looked like lace, and then they all turned yellow and lay on the ground."

"Cabbages are a very hard thing to grow. You should start with something easier." Simon left the table and went to the window. "Point me out where you had your garden."

"Along the fence. That's where they had it before."

"That is no good, it's too close to the walnut tree. Walnut trees are bad for the soil."

"I didn't know that."

"Well, it's true. You should have it nearer the house. Tomorrow I will dig up a garden for you. You'll need a lot of fertilizer. Now. Sheep manure is the very best fertilizer. Do you know anyone around here who has sheep? We will get several sacks of sheep manure and draw up a plan of what to plant, though it's too early yet, there could still be frost. You can start some things indoors, from seed. Tomatoes."

"I thought you had to go back on the morning bus," Rose said. They had driven up in her car.

"Monday is a light day. I will phone up and cancel. I'll tell the girls in the office to say I have a sore throat."

"Sore throat?"

"Something like that."

"It's good that you're here," said Rose truthfully. "Otherwise I'd be spending my time thinking about that boy. I'd be trying not to, but it would keep coming at me. In unprotected moments. I would have been in a state of humiliation."

"That's a pretty small thing to get into a state of humiliation about."

"So I see. It doesn't take much with me."

"Learn not to be so thin-skinned," said Simon, as if he were taking her over, in a sensible way, along with the house and garden. "Radishes. Leaf lettuce. Onions. Potatoes. Do you eat potatoes?"

Before he left they drew up a plan of the garden. He dug and worked the soil for her, though he had to content himself with cow manure. Rose had to go to work, on Monday, but kept him in her mind all day. She saw him digging in the garden. She saw him naked peering down the cellarway. A short, thick man, hairy, warm, with a crumpled comedian's face. She knew what he would say when she got home. He would say, "I hope I done it to your satisfaction, mum," and yank a forelock.

That was what he did, and she was so delighted she cried out, "Oh Simon, you idiot, you're the man for my life!" Such was the privilege, the widespread sunlight of the moment, that she did not reflect that saying this might be unwise.

In the middle of the week she went to the store, not to buy anything, but to get her fortune told. The woman looked in her cup and said, "Oh, you! You've met the man who will change everything."

"Yes, I think so."

"He will change your life. Oh, Lord. You won't stay here. I see fame. I see water."

"I don't know about that. I think he wants to insulate my house."
"The change has begun already."
"Yes. I know it has. Yes."

She could not remember what they had said about Simon coming again. She thought that he was coming on the weekend. She expected him, and she went out and bought groceries, not at the local store this time but at a supermarket several miles away. She hoped the woman at the store wouldn't see her carrying the grocery bags into the house. She had wanted fresh vegetables and steak and imported black cherries, and Camembert and pears. She had bought wine, too, and a pair of sheets covered with stylish garlands of blue and yellow flowers. She was thinking her pale haunches would show up well against them.

On Friday night she put the sheets on the bed and the cherries in a blue bowl. The wine was chilling, the cheese was getting soft. Around nine o'clock came the loud knock, the expected joking knock on the door. She was surprised that she hadn't heard his car.

"Felt lonesome," said the woman from the store. "So I just thought I'd drop in and—oh-oh. You're expecting your company."

"Not really," Rose said. Her heart had started thumping joyfully when she heard the knock and was thumping still. "I don't know when he's arriving here," she said. "Maybe tomorrow."

"Bugger of a rain."

The woman's voice sounded hearty and practical, as if Rose might need distracting or consoling.

"I just hope he isn't driving in it, then," Rose said.

"No sir, you wouldn't want him driving in it."

The woman ran her fingers through her short gray hair, shaking the rain out, and Rose knew she ought to offer her something. A glass of wine? She might become mellow and talkative, wanting to stay and finish the bottle. Here was a person Rose had talked to, plenty of times, a friend of sorts, somebody she would have claimed to like, and she could hardly be bothered to acknowledge her. It would have been the same at that moment with anyone who was not Simon. Anyone else seemed accidental and irritating.

Rose could see what was coming. All the ordinary delights, consolations, diversions, of life would be rolled up and packed away; the pleasure found in food, lilacs, music, thunder in the night, would vanish. Nothing would do anymore but to lie under Simon, nothing would do but to give way to pangs and convulsions.

She decided on tea. She thought she might as well put the time to use by having another go at her future.

"It's not clear," the woman said.

"What's not?"

"I'm not able to get anything in focus tonight. That happens. No, to be honest, I can't locate him."

"Can't locate him?"

"In your future. I'm beat."

Rose thought she was saying this out of ill-will, out of jealousy.

"Well, I'm not just concerned about him."

"Maybe I could do better if you had a possession of his, just let me have it to hang on to. Anything he had his hands on, do you have that?"

"Me," said Rose. A cheap boast, at which the fortune-teller was obliged to laugh.

"No, seriously."

"I don't think so. I threw his cigarette butts out."

After the woman had gone, Rose sat up waiting. Soon it was midnight. The rain came down hard. The next time she looked it was twenty to two. How could time so empty pass so quickly? She put out the lights because she didn't want to be caught sitting up. She undressed, but couldn't lie down on the fresh sheets. She sat on in the kitchen, in the dark. From time to time she made fresh tea. Some light from the street light at the corner came into the room. The village had bright new mercury vapor lights. She could see that light, a bit of the store, the church steps across the road. The church no longer served the discreet and respectable Protestant sect that had built it, but proclaimed itself a Temple of Nazareth, also a Holiness Center, whatever that might be. Things were more askew here than Rose had noticed before. No retired farmers lived in these houses; in fact there were no farms to retire from, just the poor fields covered with juniper. People worked thirty or forty miles away, in factories, in the Provincial Mental Hospital, or they didn't work at all, they lived a mysterious life on the borders of criminality or a life of orderly craziness in the shade of the Holiness Center. People's lives were surely more desperate than they used to be, and what could be more desperate than a woman of Rose's age, sitting up all night in her dark kitchen waiting for her lover? And this was a situation she had created, she had done it all herself, it seemed she never learned any lessons at all. She had turned Simon into the peg on which her hopes were hung and she could never manage now to turn him back into himself.

The mistake was in buying the wine, she thought, and the sheets and the cheese and the cherries. Preparations court disaster. She hadn't realized that till she opened the door and the commotion of her heart turned from merriment to dismay, like the sound of a tower full of bells turned comically (but not for Rose) into a rusty foghorn.

Hour after hour in the dark and the rain she foresaw what could happen. She could wait through the weekend, fortifying herself with excuses and sickening with doubt, never leaving the house in case the phone might ring. Back at work on Monday, dazed but slightly comforted by the real world, she would get up the courage to write him a note, in care of the classics department.

"I was thinking we might plant the garden next weekend. I have bought a great array of seeds (a lie, but she would buy them, if she heard from him). Do let me know if you're coming, but don't worry if you've made other plans."

Then she would worry: did it sound too offhand, with that mention of other plans? Wouldn't it be too pushy, if she didn't tack that on? All her confidence, her lightness of heart, would have leaked away, but she would try to counterfeit it.

"If it's too wet to work in the garden we could always go for a drive. Maybe we could shoot some groundhogs. Best, Rose."

Then a further time of waiting, for which the weekend would have been only a casual trial run, a haphazard introduction to the serious, commonplace, miserable ritual. Putting her hand into the mailbox and drawing the mail out without looking at it, refusing to leave the college until five o'clock, putting a cushion against the telephone to block her view of it; pretending inattention. Watch-pot thinking. Sitting up late at night, drinking, never getting quite sick enough of this foolishness to give up on it because the waiting would be interspersed with such green and springlike reveries, such convincing arguments as to his intentions. These would be enough, at some point, to make her decide that he must have been taken ill, he would never have deserted her otherwise. She would phone the Kingston Hospital, ask about his condition, be told that he was not a patient. After that would come the day she went into the college library, picked up back copies of the Kingston paper, searched the obituaries to discover if he had by any chance dropped dead. Then, giving in utterly, cold and shaking, she would call him at the university. The girl in his office would say he was gone. Gone to Europe, gone to California; he had only been teaching there for a single term. Gone on a camping trip, gone to get married.

Or she might say, "Just a minute, please," and turn Rose over to him, just like that.

"Yes?"

"Simon?"

"Yes."

"It's Rose."

"Rose?"

It wouldn't be as drastic as that. It would be worse.

"I've been meaning to call you," he would say, or, "Rose, how *are* you?" or even, "How is that garden?"

Better lose him now. But going by the phone she put her hand on it, to see if it was warm, maybe, or to encourage it.

Before it began to get light Monday morning she packed what she thought she would need into the back of the car, and locked the house, with the Camembert still weeping on the kitchen counter; she drove off in a westerly direction. She meant to be gone a couple of days, until she came to her senses and could face the sheets and the patch of readied earth and the place behind the bed where she had put her hand to feel the draft. (Why did she bring her boots and her winter coat, if this was the case?) She wrote a letter to the college—she could lie beautifully in letters, though not on the phone—in which she said that she had been called to Toronto by the terminal illness of a dear friend. (Perhaps she didn't lie so beautifully after all, perhaps she overdid it.) She had been awake almost the whole weekend, drinking, not so very much, but steadily. *I'm not having any of it,* she said out loud, very seriously and emphatically, as she loaded the car. And as she crouched in the front seat, writing the letter, which she could more comfortably have written in the house, she thought how many crazy letters she had written, how many overblown excuses she had found, having to leave a place, or being afraid to leave a place, on account of some man. Nobody knew the extent of her foolishness, friends who had known her twenty years didn't know half of the flights she had been on, the money she had spent, and the risks she had taken.

Here she was, she thought a bit later, driving a car, shutting down the windshield wipers as the rain finally let up on a Monday morning at ten o'clock, stopping for gas, stopping to get a transfer of money, now that the banks were open; she was competent and cheery, she remembered what to do, who would guess what mortifications, memories of mortification, predictions, were beating in her head? The most mortifying thing of all was simply hope, which burrows so deceitfully at first, masks itself cunningly, but not for long. In a week's time it can be out trilling and twittering and singing hymns at heaven's gate. And it was busy even now, telling her that Simon might be turning into her driveway at this very moment, might be standing at her door with his hands together, praying, mocking, apologizing. *Memento mori.*

Even so, even if that were true, what would happen some day, some morning? Some morning she could wake up and she would know by his breathing that he was awake beside her and not touching her, and that she was not supposed to touch him. So much female touching is asking (this is what she would have learned, or learned again, from him); women's tenderness is greedy, their sensuality is dishonest. She would lie there wishing she had some plain defect, something her shame could curl around and protect. As it was, she would have to be ashamed of, burdened by, the whole physical fact of herself, the whole outspread naked digesting putrefying fact. Her flesh could seem disastrous; thick and porous, gray and spotty. His body would not be in question, it never would be; he would be the one who condemned and forgave and how could she ever know if he would forgive her again? *Come here,* he could tell her, or *go away.* Never since Patrick had she been the free person, the one with that power; maybe she had used it all up, all that was coming to her.

Or she might hear him at a party, saying, "And then I knew I'd be all right, I knew it was a lucky sign." Telling his story to some tarty unworthy girl in a leopard-spotted silk, or—far worse—to a gentle long-haired girl in an embroidered smock, who would lead him by the hand, sooner or later, through a doorway into a room or landscape where Rose couldn't follow.

Yes, but wasn't it possible nothing like that would happen, wasn't it possible there'd be nothing but kindness, and sheep manure, and deep spring nights with the frogs singing? A failure to appear, on the first weekend, or to telephone, might have meant nothing but a different timetable; no ominous sign at all. Thinking like this, every twenty miles or so, she slowed, even looked for a place to turn around. Then she did not do it, she speeded up, thinking she would drive a little further to make sure her head was clear. Thoughts of herself sitting in the kitchen, images of loss, poured over her again. And so it was, back and forth, as if the rear end of the car was held by a magnetic force, which ebbed and strengthened, ebbed and strengthened again, but the strength was never quite enough to make her turn, and after a while she became almost impersonally curious, seeing it as a real physical force and wondering if it was getting weaker, as she drove, if at some point far ahead the car and she would leap free of it, and she would recognize the moment when she left its field.

So she kept driving. Muskoka; the Lakehead; the Manitoba border. Sometimes she slept in the car, pulled off to the side of the road for an hour or so. In Manitoba it was too cold to do that; she checked into a motel. She ate in roadside restaurants. Before she entered a restaurant she combed her hair and made up her face and put on that distant, dreamy, shortsighted look women wear when they think some man may be watching them. It was too much to say that she really expected Simon to be there, but it seemed she did not entirely rule him out.

The force did weaken, with distance. It was as simple as that, though the distance, she thought afterward, would have to be covered by car, or by bus, or bicycle; you couldn't get the same results by flying. In a prairie town within sight of the Cypress Hills she recognized the change. She had driven all night until the sun came up behind her and she felt calm and clearheaded as you do at such times. She went into a café and ordered coffee and fried eggs. She sat at the counter looking at the usual things there are behind café counters—the coffeepots and the bright, probably stale pieces of lemon and raspberry pie, the thick glass dishes they put ice cream or jello in. It was those dishes that told her of her changed state. She could not have said she found them shapely, or eloquent, without misstating the case. All she could have said was that she saw them in a way that wouldn't be possible to a person in any stage of love. She felt their solidity with a convalescent gratitude whose weight settled comfortably into her brains and feet. She realized then that she had come into this café without the least farfetched idea of Simon, so it seemed the world had stopped being a stage where she might meet him, and gone back to being itself. During that bountifully clear half hour before her breakfast made her so sleepy she had to get to a motel, where she fell asleep with her clothes on and the curtains ópen to the sun, she thought how love removes the world for you, and just as surely when it's going well as when it's going badly. This shouldn't have been, and wasn't, a surprise to her; the surprise was that she so much wanted, required, everything to be there for her, thick and plain as ice cream dishes, so that it seemed to her it might not be the disappointment, the losses, the dissolution, she had been running from, any more than the opposite of those things: the celebration and shock of love, the dazzling alteration. Even if that was safe, she couldn't accept it. Either way you were robbed of something—a private balance spring, a little dry kernel of probity. So she thought.

She wrote to the college that while in Toronto attending the deathbed of her friend she had run into an old acquaintance who had offered her a job on the west coast, and that she was going there immediately. She supposed they could make trouble for her but she also supposed, rightly, that they would not bother, since the terms of her employment, and particularly her pay, were not quite regular. She wrote to the agency from which she rented the house; she wrote to the woman at the store, good luck and good-bye. On the Hope-Princeton highway she got out of the car and stood in the cool rain of the coastal mountains. She felt relatively safe, and exhausted, and sane, though she knew she had left some people behind who would not agree with that.

Luck was with her. In Vancouver she met a man she knew who was casting a new television series. It was to be produced on the west coast and concerned a family, or pseudo-family, of eccentrics and drifters using an old house on Salt Spring Island as their home or headquarters. Rose got the role of the woman who owned the house, the pseudo-mother. Just as she had said in the letter; a job on the west coast, possibly the best job she had ever had. Some special makeup techniques, aging techniques, had to be used on her face; the makeup man joked that if the series was a success, and ran for a few years, these techniques would not be necessary.

A word everybody at the coast was using was *fragile*. They spoke of feeling fragile today, of being in a fragile state. Not me, Rose said, I am getting a distinct feeling of being made of old horsehide. The wind and sun on the prairies had browned and roughened her skin. She slapped her creased brown neck, to emphasize the word *horsehide*. She was already beginning to adopt some of the turns of phrase, the mannerisms, of the character she was to play.

A year or so later Rose was out on the deck of one of the B.C. ferries, wearing a dingy sweater and a head scarf. She had to creep around among the lifeboats, keeping an eye on a pretty young girl who was freezing in cut-off jeans and a halter. According to the script, the woman Rose played was afraid this young girl meant to jump off the boat because she was pregnant.

Filming this scene, they collected a sizeable crowd. When they broke and walked toward the sheltered part of the deck, to put on their coats and drink coffee, a woman in the crowd reached out and touched Rose's arm.

"You won't remember me," she said, and in fact Rose did not remember her. Then this woman began to talk about Kingston, the couple who had given the party, even about the death of Rose's cat. Rose recognized her as the woman who had been doing the paper on suicide. But she looked quite different; she was wearing an expensive beige pantsuit, a beige and white scarf around her hair; she was no longer fringed and soiled and stringy and mutinous-looking. She introduced a husband, who grunted at Rose as if to say that if she expected him to make a big fuss about her, she had another think coming. He moved away and the woman said, "Poor Simon. You know he died."

Then she wanted to know if they were going to be shooting any more scenes. Rose knew why she asked. She wanted to get into the background or even the foreground of these scenes so that she could call up her friends and tell them to watch her. If she called the people who had been at that party she would have to say that she knew the series was utter tripe but that she had been persuaded to be in a scene, for the fun of it.

"Died?"

The woman took off her scarf and the wind blew her hair across her face.

"Cancer of the pancreas," she said, and turned to face the wind so that she could put the scarf on again, more to her satisfaction. Her voice seemed to Rose knowledgeable and sly. "I don't know how well you knew him," she said. Was that to make Rose wonder how well *she* knew him? That slyness could ask for help, as well as measure victories; you could be sorry for her perhaps, but never trust her. Rose was thinking this instead of thinking about what she had told her. "So sad," she said, businesslike now, as she tucked her chin in, knotting the scarf. "Sad. He had it for a long time."

Somebody was calling Rose's name; she had to go back to the scene. The girl didn't throw herself into the sea. They didn't have things like that happening in the series. Such things always threatened to happen but they didn't happen, except now and then to peripheral and unappealing characters. People watching trusted that they would be protected from predictable disasters, also from those shifts of emphasis that throw the story line open to question, the disarrangements which demand new judgments and solutions, and throw the windows open on inappropriate unforgettable scenery.

Simon's dying struck Rose as that kind of disarrangement. It was preposterous, it was unfair, that such a chunk of information should have been left out, and that Rose even at this late date could have thought herself the only person who could seriously lack power.

Spelling

In the store, in the old days, Flo used to say she could tell when some woman was going off the track. Special headgear or footwear were often the first giveaways. Galoshes flopping open on a summer day. Rubber boots they slopped around in, or men's workboots. They might say it was on account of corns, but Flo knew better. It was deliberate, it was meant to tell. Next might come the old felt hat, the torn raincoat worn in all weathers, the trousers held up at the waist with twine, the dim shredded scarves, the layers of ravelling sweaters.

Mothers and daughters often the same way. It was always in them. Waves of craziness, always rising, irresistible as giggles, from some place deep inside, gradually getting the better of them.

They used to come telling Flo their stories. Flo would string them along. "Is that so?" she would say. "Isn't that a shame?"

My vegetable grater is gone and I know who took it.

There is a man comes and looks at me when I take my clothes off at night. I pull the blind down and he looks through the crack.

Two hills of new potatoes stolen. A jar of whole peaches. Some nice ducks' eggs.

One of those women they took to the County Home at last. The first thing they did, Flo said, was give her a bath. The next thing they did was cut off her hair, which had grown out like a haystack. They expected to find anything in it, a dead bird or maybe a nest of baby mouse skeletons. They did find burrs and leaves and a bee that must have got caught and buzzed itself to death. When they had cut down far enough they found a cloth hat. It had rotted on her head and the hair had just pushed up through it, like grass through wire.

Flo had got into the habit of keeping the table set for the next meal, to save trouble. The plastic cloth was gummy, the outline of the plate and saucer plain on it as the outline of pictures on a greasy wall. The refrigerator was full of sulfurous scraps, dark crusts, furry oddments. Rose got to work cleaning, scraping, scalding. Sometimes Flo came lumbering through on her two canes. She might ignore Rose's presence altogether, she might tip the jug of maple syrup up against her mouth and drink it like wine. She loved sweet things now, craved them. Brown sugar by the spoonful, maple syrup, tinned puddings, jelly, globs of sweetness to slide down her throat. She had given up smoking, probably for fear of fire.

Another time she said, "What are you doing in there behind the counter? You ask me what you want, and I'll get it." She thought the kitchen was the store.

"I'm *Rose,*" Rose said in a loud, slow voice. "We're in the *kitchen.* I'm cleaning up the *kitchen.*"

The old arrangement of the kitchen: mysterious, personal, eccentric. Big pan in the oven, medium-sized pan under the potato pot on the corner shelf, little pan hanging on the nail by the sink. Colander under the sink. Dishrags, newspaper clippings, scissors, muffin tins, hanging on various nails. Piles of bills and letters on the sewing machine, on the telephone shelf. You would think someone had set them down a day or two ago, but they were years old. Rose had come across some letters written by herself, in a forced and spritely style. False messengers; false connections, with a lost period of her life.

"Rose is away," Flo said. She had a habit now of sticking her bottom lip out, when she was displeased or perplexed. "Rose got married."

The second morning Rose got up and found that a gigantic stirring-up had occurred in the kitchen, as if someone had wielded a big shaky spoon. The big pan was lodged behind the refrigerator; the egg lifter was in with the towels, the bread knife was in the flour bin and the roasting pan wedged in the pipes under the sink. Rose made Flo's

breakfast porridge and Flo said, "You're that woman they were sending to look after me."

"Yes."

"You aren't from around here?"

"No."

"I haven't got money to pay you. They sent you, they can pay you."

Flo spread brown sugar over her porridge until the porridge was entirely covered, then patted the sugar smooth with her spoon.

After breakfast she spied the cutting board, which Rose had been
using when she cut bread for her own toast. "What is this thing doing
here getting in our road?" said Flo authoritatively, picking it up and
marching off—as well as anybody with two canes could march—to
hide it somewhere, in the piano bench or under the back steps.

Years ago, Flo had had a little glassed-in side porch built on to the
house. From there she could watch the road just as she used to watch
from behind the counter of the store (the store window was now
boarded up, the old advertising signs painted over). The road wasn't
the main road out of Hanratty through West Hanratty to the Lake
anymore; there was a highway bypass. And it was paved, now, with
wide gutters, new mercury vapor street lights. The old bridge was gone
and a new, wide bridge, much less emphatic, had taken its place. The
change from Hanratty to West Hanratty was hardly noticeable. West
Hanratty had got itself spruced up with paint and aluminum siding;
Flo's place was about the only eyesore left.

What were the things Flo put up to look at, in her little porch,
where she had been sitting for years now with her joints and arteries
hardening?

A calendar with a picture of a puppy and a kitten on it. Faces
turned toward each other so that the noses touched, and the space between the two bodies made a heart.

A photograph, in color, of Princess Anne as a child.

A Blue Mountain pottery vase, gift from Brian and Phoebe, with
three yellow plastic roses in it, vase and roses bearing several seasons'
sifting of dust.

Six shells from the Pacific coast, sent home by Rose but not gathered by her, as Flo believed, or had once believed. Bought on a vaca-

tion in the state of Washington. They were an impulse item in a plastic bag by the cashier's desk in a tourist restaurant.

THE LORD IS MY SHEPHERD, in black cutout scroll with a sprinkling of glitter. Free gift from a dairy.

Newspaper photograph of seven coffins in a row. Two large and five small. Parents and children, all shot by the father in the middle of the night, for reasons nobody knew, in a farmhouse out in the country. That house was not easy to find but Flo had seen it. Neighbors took her, on a Sunday drive, in the days when she was using only one cane. They had to ask directions at a gas station on the highway, and again at a crossroads store. They were told that many people had asked the same questions, had been equally determined. Though Flo had to admit there was nothing much to see. A house like any other. The chimney, the windows, the shingles, the door. Something that could have been a dish towel, or a diaper, that nobody had felt like taking in, left to rot on the line.

Rose had not been back to see Flo for nearly two years. She had been busy, she had been traveling with small companies, financed by grants, putting on plays or scenes from plays, or giving readings, in high school auditoriums and community halls, all over the country. It was part of her job to go on local television chatting about these productions, trying to drum up interest, telling amusing stories about things that had happened during the tour. There was nothing shameful about any of this, but sometimes Rose was deeply, unaccountably ashamed. She did not let her confusion show. When she talked in public she was frank and charming; she had a puzzled, diffident way of leading into her anecdotes, as if she were just now remembering, had not told them a hundred times already. Back in her hotel room, she often shivered and moaned, as if she were having an attack of fever. She blamed it on exhaustion, or her approaching menopause. She couldn't remember any of the people she had met, the charming, interesting people who had invited her to dinner and to whom, over drinks in various cities, she had told intimate things about her life.

Neglect in Flo's house had turned a final corner, since Rose saw it last. The rooms were plugged up with rags and papers and dirt. Pull a blind to let some light in, and the blind comes apart in your hand. Shake a curtain and the curtain falls to rags, letting loose a choking dust. Put a hand into a drawer and it sinks into something soft and dark and rubbishy.

We hate to write bad news but it looks like she has got past where she can look after herself. We try to look in on her but we are not so young ourselves anymore so it looks like maybe the time has come.

The same letter, more or less, had been written to Rose and to her half brother, Brian, who was an engineer, living in Toronto. Rose had just come back from her tour. She had assumed that Brian and his wife, Phoebe, whom she saw seldom, were keeping in touch with Flo. After all, Flo was Brian's mother, Rose's stepmother. And it turned out that they had been keeping in touch, or so they thought. Brian had recently been in South America but Phoebe had been phoning Flo every Sunday night. Flo had little to say but she had never talked to Phoebe anyway; she had said she was fine, everything was fine, she had offered some information about the weather. Rose had observed Flo on the telephone, since she came home, and she saw how Phoebe could have been deceived. Flo spoke normally, she said hello, fine, that was a big storm we had last night, yes, the lights were out here for hours. If you didn't live in the neighborhood you wouldn't realize there hadn't been any storm.

It wasn't that Rose had entirely forgotten Flo in those two years. She had fits of worry about her. It was just that for some time now she had been between fits. One time the fit had come over her in the middle of a January storm, she had driven two hundred miles through blizzards, past ditched cars, and when she finally parked on Flo's street, finally tramped up the walk Flo had not been able to shovel, she was full of relief for herself and concern for Flo, a general turmoil of feelings both anxious and pleasurable. Flo opened the door and gave a bark of warning.

"You can't park there!"

"What?"

"Can't park there!"

Flo said there was a new bylaw; no parking on the streets during the winter months.

"You'll have to shovel out a place."

Of course Rose had an explosion.

"If you say one more word right now I'll get in the car and drive back."

"Well you can't park—"

"One more word!"

"Why do you have to stand here and argue with the cold blasting into the house?"

Rose stepped inside. Home.

That was one of the stories she told about Flo. She did it well; her own exhaustion and sense of virtue; Flo's bark, her waving cane, her fierce unwillingness to be the object of anybody's rescue.

After she read the letter Rose had phoned Phoebe, and Phoebe had asked her to come to dinner, so they could talk. Rose resolved to behave well. She had an idea that Brian and Phoebe moved in a permanent cloud of disapproval of her. She thought that they disapproved of her success, limited and precarious and provincial though it might be, and that they disapproved of her even more when she failed. She also knew it was not likely they would have her on their minds so much, or feel anything so definite.

She put on a plain skirt and an old blouse, but at the last minute changed into a long dress, made of thin red and gold cotton from India, the very thing that would justify their saying that Rose was always so theatrical.

Nevertheless she made up her mind as she usually did that she would speak in a low voice, stick to facts, not get into any stale and silly arguments with Brian. And as usual most of the sense seemed to fly out of her head as soon as she entered their house, was subjected to their calm routines, felt the flow of satisfaction, self-satisfaction, perfectly justified self-satisfaction, that emanated from the very bowls and draperies. She was nervous, when Phoebe asked her about her tour, and Phoebe was a bit nervous too, because Brian sat silent, not exactly frowning but indicating that the frivolity of the subject did not please him. In Rose's presence Brian had said more than once that he had no use for people in her line of work. But he had no use for a good many people. Actors, artists, journalists, rich people (he would never admit to being one himself), the entire Arts faculty of universities. Whole classes and categories, down the drain. Convicted of woolly-mindedness, and showy behavior; inaccurate talk, many excesses. Rose did not know if he spoke the truth or if this was something he had to say in front of her. He offered the bait of his low-voiced contempt; she rose to it; they had fights, she had left his house in tears. And underneath all this, Rose felt, they loved each other. But they could never stop the old, old competition; who is the better person, who has chosen the better work? What were they looking for? Each other's good opinion, which perhaps they meant to grant, in full, but not yet. Phoebe, who was a calm and dutiful woman with a great talent for normalizing things (the very opposite of their family talent for blowing things up), would serve food and pour coffee and regard them with a polite puzzlement; their contest, their vulnerability, their hurt, perhaps seemed as odd to her as the antics of comic-strip characters who stick their fingers into light sockets.

"I always wished Flo could have come back for another visit with us," Phoebe said. Flo had come once, and asked to be taken home after three days. But afterward it seemed to be a pleasure to her, to sit and list the things Brian and Phoebe owned, the features of their house. Brian and Phoebe lived quite unostentatiously, in Don Mills, and the things Flo dwelt on—the door chimes, the automatic garage doors, the swimming pool—were among the ordinary suburban acquisitions. Rose had said as much to Flo who believed that she, Rose, was jealous.

"You wouldn't turn them down if you was offered."

"Yes I would."

That was true, Rose believed it was true, but how could she ever explain it to Flo or anybody in Hanratty? If you stay in Hanratty and do not get rich it is all right because you are living out your life as was intended, but if you go away and do not get rich, or, like Rose, do not remain rich, then what was the point?

After dinner Rose and Brian and Phoebe sat in the backyard beside the pool, where the youngest of Brian and Phoebe's four daughters was riding an inflated dragon. Everything had gone amicably, so far. It had been decided that Rose would go to Hanratty, that she would make arrangements to get Flo into the Wawanash County Home. Brian had already made inquiries about it, or his secretary had, and he said that it seemed not only cheaper but better run, with more facilities, than any private nursing home.

"She'll probably meet old friends there," Phoebe said.

Rose's docility, her good behavior, was partly based on a vision she had been building up all evening, and would never reveal to Brian and Phoebe. She pictured herself going to Hanratty and looking after Flo, living with her, taking care of her for as long as was necessary. She thought how she would clean and paint Flo's kitchen, patch the shingles over the leaky spots (that was one of the things the letter had mentioned), plant flowers in the pots, and make nourishing soup. She wasn't so far gone as to imagine Flo fitting comfortably into this picture, settling down to a life of gratitude. But the crankier Flo got, the milder and more patient Rose would become, and who, then, could accuse her of egotism and frivolity?

This vision did not survive the first two days of being home.

Would you like a pudding?" Rose said.

"Oh, I don't care."

The elaborate carelessness some people will show, the gleam of hope, on being offered a drink.

Rose made a trifle. Berries, peaches, custard, cake, whipped cream and sweet sherry.

Flo ate half the bowlful. She dipped in greedily, not bothering to transfer a portion to a smaller bowl.

"That was lovely," she said. Rose had never heard such an admission of grateful pleasure from her. "Lovely," said Flo and sat remembering, appreciating, belching a little. The suave dreamy custard, the nipping berries, robust peaches, luxury of sherry-soaked cake, munificence of whipped cream.

Rose thought that she had never done anything in her life that came as near pleasing Flo as this did.

"I'll make another soon."

Flo recovered herself. "Oh well. You do what you like."

Rose drove out to the County Home. She was conducted through it. She tried to tell Flo about it when she came back.

"Whose home?" said Flo.

"No, the *County* Home."

Rose mentioned some people she had seen there. Flo would not admit to knowing any of them. Rose spoke of the view and the pleasant rooms. Flo looked angry; her face darkened and she stuck out her lip. Rose handed her a mobile she had bought for fifty cents in the County Home Crafts Center. Cutout birds of blue and yellow paper were bobbing and dancing, on undetectable currents of air.

"Stick it up your arse," said Flo.

Rose put the mobile up in the porch and said she had seen the trays coming up, with supper on them.

"They go to the dining room if they're able, and if they're not they have trays in their rooms. I saw what they were having.

"Roast beef, well done, mashed potatoes and green beans, the frozen not the canned kind. Or an omelette. You could have a mushroom omelette or a chicken omelette or a plain omelette, if you liked."

"What was for dessert?"

"Ice cream. You could have sauce on it."

"What kind of sauce was there?"

"Chocolate. Butterscotch. Walnut."

"I can't eat walnuts."

"There was marshmallow too."

Out at the Home the old people were arranged in tiers. On the first floor were the bright and tidy ones. They walked around, usually with the help of canes. They visited each other, played cards. They had singsongs and hobbies. In the Crafts Center they painted pictures, hooked rugs, made quilts. If they were not able to do things like that they could make rag dolls, mobiles like the one Rose bought, poodles and snowmen which were constructed of Styrofoam balls, with sequins for eyes; they also made silhouette pictures by placing thumbtacks on traced outlines: knights on horseback, battleships, airplanes, castles.

They organized concerts; they held dances; they had checker tournaments.

"Some of them say they are the happiest here they have ever been in their lives."

Up one floor there was more television watching, there were more wheelchairs. There were those whose heads drooped, whose tongues lolled, whose limbs shook uncontrollably. Nevertheless sociability was still flourishing, also rationality, with occasional blanks and absences.

On the third floor you might get some surprises.

Some of them up there had given up speaking.

Some had given up moving, except for odd jerks and tosses of the head, flailing of the arms, that seemed to be without purpose or control.

Nearly all had given up worrying about whether they were wet or dry.

Bodies were fed and wiped, taken up and tied in chairs, untied and put to bed. Taking in oxygen, giving out carbon dioxide, they continued to participate in the life of the world.

Crouched in her crib, diapered, dark as a nut, with three tufts of hair like dandelion floss sprouting from her head, an old woman was making loud shaky noises.

"Hello Aunty," the nurse said. "You're spelling today. It's lovely weather outside." She bent to the old woman's ear. "Can you spell weather?"

This nurse showed her gums when she smiled, which was all the time; she had an air of nearly demented hilarity.

"Weather," said the old woman. She strained forward, grunting, to get the word. Rose thought she might be going to have a bowel movement. "W-E-A-T-H-E-R."

That reminded her.

"Whether. W-H-E-T-H-E-R."

So far so good.

"Now you say something to her," the nurse said to Rose.

The words in Rose's mind were for a moment all obscene or despairing.

But without prompting came another.

"Forest. F-O-R-E-S-T."

"Celebrate," said Rose suddenly.

"C-E-L-E-B-R-A-T-E."

You had to listen very hard to make out what the old woman was saying, because she had lost much of the power to shape sounds. What she said seemed to come not from her mouth or her throat, but from deep in her lungs and belly.

"Isn't she a wonder," the nurse said. "She can't see and that's the only way we can tell she can hear. Like if you say, 'Here's your dinner,' she won't pay any attention to it, but she might start spelling *dinner*.

"Dinner," she said, to illustrate, and the old woman picked it up. "D-I-N-N . . ." Sometimes a long wait, a long wait between letters. It seemed she had only the thinnest thread to follow, meandering through that emptiness or confusion that nobody on this side can do more than guess at. But she didn't lose it, she followed it through to the end, however tricky the word might be, or cumbersome. Finished. Then she was sitting waiting; waiting, in the middle of her sightless eventless day, till up from somewhere popped another word. She would encompass it, bend all her energy to master it. Rose wondered what the words were like, when she held them in her mind. Did they carry their usual meaning, or any meaning at all? Were they like words in dreams or in the minds of young children, each one marvelous and distinct and alive as a new animal? This one limp and clear, like a jellyfish, that one hard and mean and secretive, like a horned snail. They could be austere and comical as top hats, or smooth and lively and flattering as ribbons. A parade of private visitors, not over yet.

Something woke Rose early the next morning. She was sleeping in the little porch, the only place in Flo's house where the smell was bearable. The sky was milky and brightening. The trees across the river—due to be cut down soon, to make room for a trailer park—were hunched against the dawn sky like shaggy dark animals, like buffalo. Rose had been dreaming. She had been having a dream obviously connected with her tour of the Home the day before.

Someone was taking her through a large building where there were people in cages. Everything was dim and cobwebby at first, and Rose was protesting that this seemed a poor arrangement. But as she went on the cages got larger and more elaborate, they were like enormous wicker birdcages, Victorian birdcages, fancifully shaped and decorated. Food was being offered to the people in the cages and Rose examined it, saw that it was choice; chocolate mousse, trifle, Black Forest cake. Then in one of the cages Rose spotted Flo, who was handsomely seated on a thronelike chair, spelling out words in a clear authoritative voice (what the words were, Rose, wakening, could not remember) and looking pleased with herself, for showing powers she had kept secret till now.

Rose listened to hear Flo breathing, stirring, in her rubble-lined room. She heard nothing. What if Flo had died? Suppose she had died at the very moment she was making her radiant, satisfied appearance in Rose's dream? Rose hurried out of bed, ran barefoot to Flo's

room. The bed there was empty. She went into the kitchen and found
Flo sitting at the table, dressed to go out, wearing the navy blue summer coat and matching turban hat she had worn to Brian's and
Phoebe's wedding. The coat was rumpled and in need of cleaning, the
turban was crooked.

"Now I'm ready for to go," Flo said.

"Go where?"

"Out there," said Flo, jerking her head. "Out to the whattayacallit.
The Poorhouse."

"The Home," said Rose. "You don't have to go today."

"They hired you to take me, now you get a move on and take me,"
Flo said.

"I'm not hired. I'm Rose. I'll make you a cup of tea."

"You can make it. I won't drink it."

She made Rose think of a woman who had started in labor. Such
was her concentration, her determination, her urgency. Rose thought
Flo felt her death moving in her like a child, getting ready to tear her.
So she gave up arguing, she got dressed, hastily packed a bag for Flo,
got her to the car and drove her out to the Home, but in the matter of
Flo's quickly tearing and relieving death she was mistaken.

Some time before this, Rose had been in a play, on national television. *The Trojan Women*. She had no lines, and in fact she was in the
play simply to do a favor for a friend, who had got a better part elsewhere. The director thought to liven all the weeping and mourning by
having the Trojan women go bare-breasted. One breast apiece, they
showed, the right in the case of royal personages such as Hecuba and
Helen; the left, in the case of ordinary virgins or wives, such as Rose.
Rose didn't think herself enhanced by this exposure—she was getting
on, after all, her bosom tended to flop—but she got used to the idea.
She didn't count on the sensation they would create. She didn't think
many people would be watching. She forgot about those parts of the
country where people can't exercise their preference for quiz shows,
police-car chases, American situation comedies, and are compelled to
put up with talks on public affairs and tours of art galleries and ambi-
tious offerings of drama. She did not think they would be so amazed,
either, now that every magazine rack in every town was serving up
slices and cutlets of bare flesh. How could such outrage fasten on the

Trojan ladies' sad-eyed collection, puckered with cold then running with sweat under the lights, badly and chalkily made-up, all looking rather foolish without their mates, rather pitiful and unnatural, like tumors?

Flo took to pen and paper over that, forced her still swollen fingers, crippled almost out of use with arthritis, to write the word *Shame*. She wrote that if Rose's father had not been dead long ago he would now wish that he was. That was true. Rose read the letter, or part of it, out loud to some friends she was having for dinner. She read it for comic effect, and dramatic effect, to show the gulf that lay behind her, though she did realize, if she thought about it, that such a gulf was nothing special. Most of her friends, who seemed to her ordinarily hard-working, anxious, and hopeful people, could lay claim to being disowned or prayed for, in some disappointed home.

Halfway through she had to stop reading. It wasn't that she thought how shabby it was, to be exposing and making fun of Flo this way. She had done it often enough before; it was no news to her that it was shabby. What stopped her was, in fact, that gulf; she had a fresh and overwhelming realization of it, and it was nothing to laugh about. These reproaches of Flo's made as much sense as a protest about raising umbrellas, a warning against eating raisins. But they were painfully, truly, meant; they were all a hard life had to offer. Shame on a bare breast.

Another time, Rose was getting an award. So were several other people. A reception was being held, in a Toronto hotel. Flo had been sent an invitation, but Rose had never thought that she would come. She had thought she should give someone's name, when the organizers asked about relatives, and she could hardly name Brian and Phoebe. Of course it was possible that she did, secretly, want Flo to come, wanted to show Flo, intimidate her, finally remove herself from Flo's shade. That would be a natural thing to want to do.

Flo came down on the train, unannounced. She got to the hotel. She was arthritic then, but still moving without a cane. She had always been decently, soberly, cheaply, dressed, but now it seemed she had spent money and asked advice. She was wearing a mauve and purple checked pants suit, and beads like strings of white and yellow popcorn. Her hair was covered by a thick gray-blue wig, pulled low on her forehead like a woollen cap. From the vee of the jacket, and its too-short sleeves, her neck and wrists stuck out brown and warty as if covered with bark. When she saw Rose she stood still. She seemed to be waiting—not just for Rose to go over to her but for her feelings about the scene in front of her to crystallize.

Soon they did.

"Look at the nigger!" said Flo in a loud voice, before Rose was anywhere near her. Her tone was one of simple, gratified astonishment, as if she had been peering down the Grand Canyon or seen oranges growing on a tree.

She meant George, who was getting one of the awards. He turned around, to see if someone was feeding him a comic line. And Flo did look like a comic character, except that her bewilderment, her authenticity, were quite daunting. Did she note the stir she had caused? Possibly. After that one outburst she clammed up, would not speak again except in the most grudging monosyllables, would not eat any food or drink any drink offered her, would not sit down, but stood astonished and unflinching in the middle of that gathering of the bearded and beaded, the unisexual and the unashamedly un-Anglo-Saxon, until it was time for her to be taken to her train and sent home.

Rose found that wig under the bed, during the horrifying cleanup that followed Flo's removal. She took it out to the Home, along with some clothes she had washed or had dry-cleaned, and some stockings, talcum powder, cologne, that she had bought. Sometimes Flo seemed to think Rose was a doctor, and she said, "I don't want no woman doctor, you can just clear out." But when she saw Rose carrying the wig she said, "Rose! What is that you got in your hands, is it a dead gray squirrel?"

"No," said Rose, "it's a wig."

"What?"

"A wig," said Rose, and Flo began to laugh. Rose laughed too. The wig did look like a dead cat or squirrel, even though she had washed and brushed it; it was a disturbing-looking object.

"My God, Rose, I thought what is she doing bringing me a dead squirrel! If I put it on somebody'd be sure to take a shot at me."

Rose stuck it on her own head, to continue the comedy, and Flo laughed so that she rocked back and forth in her crib.

When she got her breath Flo said, "What am I doing with these damn sides up on my bed? Are you and Brian behaving yourselves? Don't fight, it gets on your father's nerves. Do you know how many gallstones they took out of me? Fifteen! One as big as a pullet's egg. I got them somewhere. I'm going to take them home." She pulled at the sheets searching. "They were in a bottle."

"I've got them already," said Rose. "I took them home."

"Did you? Did you show your father?"

"Yes."

"Oh, well, that's where they are then," said Flo, and she lay down and closed her eyes.

Who Do You Think
You Are?

There were some things Rose and her brother Brian could safely talk about, without running aground on principles or statements of position, and one of them was Milton Homer. They both remembered that when they had measles and there was a quarantine notice put up on the door—this was long ago, before their father died and before Brian went to school—Milton Homer came along the street and read it. They heard him coming over the bridge and as usual he was complaining loudly. His progress through town was not silent unless his mouth was full of candy; otherwise he would be yelling at dogs and bullying the trees and telephone poles, mulling over old grievances.

"And I did not and I did not and I did not!" he yelled, and hit the bridge railing.

Rose and Brian pulled back the quilt that was hung over the window to keep the light out, so they would not go blind.

"Milton Homer," said Brian appreciatively.

Milton Homer then saw the notice on the door. He turned and mounted the steps and read it. He could read. He would go along the main street reading all the signs out loud.

Rose and Brian remembered this and they agreed that it was the side door, where Flo later stuck on the glassed-in porch; before that there was only a slanting wooden platform, and they remembered Milton Homer standing on it. If the quarantine notice was there and not on the front door, which led into Flo's store, then the store must have been open; that seemed odd, and could only be explained by Flo's having bullied the Health Officer. Rose couldn't remember; she could only remember Milton Homer on the platform with his big head on one side and his fist raised to knock.

"Measles, huh?" said Milton Homer. He didn't knock, after all; he stuck his head close to the door and shouted, "Can't scare me!" Then he turned around but did not leave the yard. He walked over to the swing, sat down, took hold of the ropes and began moodily, then with mounting and ferocious glee, to give himself a ride.

"Milton Homer's on the swing, Milton Homer's on the swing!" Rose shouted. She had run from the window to the stairwell.

Flo came from wherever she was to look out the side window.

"He won't hurt it," said Flo surprisingly. Rose had thought she would chase him with the broom. Afterward she wondered: could Flo have been frightened? Not likely. It would be a matter of Milton Homer's privileges.

"I can't sit on the seat after Milton Homer's sat on it!"

"You! You go on back to bed."

Rose went back into the dark smelly measles room and began to tell Brian a story she thought he wouldn't like.

"When you were a baby, Milton Homer came and picked you up."

"He did not."

"He came and held you and asked what your name was. I remember."

Brian went out to the stairwell.

"Did Milton Homer come and pick me up and ask what my name was? Did he? When I was a baby?"

"You tell Rose he did the same for her."

Rose knew that was likely, though she hadn't been going to mention it. She didn't really know if she remembered Milton Homer holding Brian, or had been told about it. Whenever there was a new baby in a house, in that recent past when babies were still being born at home, Milton Homer came as soon as possible and asked to see the baby, then asked its name, and delivered a set speech. The speech was to the effect that if the baby lived, it was to be hoped it would lead a Christian life, and if it died, it was to be hoped it would go straight to Heaven. The same idea as baptism, but Milton did not call on the Father or the Son or do any business with water. He did all this on his own authority. He seemed to be overcome by a stammer he did not have at other times, or else he stammered on purpose in order to give his pronouncements more weight. He opened his mouth wide and rocked back and forth, taking up each phrase with a deep grunt.

"And *if* the Baby—*if* the Baby—*if* the Baby—*lives*—"

Rose would do this years later, in her brother's living room, rocking back and forth, chanting, each *if* coming out like an explosion, leading up to the major explosion of *lives*.

"He will live a—good life—and he will—and he will—and he will—*not* sin. He will lead a *good life*—a *good life*—and he will *not sin.* He will *not sin!*

"And if the baby—if the baby—if the baby—*dies*—"

"Now that's enough. That's enough, Rose," said Brian, but he laughed. He could put up with Rose's theatrics when they were about Hanratty.

"How can you remember?" said Brian's wife Phoebe, hoping to stop Rose before she went on too long and roused Brian's impatience. "Did you see him do it? That often?"

"Oh no," said Rose, with some surprise. "I didn't see him do it. What I saw was Ralph Gillespie *doing* Milton Homer. He was a boy in school. Ralph."

Milton Homer's other public function, as Rose and Brian remembered it, was to march in parades. There used to be plenty of parades in Hanratty. The Orange Walk, on the Twelfth of July; the High School Cadet Parade, in May; the schoolchildren's Empire Day Parade; the Legion's Church Parade; the Santa Claus Parade; the Lions Club Old-Timers' Parade. One of the most derogatory things that could be said about anyone in Hanratty was that he or she was fond of parading around, but almost every soul in town—in the town proper, not West Hanratty, that goes without saying—would get a chance to march in public in some organized and approved affair. The only thing was that you must never look as if you were enjoying it; you had to give the impression of being called forth out of preferred obscurity, ready to do your duty and gravely preoccupied with whatever notions the parade celebrated.

The Orange Walk was the most splendid of all the parades. King Billy at the head of it rode a horse as near pure white as could be found, and the Black Knights at the rear, the noblest rank of Orangemen—usually thin, and poor, and proud and fanatical old farmers—rode dark horses and wore the ancient father-to-son top hats and swallowtail coats. The banners were all gorgeous silks and embroideries, blue and gold, orange and white, scenes of Protestant triumph, lilies and open Bibles, mottoes of godliness and honor and flaming bigotry. The ladies came beneath their sunshades, Orangemen's wives and daughters all wearing white for purity. Then the bands, the fifes and drums, and gifted step-dancers performing on a clean hay wagon as a movable stage.

Also, there came Milton Homer. He could show up anywhere in the parade and he varied his place in it from time to time, stepping out behind King Billy or the Black Knights or the step-dancers or the shy orange-sashed children who carried the banners. Behind the Black Knights he would pull a dour face, and hold his head as if a top hat was riding on it; behind the ladies he wiggled his hips and diddled an imaginary sunshade. He was a mimic of ferocious gifts and terrible energy. He could take the step-dancers' tidy show and turn it into an idiot's prance, and still keep the beat.

The Orange Walk was his best opportunity, in parades, but he was conspicuous in all of them. Head in the air, arms whipping out, snootily in step, he marched behind the commanding officer of the Legion. On Empire Day he provided himself with a Red Ensign and a Union Jack, and kept them going like whirligigs above his head. In the Santa Claus parade he snatched candy meant for children; he did not do it for a joke.

You would think that somebody in authority in Hanratty would have put an end to this. Milton Homer's contribution to any parade was wholly negative, designed, if Milton Homer could have designed anything, just to make the parade look foolish. Why didn't the organizers and the paraders make an effort to keep him out? They must have decided that was easier said than done. Milton lived with his two old-maid aunts, his parents being dead, and nobody would have liked to ask the two old ladies to keep him home. It must have seemed as if they had enough on their hands already. How could they keep him in, once he had heard the band? They would have to lock him up, tie him down. And nobody wanted to haul him out and drag him away once things began. His protests would have ruined everything. There wasn't any doubt that he would protest. He had a strong, deep voice and he was a strong man, though not very tall. He was about the size of Napoleon. He had kicked through gates and fences when people tried to shut him out of their yards. Once he had smashed a child's wagon on the sidewalk, simply because it was in his way. Letting him participate must have seemed the best choice, under the circumstances.

Not that it was done as the best of bad choices. Nobody looked askance at Milton in a parade; everybody was used to him. Even the Commanding Officer would let himself be mocked, and the Black Knights with their old black grievances took no notice. People just said, "Oh, there's Milton," from the sidewalk. There wasn't much laughing at him, though strangers in town, city relatives invited to watch the parade, might point him out and laugh themselves silly, thinking he was there officially and for purposes of comic relief, like the clowns who were actually young businessmen, unsuccessfully turning cartwheels.

"Who is that?" the visitors said, and were answered with nonchalance and a particularly obscure sort of pride.

"That's just Milton Homer. It wouldn't be a parade without Milton Homer."

The village idiot," said Phoebe, trying to comprehend these things, with her inexhaustible unappreciated politeness, and both Rose and Brian said that they had never heard him described that way. They had never thought of Hanratty as a village. A village was a cluster of picturesque houses around a steepled church on a Christmas card. Villagers were the costumed chorus in the high school operetta. If it was necessary to describe Milton Homer to an outsider, people would say that he was "not all there." Rose had wondered, even at that time, what was the part that wasn't there? She still wondered. Brains, would be the easiest answer. Milton Homer must surely have had a low I.Q. Yes; but so did plenty of people, in Hanratty and out of it, and they did not distinguish themselves as he did. He could read without difficulty, as shown in the case of the quarantine sign; he knew how to count his change, as evidenced in many stories about how people had tried to cheat him. What was missing was a sense of precaution, Rose thought now. Social inhibition, though there was no such name for it at that time. Whatever it is that ordinary people lose when they are drunk, Milton Homer never had, or might have chosen not to have—and this is what interests Rose—at some point early in life. Even his expressions, his everyday looks, were those that drunks wear in theatrical extremity—goggling, leering, drooping looks that seemed boldly calculated, and at the same time helpless, involuntary; is such a thing possible?

The two ladies Milton Homer lived with were his mother's sisters. They were twins; their names were Hattie and Mattie Milton, and they were usually called Miss Hattie and Miss Mattie, perhaps to detract from any silly sound their names might have had otherwise. Milton had been named after his mother's family. That was a common practice, and there was probably no thought of linking together the names of two great poets. That coincidence was never mentioned and was perhaps not noticed. Rose did not notice it until one day in high school when the boy who sat behind her tapped her on the shoulder and showed her what he had written in his English book. He had stroked out the word *Chapman's* in the title of a poem and inked in the word *Milton*, so that the title now read: *On First Looking into Milton Homer*.

Any mention of Milton Homer was a joke, but this changed title was also a joke because it referred, rather weakly, to Milton Homer's more scandalous behavior. The story was that when he got behind somebody in a line-up at the Post Office or a movie theater, he would open his coat and present himself, then lunge and commence rubbing. Though of course he wouldn't get that far; the object of his passion would have ducked out of his way. Boys were said to dare each other to get him into position, and stay close ahead of him until the very last moment, then jump aside and reveal him in dire importunity.

It was in honor of this story—whether it was true or not, had happened once under provocation, or kept happening all the time—that ladies crossed the street when they saw Milton coming, that children were warned to stay clear of him. *Just don't let him monkey around* was what Flo said. He was allowed into houses on those ritual occasions when there was a new baby—with hospital births getting commoner, those occasions diminished—but at other times the doors were locked against him. He would come and knock, and kick the door panels, and go away. But he was let have his way in yards, because he didn't take things, and could do so much damage if offended.

Of course, it was another story altogether when he appeared with one of his aunts. At those times he was hangdog-looking, well-behaved; his powers and his passions, whatever they were, all banked and hidden. He would be eating candy the aunt had bought him, out of a paper bag. He offered it when told to, though nobody but the most greedy person alive would touch what might have been touched by Milton Homer's fingers or blessed by his spittle. The aunts saw that he got his hair cut; they did their best to keep him presentable. They washed and ironed and mended his clothes, sent him out in his raincoat and rubbers, or knitted cap and muffler, as the weather indicated. Did they know how he conducted himself when out of their sight? They must have heard, and if they heard they must have suffered, being people of pride and Methodist morals. It was their grandfather who had started the flax mill in Hanratty and compelled all his employees to spend their Saturday nights at a Bible Class he himself conducted. The Homers, too, were decent people. Some of the Homers were supposed to be in favor of putting Milton away but the Milton ladies wouldn't do it. Nobody suggested they refused out of tender-heartedness.

"They won't put him in the Asylum, they're too proud."

Miss Hattie Milton taught at the high school. She had been teaching there longer than all the other teachers combined and was more important than the Principal. She taught English—the alteration in the poem was the more daring and satisfying because it occurred under her nose—and the thing she was famous for was keeping order. She did this without apparent effort, through the force of her large-bosomed, talcumed, spectacled, innocent and powerful presence, and her refusal to see that there was any difference between teenagers (she did not use the word) and students in Grade Four. She assigned a lot of memory work. One day she wrote a long poem on the board and said that everyone was to copy it out, then learn it off by heart, and the next day recite it. This was when Rose was in her third or fourth year at high school and she did not believe these instructions were to be taken literally. She learned poetry with ease; it seemed reasonable to her to skip the first step. She read the poem and learned it, verse by verse, then said it over a couple of times in her head. While she was doing this Miss Hattie asked her why she wasn't copying.

Rose replied that she knew the poem already, though she was not perfectly sure that this was true.

"Do you really?" said Miss Hattie. "Stand up and face the back of the room."

Rose did so, trembling for her boast.

"Now recite the poem to the class."

Rose's confidence was not mistaken. She recited without a hitch. What did she expect to follow? Astonishment and compliments, and unaccustomed respect?

"Well, you may know the poem," Miss Hattie said, "but that is no excuse for not doing what you were told. Sit down and write it in your book. I want you to write every line three times. If you don't get finished you can stay after four."

Rose did have to stay after four, of course, raging and writing while Miss Hattie got out her crocheting. When Rose took the copy to her desk Miss Hattie said mildly enough but with finality, "You can't go thinking you are better than other people just because you can learn poems. Who do you think you are?"

This was not the first time in her life Rose had been asked who she thought she was; in fact the question had often struck her like a monotonous gong and she paid no attention to it. But she understood, afterward, that Miss Hattie was not a sadistic teacher; she had refrained from saying what she now said in front of the class. And she was not vindictive; she was not taking revenge because she had not believed Rose had been proved wrong. The lesson she was trying to teach here was more important to her than any poem, and one she truly believed Rose needed. It seemed that many other people believed she needed it, too.

The whole class was invited, at the end of the senior year, to a lantern slide show at the Miltons' house. The lantern slides were of China, where Miss Mattie, the stay-at-home twin, had been a missionary in her youth. Miss Mattie was very shy, and she stayed in the background, working the slides, while Miss Hattie commented. The lantern slides showed a yellow country, much as expected. Yellow hills and sky, yellow people, rickshaws, parasols, all dry and papery-looking, fragile, unlikely, with black zigzags where the paint had cracked, on the temples, the roads and faces. At this very time, the one and only time Rose sat in the Miltons' parlor, Mao was in power in China and the Korean War was under way, but Miss Hattie made no concessions to history, any more than she made concessions to the fact that the members of her audience were eighteen and nineteen years old.

"The Chinese are heathens," Miss Hattie said. "That is why they have beggars."

There was a beggar, kneeling in the street, arms outstretched to a rich lady in a rickshaw, who was not paying any attention to him.

"They do eat things we wouldn't touch," Miss Hattie said. Some Chinese were pictured poking sticks into bowls. "But they eat a better diet when they become Christians. The first generation of Christians is an inch and a half taller."

Christians of the first generation were standing in a row with their mouths open, possibly singing. They wore black and white clothes.

After the slides, plates of sandwiches, cookies, tarts were served. All were homemade and very good. A punch of grape juice and ginger ale was poured into paper cups. Milton sat in a corner in his thick tweed suit, a white shirt and a tie, on which punch and crumbs had already been spilled.

"Some day it will just blow up in their faces," Flo had said darkly, meaning Milton. Could that be the reason people came, year after year, to see the lantern slides and drink the punch that all the jokes were about? To see Milton with his jowls and stomach swollen as if with bad intentions, ready to blow? All he did was stuff himself at an unbelievable rate. It seemed as if he downed date squares, hermits, Nanaimo bars and fruit drops, butter tarts and brownies, whole, the way a snake will swallow frogs. Milton was similarly distended.

Methodists were people whose power in Hanratty was passing, but slowly. The days of the compulsory Bible Class were over. Perhaps the Miltons didn't know that. Perhaps they knew it but put a heroic face on their decline. They behaved as if the requirements of piety hadn't changed and as if its connection with prosperity was unaltered. Their brick house, with its overstuffed comfort, their coats with collars of snug dull fur, seemed proclaimed as a Methodist house, Methodist clothing, inelegant on purpose, heavy, satisfactory. Everything about them seemed to say that they had applied themselves to the world's work for God's sake, and God had not let them down. For God's sake the hall floor shone with wax around the runner, the lines were drawn perfectly with a straight pen in the account book, the begonias flourished, the money went into the bank.

But mistakes were made, nowadays. The mistake the Milton ladies made was in drawing up a petition to be sent to the Canadian Broadcasting Corporation, asking for the removal from the air of the programs that interfered with church-going on Sunday nights: Edgar Bergen and Charlie McCarthy; Jack Benny; Fred Allen. They got the minister to speak about their petition in church—this was in the United Church, where Methodists had been outnumbered by Presbyterians and Congregationalists, and it was not a scene Rose witnessed, but had described to her by Flo—and afterward they waited, Miss Hattie and Miss Mattie, one on each side of the outgoing stream, intending to deflect people and make them sign the petition, which was set up on a little table in the church vestibule. Behind the table Milton Homer was sitting. He had to be there; they never let him get out of going to church on Sunday. They had given him a job to keep him busy; he was to be in charge of the fountain pens, making sure they were full and handing them to signers.

That was the obvious part of the mistake. Milton had got the idea of drawing whiskers on himself, and had done so, without the help of a mirror. Whiskers curled out over his big sad cheeks, up toward his bloodshot foreboding eyes. He had put the pen in his mouth, too, so that ink had blotched his lips. In short, he had made himself so comical a sight that the petition which nobody really wanted could be treated as a comedy, too, and the power of the Milton sisters, the flax-mill Methodists, could be seen as a leftover dribble. People smiled and slid past; nothing could be done. Of course the Milton ladies didn't scold Milton or put on any show for the public, they just bundled him up with their petition and took him home.

"That was the end of them thinking they could run things," Flo
said. It was hard to tell, as always, what particular defeat—was it that
of religion or pretension?—she was so glad to see.

The boy who showed Rose the poem in Miss Hattie's own English
class in Hanratty High School was Ralph Gillespie, the same boy who
specialized in Milton Homer imitations. As Rose remembered it, he
hadn't started on the imitations at the time he showed her the poem.
They came later, during the last few months he was in school. In most
classes he sat ahead of Rose or behind her, due to the alphabetical
closeness of their names. Beyond this alphabetical closeness they did
have something like a family similarity, not in looks but in habits or
tendencies. Instead of embarrassing them, as it would have done if
they had really been brother and sister, this drew them together in
helpful conspiracy. Both of them lost or mislaid, or never adequately
provided themselves with, all the pencils, rulers, erasers, pen nibs,
ruled paper, graph paper, the compass, dividers, protractor, necessary
for a successful school life; both of them were sloppy with ink, subject
to spilling and blotting mishaps; both of them were negligent about
doing homework but panicky about not having done it. So they did
their best to help each other out, sharing whatever supplies they had,
begging from their more provident neighbors, finding someone's
homework to copy. They developed the comradeship of captives, of
soldiers who have no heart for the campaign, wishing only to survive
and avoid action.

That wasn't quite all. Their shoes and boots became well ac-
quainted, scuffling and pushing in friendly and private encounter,
sometimes resting together a moment in tentative encouragement;
this mutual kindness particularly helped them through those moments
when people were being selected to do mathematics problems on the
blackboard.

Once Ralph came in after noon hour with his hair full of snow. He
leaned over and shook the snow onto Rose's desk, saying, "Do you
have those dandruff blues?"

"No. Mine's white."

This seemed to Rose a moment of some intimacy, with its physical
frankness, its remembered childhood joke. Another day at noon hour,

before the bell rang, she came into the classroom and found him, in a ring of onlookers, doing his Milton Homer imitation. She was surprised and worried; surprised because his shyness in class had always equalled hers and had been one of the things that united them; worried that he might not be able to bring it off, might not make them laugh. But he was very good; his large, pale, good-natured face took on the lumpy desperation of Milton's; his eyes goggled and his jowls shook and his words came out in a hoarse hypnotized singsong. He was so successful that Rose was amazed, and so was everybody else. From that time on Ralph began to do imitations; he had several, but Milton Homer was his trademark. Rose never quite got over a comradely sort of apprehension on his behalf. She had another feeling as well, not envy but a shaky sort of longing. She wanted to do the same. Not Milton Homer; she did not want to do Milton Homer. She wanted to fill up in that magical, releasing way, transform herself; she wanted the courage and the power.

Not long after he started publicly developing these talents he had, Ralph Gillespie dropped out of school. Rose missed his feet and his breathing and his finger tapping her shoulder. She met him sometimes on the street but he did not seem to be quite the same person. They never stopped to talk, just said hello and hurried past. They had been close and conspiring for years, it seemed, maintaining their spurious domesticity, but they had never talked outside of school, never gone beyond the most formal recognition of each other, and it seemed they could not, now. Rose never asked him why he had dropped out; she did not even know if he had found a job. They knew each other's necks and shoulders, heads and feet, but were not able to confront each other as full-length presences.

After a while Rose didn't see him on the street anymore. She heard that he had joined the Navy. He must have been just waiting till he was old enough to do that. He had joined the Navy and gone to Halifax. The war was over, it was only the peacetime Navy. Just the same it was odd to think of Ralph Gillespie, in uniform, on the deck of a destroyer, maybe firing off guns. Rose was just beginning to understand that the boys she knew, however incompetent they might seem, were going to turn into men, and be allowed to do things that you would think required a lot more talent and authority than they could have.

There was a time, after she gave up the store and before her arthritis became too crippling, during which Flo went out to Bingo games and sometimes played cards with her neighbors at the Legion Hall. When Rose was home on a visit conversation was difficult, so she would ask Flo about the people she saw at the Legion. She would ask for news of her own contemporaries, Horse Nicholson, Runt Chesterton, whom she could not really imagine as grown men; did Flo ever see them?

"There's one I see and he's around there all the time. Ralph Gillespie."

Rose said that she had thought Ralph Gillespie was in the Navy.

"He was, but he's back home now. He was in an accident."

"What kind of accident?"

"I don't know. It was in the Navy. He was in a Navy hospital three solid years. They had to rebuild him from scratch. He's all right now except he walks with a limp, he sort of drags the one leg."

"That's too bad."

"Well, yes. That's what I say. I don't hold any grudge against him but there's some up there at the Legion that do."

"Hold a grudge?"

"Because of the pension," said Flo, surprised and rather contemptuous of Rose for not taking into account so basic a fact of life, and so natural an attitude, in Hanratty. "They think, well, he's set for life. I say he must've suffered for it. Some people say he gets a lot but I don't believe it. He doesn't need much, he's all on his own. One thing, if he suffers pain he don't let on. Like me. I don't let on. Weep and you weep alone. He's a good darts player. He'll play anything that's going. And he can imitate people to the life."

"Does he still do Milton Homer? He used to do Milton Homer at school."

"He does him. Milton Homer. He's comical at that. He does some others too."

"Is Milton Homer still alive? Is he still marching in parades?"

"Sure he's still alive. He's quietened down a lot, though. He's out there at the County Home and you can see him on a sunny day down by the highway keeping an eye on the traffic and licking up an ice cream cone. Both the old ladies is dead."

"So he isn't in the parades anymore?"

"There isn't the parades to be in. Parades have fallen off a lot. All the Orangemen are dying out and you wouldn't get the turnout, anyway, people'd rather stay home and watch TV."

On later visits Rose found that Flo had turned against the Legion.

"I don't want to be one of those old crackpots," she said.

"What old crackpots?"

"Sit around up there telling the same stupid yarns and drinking beer. They make me sick."

This was very much in Flo's usual pattern. People, places, amusements, went abruptly in and out of favor. The turnabouts had become more drastic and frequent with age.

"Don't you like any of them anymore? Is Ralph Gillespie still going there?"

"He still is. He likes it so well he tried to get himself a job there. He tried to get the part-time bar job. Some people say he got turned down because he already has the pension, but I think it was because of the way he carries on."

"How? Does he get drunk?"

"You couldn't tell if he was, he carries on just the same, imitating, and half the time he's imitating somebody that the newer people that's come to town, they don't know even who the person was, they just think it's Ralph being idiotic."

"Like Milton Homer?"

"That's right. How do they know it's supposed to be Milton Homer and what was Milton Homer like? They don't know. Ralph don't know when to stop. He Milton Homer'd himself right out of a job."

After Rose had taken Flo to the County Home—she had not seen Milton Homer there, though she had seen other people she had long believed dead—and was staying to clean up the house and get it ready for sale, she herself was taken to the Legion by Flo's neighbors, who thought she must be lonely on a Saturday night. She did not know how to refuse, so she found herself sitting at a long table in the basement of the hall, where the bar was, just at the time the last sunlight was coming across the fields of beans and corn, across the gravel parking lot and through the high windows, staining the plywood walls. All around the walls were photographs, with names lettered by hand and taped to the frames. Rose got up to have a look at them. The Hundred and Sixth, just before embarkation, 1915. Various heroes of that war, whose names were carried on by sons and nephews, but whose existence had not been known to her before. When she came back to the table a card game had started. She wondered if it had been a disruptive thing to do, getting up to look at the pictures. Probably nobody ever looked at them; they were not for looking at; they were just there, like the plywood on the walls. Visitors, outsiders, are always looking at things, always taking an interest, asking who was this, when was that, trying to liven up the conversation. They put too much in; they want too much out. Also, it could have looked as if she was parading around the room, asking for attention.

A woman sat down and introduced herself. She was the wife of one of the men playing cards. "I've seen you on television," she said. Rose was always a bit apologetic when somebody said this; that is, she had to control what she recognized in herself as an absurd impulse to apologize. Here in Hanratty the impulse was stronger than usual. She was aware of having done things that must seem high-handed. She remembered her days as a television interviewer, her beguiling confidence and charm; here as nowhere else they must understand how that was a sham. Her acting was another matter. The things she was ashamed of were not what they must think she was ashamed of; not a flopping bare breast, but a failure she couldn't seize upon or explain.

This woman who was talking to her did not belong to Hanratty. She said she had come from Sarnia when she was married, fifteen years ago.

"I still find it hard to get used to. Frankly I do. After the city. You look better in person than you do in that series."

"I should hope so," said Rose, and told about how they made her up. People were interested in things like that and Rose was more comfortable, once the conversation got on to technical details.

"Well, here's old Ralph," the woman said. She moved over, making room for a thin, gray-haired man holding a mug of beer. This was Ralph Gillespie. If Rose had met him on the street she would not have recognized him, he would have been a stranger to her, but after she had looked at him for a moment he seemed quite unchanged to her, unchanged from himself at seventeen or fifteen, his gray hair which had been light brown still falling over his forehead, his face still pale and calm and rather large for his body, the same diffident, watchful, withholding look. But his body was thinner and his shoulders seemed to have shrunk together. He wore a short-sleeved sweater with a little collar and three ornamental buttons; it was light blue with beige and yellow stripes. This sweater seemed to Rose to speak of aging jauntiness, a kind of petrified adolescence. She noticed that his arms were old and skinny and that his hands shook so badly that he used both of them to raise the glass of beer to his mouth.

"You're not staying around here long, are you?" said the woman who had come from Sarnia.

Rose said that she was going to Toronto tomorrow, Sunday, night.

"You must have a busy life," the woman said, with a large sigh, an honest envy that in itself would have declared out-of-town origins.

Rose was thinking that on Monday at noon she was to meet a man for lunch and to go to bed. This man was Tom Shepherd, whom she had known for a long time. At one time he had been in love with her, he had written love letters to her. The last time she had been with him, in Toronto, when they were sitting up in bed afterward drinking gin and tonic—they always drank a good deal when they were together—Rose suddenly thought, or knew, that there was somebody now, some woman he was in love with and was courting from a distance, probably writing letters to, and that there must have been another woman he was robustly bedding, at the time he was writing letters to her. Also, and all the time, there was his wife. Rose wanted to ask him about this; the necessity, the difficulties, the satisfactions. Her interest was friendly and uncritical but she knew, she had just enough sense to know, that the question would not do.

The conversation in the Legion had turned on lottery tickets, Bingo games, winnings. The men playing cards—Flo's neighbor among them—were talking about a man who was supposed to have won ten thousand dollars, and never publicized the fact, because he had gone bankrupt a few years before and owed so many people money.

One of them said that if he had declared himself bankrupt, he didn't owe the money anymore.

"Maybe he didn't owe it then," another said. "But he owes it now. The reason is, he's got it now."

This opinion was generally favored.

Rose and Ralph Gillespie looked at each other. There was the same silent joke, the same conspiracy, comfort; the same, the same.

"I hear you're quite a mimic," Rose said.

That was wrong; she shouldn't have said anything. He laughed and shook his head.

"Oh, come on. I hear you do a sensational Milton Homer."

"I don't know about that."

"Is he still around?"

"Far as I know he's out at the County Home."

"Remember Miss Hattie and Miss Mattie? They had the lantern slide show at their house."

"Sure."

"My mental picture of China is still pretty well based on those slides."

Rose went on talking like this, though she wished she could stop. She was talking in what elsewhere might have been considered an amusing, confidential, recognizably and meaninglessly flirtatious style. She did not get much response from Ralph Gillespie, though he seemed attentive, even welcoming. All the time she talked, she was wondering what he wanted her to say. He did want something. But he would not make any move to get it. Her first impression of him, as boyishly shy and ingratiating, had to change. That was his surface. Underneath he was self-sufficient, resigned to living in bafflement, perhaps proud. She wished that he would speak to her from that level, and she thought he wished it, too, but they were prevented.

But when Rose remembered this unsatisfactory conversation she seemed to recall a wave of kindness, of sympathy and forgiveness, though certainly no words of that kind had been spoken. That peculiar shame which she carried around with her seemed to have been eased. The thing she was ashamed of, in acting, was that she might have been paying attention to the wrong things, reporting antics, when there was always something further, a tone, a depth, a light, that she couldn't get and wouldn't get. And it wasn't just about acting she suspected this. Everything she had done could sometimes be seen as a mistake. She had never felt this more strongly than when she was talking to Ralph Gillespie, but when she thought about him afterward her mistakes appeared unimportant. She was enough a child of her time to wonder if what she felt about him was simply sexual warmth, sexual curiosity; she did not think it was. There seemed to be feelings which could only be spoken of in translation; perhaps they could only be acted on in translation; not speaking of them and not acting on them is the right course to take because translation is dubious. Dangerous, as well.

For these reasons Rose did not explain anything further about Ralph Gillespie to Brian and Phoebe when she recalled Milton Homer's ceremony with babies or his expression of diabolical happiness on the swing. She did not even mention that he was dead. She knew he was dead because she still had a subscription to the Hanratty paper. Flo had given Rose a seven-year subscription on the last Christmas when she felt obliged to give Christmas presents; characteristically, Flo said that the paper was just for people to get their names in and hadn't anything in it worth reading. Usually Rose turned the pages quickly and put the paper in the firebox. But she did see the story about Ralph which was on the front page.

FORMER NAVY MAN DIES

Mr. Ralph Gillespie, Naval Petty Officer, retired, sustained fatal head injuries at the Legion Hall on Saturday night last. No other person was implicated in the fall and unfortunately several hours passed before Mr. Gillespie's body was discovered. It is thought that he mistook the basement door for the exit door and lost his balance, which was precarious due to an old injury suffered in his naval career which left him partly disabled.

The paper went on to give the names of Ralph's parents, who were apparently still alive, and of his married sister. The Legion was taking charge of the funeral services.

Rose didn't tell this to anybody, glad that there was one thing at least she wouldn't spoil by telling, though she knew it was lack of material as much as honorable restraint that kept her quiet. What could she say about herself and Ralph Gillespie, except that she felt his life, close, closer than the lives of men she'd loved, one slot over from her own?